E. Jane Gay

The new Yankee Doodle

being an account of the little difficulty in the family of Uncle Sam

E. Jane Gay

The new Yankee Doodle
being an account of the little difficulty in the family of Uncle Sam

ISBN/EAN: 9783337414122

Printed in Europe, USA, Canada, Australia, Japan

Cover: Foto ©Andreas Hilbeck / pixelio.de

More available books at **www.hansebooks.com**

THE

NEW YANKEE DOODLE:

BEING AN ACCOUNT OF

THE LITTLE DIFFICULTY

IN THE

FAMILY OF UNCLE SAM.

BY

TRUMAN TRUMBULL, A. M.

New York:

WM. OLAND BOURNE, No. 12 CENTRE STREET
OFFICE OF THE "SOLDIER'S FRIEND;"
THE AMERICAN NEWS COMPANY,
119 & 121 NASSAU STREET.
1868.

TO

THE DEFENDERS OF THE FLAG,

ON SHIP AND SHORE,

AND TO

ALL WHO LOVE FREEDOM AND UNION,

THESE PAGES

ARE DEDICATED BY

THE AUTHOR.

PREFACE.

THE author of this volume has endeavored to give a truthful impression of the Rebellion as it appeared to the loyal public.

He does not pretend to give a *History* of the War, or to do *justice* to any one of the thousand noble men who volunteered to fight the monster-treason, and who, with a hearty free will, dealt out sturdy blows until it lay writhing in its death-throes. He hopes that he has done injustice to none of those who bore fatigue, and wounds, and insult, imprisonment, cold, hunger, and death, in order that Union might be perpetual, and Freedom made universal wherever the national emblem floats in the sunshine of heaven.

T. T.

CONTENTS.

CHAPTER VII.

CHAPTER VIII.

CHAPTER IX.

CHAPTER X.

CHAPTER XI.

CHAPTER XII.

CHAPTER XIII.

CHAPTER XIV.

CHAPTER XV.

CHAPTER XVI.

CHAPTER XVII.

CHAPTER XVIII.

CHAPTER XIX.

CHAPTER XX.

CHAPTER XXI.

CHAPTER XXII.

CHAPTER XXIII.

CHAPTER XXIV.

CHAPTER XXV.

CHAPTER XXVI.

CHAPTER XXVII.

CHAPTER XXVIII.

CHAPTER XXIX.

CHAPTER XXX.

CHAPTER XXXI.

CHAPTER XXXII.

CHAPTER XXXIII.

CHAPTER XXXIV.

CHAPTER XXXV.

CHAPTER XXXVI.

CHAPTER XXXVII.

CHAPTER XXXVIII.

CHAPTER XXXIX.

CHAPTER XL.

CHAPTER XLI.

CHAPTER XLII.

CHAPTER XLIII.

CHAPTER XLIV.

CHAPTER XLV.

CHAPTER XLVI.

CHAPTER XLVII.

CHAPTER XLVIII.

CHAPTER XLIX.

CHAPTER L.

CHAPTER LI.

CHAPTER LII.

CHAPTER LIII.

CHAPTER LIV.

CHAPTER LV.

THE

NEW YANKEE DOODLE.

———◆◆◆———

CHAPTER I.

ONCE on a time King Jeff sat down,
    Beside a brandy smash, sir,
And said to Messrs. Cobb and Floyd,
    "It's time to make a dash, sir.
Our little plan," says he, "will fail
    If we should keep it longer ;
We've waited thirty years and more,[1]
    We never shall be stronger.

"There's not a dollar in the chest,
    (For, Floyd, you are so handy,)
And Buck will sleep till we come down[2]
    On Yankee Doodle Dandy.
Yankee Doodle, keep it up,
    Yankee Doodle Dandy ;
We'll keep you snoozing, Mr. Buck,
    Yankee Doodle Dandy."

"But, sir," says Cobb, "what will you do,
    To keep the people quiet ;

[1] "The secession of South Carolina is not an event of a day. It is not anything produced by Mr. Lincoln's election, or by the non-execution of the Fugitive Slave Law. It has been a matter which has been gathering head for thirty years."—*Mr. Rhett in South Carolina Convention.*

[2] "By remaining in our places until 4th March, it is thought we can keep the hands of Mr. Buchanan tied," etc.—*Yulee, Jan.* 7, 1861. McPherson's History, see page 172.

(13)

Won't they upset our little plan ?"
    "I'd like to see them try it.
Why, sir! the Southern heart is fired,
    You surely have forgotten !
They *can't* hear reason if they would,
    Their ears are stuffed with cotton.

"The people South are trained too well,
    Remember, Cobb, my hearty ;
They dare not *think* like Northern men,
    They must support 'Our Party.'"
"There 's Stephens!"[1]   "Well! I own that he
    Is sort of making faces ;
But if we put him *forward horse,*
    He'll never kick the traces.

"We've got the guns,[2] our powder 's dry,
    · According to inspection ;
Keep dark awhile—be on the sly,
    Till after the election.
Old Abe is sure to be returned,
    We fixed *that* in Convention ;[3]
(But this to Democratic friends,
    Is better not to mention.)

"'Twill all work in to suit the plan,
    The Tariff and the niggers ;

---

[1] Alex. H. Stephens was among those who voted *against* the ordinance of secession in the State Convention of Georgia.

[2] "Floyd was industriously engaged, up to the date of his resignation, in sending arms and munitions of war to the seceding States."— *New York Times, Jan.* 19, 1861.

[3] "The cloud was fully charged, and the juggling revolutionists, who held the wires and could at will direct its lightnings, appeared at Charleston, broke up the Democratic Convention assembled to nominate a candidate for the Presidency, and thus secured the election of Mr. Lincoln."—*See Holt's Letter to Speed, May* 31, 1861.

And for our mercenary men,
  We 'll sprinkle a few figures.
The Border States may balk awhile,
  But they must sell their corn, sir;
We 'll coax and then precipitate,
  And clap the irons on, sir."

Then (with his finger to his nose),
  Says Jeff, "the South doth groan, sir,
That all it wants from Northern men,
  Is to be 'let alone,' sir."
So Floyd, he sent a Major down,
  To make Fort Sumter handy;
The Major *took* and *kept* the fort,[1]
  With Yankee Doodle Dandy.

Lord Pickens, then, he raved a while,
  The Major didn't hear him;
So Beauregard built up a pile
  Of earth and cannon near him.
The Major then looked out to see
  His orders fast come pouring;
But looked in vain—at Washington
  Old Buck[2] was only snoring!

All through the South the rage ran high,
  And law was much impeded;
The plotters into session went,
  And said their State *seceded.*
They trampled on the Stars and Stripes,
  But found the postage handy;[3]
And whistled Dixie, when they thought
  Of Yankee Doodle Dandy.

[1] Major Anderson evacuated Fort Moultrie and occupied Fort
Sumter, Dec. 26, 1860.   [2] James Buchanan.
[3] The mails to the rebel States stopped 31st May, 1861.

They sound the bugle, beat the drum ;
 And call the boys to muster ;
Jeff, on the sly, pulls all the wires,
 And Wigfall does the bluster.
Up in the North, Old Jonathan,[1]
 Spits out his quid, and wonders
If " ary " storm is coming on,
 Or if it only thunders.

Now by and by Sir Beauregard
 Gets stingy with the Major,
And cuts off all his beef and lard,[2]
 He 'll rue it well, I wager.
For Buck has had some awful dreams,
 And wakes up with a frown, sir ;
And to the Major corn and wine,
 A ship-load sends straight down, sir.[3]

Sir Beauregard looks very hard,
 And sees the ship a-coming ;
" Ho! he!" saith he, "that cannot be,"
 And sends a ball a-humming.
But whether shot struck ship or not,
 I 'm sure I cannot tell, sir ;
But it went booming up the North,
 Where it blew quite a spell, 'sir.

And Gunnybags did shake his head
 And talk about "conceding ;"
And ministers, to prove wrong *right,*
 Their Bibles sore were reading.

---

[1] Born in 1776.

[2] Communication between the city and Fort Sumter prohibited March 7, 1861.

[3] " Star of the West " left New.York, January 5, 1861.

And some proposed a remedy
　I'm quite ashamed to mention ;
They called John Tyler into town,[1]
　To head a Peace Convention.

*　　*　　*　　*　　*　　*

Now from the East of Tennessee,
　Starts up our " Second Andy ;"[2]
And "Treason" calls the little plot,
　On Yankee Doodle Dandy.
Yankee Doodle, keep it up,
　Yankee Doodle Dandy ;
"The traitors !—they should be strung up,"
　Says valiant Second Andy.

And Mr. Secretary Dix,[3]
　In indignation mutters :
"Those rebels down at New Orleans
　Are going to steal our cutters."
Then speaks right out to Hemphill Jones,[4]
　"The times are growing hot, sir ;
If any man hauls down our flag,
　Just shoot him on the spot, sir."

Just then there came to Washington,
　Along with Abraham Lincoln,
Old General Scott, who ne'er was caught
　A napping or a winking.
Says he, " I hate a Traitor's face
　As much as I do 'pison ;'
Give me a squad, or so, of men,
　I 'll sweep the whole horizon."

---

[1] February 5, 1861.　　　[2] Andrew Johnson of Tennessee.
[3] Secretary of the Treasury.
[4] Col. Wm. Hemphill Jones, Treasury Agent.

"But first," says Abe, "there 's Major A.'
   Is getting rather lean, sir ;
His tea is out, his bread is gone,
   His pork has ne'er a bean, sir.
The people (bless them, they 're all right,)
   Got leave of Governor Pickens
To send a cabbage, now and then,
   'And now a pair of chickens."

"Oh, yes," says Scott, "that worries me,
   It 's plain as any steeple ;
The traitors when they see the hemp,'
   Will dodge behind the people.
They 've told them, sir, that Jonathan
   Is itching for a battle,
And wants to tear their hearthstones up,
   And drive off all their cattle.

"The South, I know, is honest still,
   The traitors, sir, have made her
To work their most unholy will—
   Good God! how they 've betrayed her.
And there 's Virginny, my old State!
   (The General fell a-crying,)
She 'll be a cat's-paw, sure as fate,
   Her Washington defying."

"But, sir," says Abe, "the boy out there,
   There's no use to deny it,
Don't thrive upon his Charleston fare,
   It isn't healthy diet.
To cheer him up, I 'll send straight down
   A little keg of brandy,
I 'll never see the fellow starve,
   By—Yankee Doodle Dandy."

CHAPTER II.

SIR BEAUREGARD, he looketh hard,
  And thinks he spies a fleet;
And up jumps Pryor, all on fire,
  " *This time*[1] I 'll not retreat."
Says he, "In Old Virginny's name,
  I 'm going to send a big ball."
Then up jumps one to make a speech
  (I think his name is Wigfall);

And grasping a palmetto-tree
  To keep himself quite steady,
"Now, boys," says he, "the hour 's at hand,
  And everything is ready.
In yonder fort there 's seventy men,
  By this time lean and lanky;
Car'lina, sirs, regrets that you
  Must flog the scurvy Yankee.

"I see the chivalry are here,
  And full seven thousand strong, sir;
I 'll give three hours to take the fort—
  You 'll hardly be so long, sir.
You see that hateful striped rag,
  That 's hung so long defying;
Who 'll be the first to nail *our* flag
  Where that curs'd thing is flying?"

[1] See the Porter and Pryor Correspondence.

He said, and turned himself about,
　And went into safe quarters—
That is to say, beyond the range
　Of Yankee guns and mortars.
And then the Devil, he came up,
　And all his imps did call;
And sat them down, to gaze upon
　The opening of the ball.

Then Beauregard, he gave the word,
　He better had been dumb, sir,
For, oh! they "shot their granny" when
　They fired upon Fort Sumter.[1]
For the first gun they charged that day,
　They aimed it very ill, sir;
The shot went clear up Boston Bay!
　And lodged in Bunker Hill, sir!

*　　　*　　　*　　　*　　　*　　　*

Now Major A. was sitting down
　To eat a little snack, sir;[2]
When, bang! there came a thundering knock,
　It made the timbers crack, sir.
"Don't open yet, my gallant lads,
　(I wish I'd a potato,)
They've been to breakfast, I'll be bound,
　And can afford to wait, O.

"But while they're waiting there outside,
　Our compliments to bandy;

---

[1] The rebels opened fire from Fort Moultrie at half-past four A.M., April 12, 1861.

[2] "We took breakfast at half-past six o'clock leisurely and calmly, after which the command was divided into three reliefs."—*Tribune Account.*

Turn out the band, and play the tune,
　Called 'Yankee Doodle Dandy.' "
And as they play, the old flag swells
　Upon the startled air, sir;
And every stripe floats brave and free,
　And every star is there, sir.

The shots come booming thick and fast,
　"I pray thee do not lag, sir,"
A soldier said, "they've grazed the staff,
　They're aiming at the flag,[1] sir."
Up rose the Major, calm and pale,
　As one a great blow stuns ;
Nor spoke he, but looked at his men
　And pointed to the guns.

They man the guns, they toil like one
　Who with a single hand, sir,
Would keep a pack of wolves at bay,
　So fight they for their land, sir.
Those seventy men, I need not tell
　Their title-deeds to glory ;
For every heart, I know full well,
　Is throbbing with the story.

Nor how they gulped emotion down,
　Nor looked at one another,
As shot by shot around them fell,
　Each fired by a brother!
Nor how the Devil sat on shore,
　His spirits growing higher,

---

[1] " The aim of the enemy was principally directed at our flag-staff, from which proudly waved the Stars and Stripes. After two days' incessant firing it was shot away."—*Tribune, April* 19, 1801.

As red hot hail poured in upon
  Fort Sumter, when "on fire."[1]

Nor how he chuckled to himself,
  "Dear me! I'm of no use, sir,
To fellows, who like these can aim,
  Straight at a flag of truce, sir."
Nor how he left his imps "at cards,"[2]
  And in disgust did go, sir,
From Cummings Point, straight as a line,
  To cool off down below, sir.

Nor how these seventy weary men,
  Beleaguered in this manner,
By fire, and "full seven thousand strong,"
  Took down their Spangled Banner.
It was a "glorious bloodless" strife,
  ('Tis so, the traitors say, sir,)
They'd better lost there every life,
  Than what they lost that day, sir;

For when the Major took a ship,
  And from Car'lina started,
And carried off the Stars and Stripes,
  Her glory had departed!
But Jeff who sat in proud estate
  A self-appointed grandee,
He told them, "they had fixed the fate,
  Of Yankee Doodle Dandy."

---

1 " When the building caught fire, the enemy commenced firing hot
shot." (From Minutes of an officer in Fort Sumter.)—*Tribune, April*
19, 1861.

2 "Our troops were so cool that during the action some of the
boys at Cummings Point amused themselves with a game of cards."—
Rebel Account.

CHAPTER III.

Now, Honest Abe at Washington
  Was sweeping out the place, sir,
When, like a shot, in bolted Scott,
  With fury in his face, sir.
" Now, here 's," says he, " a pretty row,
  The traitors we must bag, sir,
For, sure as fate, the rebel pack
  Have fired upon the flag, sir ! "

" What flag ? " says Abe, a-sitting down,
  " You don't mean that at Pickens ?
Why Slemmer's not so sad a clown,
  As let Bragg play the dickens ? "
" No, no ! " says Scott, and waxing hot,
  He gave his sword a thump, sir.
" Ah ! then," says Abe, " the chaps have got
  A tartar in Fort Sumter."

" Well, well," says Scott, " that 's true or not,
  I know what they will get, sir :
For Abe, I want my squad of men,
  Before the sun is set, sir."
Then Abe, he took a pen and ink,
  (For he is mighty handy,)
And wrote a letter quick as wink,[1]
  To Yankee Doodle Dandy.

[1] April 15, 1861, President Lincoln called for 75,000 men to suppress the Rebellion.

Now when the echo of the guns
  Went rolling up the North, sir,
It stretched from Gotham clear to Maine,
  And to the West went forth, sir.
And every man throughout the land,
  Did feel a sudden thrill, sir,
And every man did silent stand
  And every pulse was still, sir.

Then with one great convulsive bound
  The nation's heart did beat, sir,
And every throb did nerve an arm,
  The traitor foe to meet, sir.
From California, through the West,
  To Maine, so bleak and sandy,
One single thought did fire the breast,
  Of Yankee Doodle Dandy.

When Abram's letter came to town,
  They read it out in meeting,
And ere the sun was half way down
  A thousand drums were beating.
That night, as Scott was going to bed
  In not the best of cheer, sir,
In at the door Abe put his head,
  Says he, "The squad is here, sir." [1]

Meanwhile, the Major up the bay,
  Brings home the " striped rag," sir,
He finds the town has blossomed out,
  Like peach trees, with the flag, sir.

---

[1] Six hundred men of the Pennsylvania militia (Col. Cake) were the first volunteers who arrived in Washington. They came in on April 18, 1861.

The Major's heart beats quick and fast,
  He sees as well as " Andy "
That Sumter's guns have waked at last
  Old Yankee Doodle Dandy.

For Jonathan has risen in haste,
  His powder-horn to fill, sir :
(It is the same his gran'sir used
  On famous Bunker Hill, sir.)
He calls his sons to leave the plough,
  The old sword buckles on, sir,
And side by side with steady tramp
  They march to Washington, sir.

Long years agone, at Lexington,
  Their fathers showed the way, sir,
To freedom ; now at Baltimore,[1]
  They celebrate the day, sir.
Sound the alarm ! ho ! minute men !
  To arms ! the brave are falling ;
The land is cursed by treason's rule,
  The oppressed for aid are calling.

---

[1] April 19, the 6th Massachusetts and 7th Pennsylvania militia had a fight with a mob in Baltimore.

4

CHAPTER IV.

Abe's letter was to Dixie sent,
  "They laughed beyond expression "[1]
When to Montgomery it went,
  Into their secret session.
"Ha! ha!" says Toombs, says he "good joke!"
  (The laugh was not so hearty,)
"Why, sir," says Keitt, "the scamp would poke
  His nose into our party."

"Ho! ho!" says Rhett, "we'll make him sweat,
  The 'ape' can only boast, sir,
For when he counts upon the North,
  He counts without his host, sir.
For Bennett there will stand *us* true,
  And Wall Street will not fail, sir,
The Democrats will nothing do
  Except to go *our* bail, sir.

"New York's too cute to go it blind,
  She lives by Southern trade, sir,
To go to war is not *her* mind,
  With Southern debts unpaid, sir.
When *she* speaks out Old Abe will cringe,
  And mind his P's and Q's, sir,
This talk of war, you'll see, will hinge
  On what *New York* will do, sir."

[1] "A quotation from President Lincoln's Proclamation was met by
shouts of derisive laughter."—*Charleston Mercury, April* 30, 1861.

Then up pops Orr; says he "He! he!
  That's good I do declare, sir;
When Abram tries to 'take the forts'
  By Jove! how he will stare, sir.
Those greedy chaps will never fight,
  They cannot *waste the time*, sir,
When Abram's army comes to light,
  I'll buy it—with a *dime*, sir."

"Haw! haw!" says Cobb, who fairly laughed
  Out louder than the rest,
"Go plant in peace, my friends," says he,
  "Virginia bares *her* breast."
Just here, in rushed young master Pryor,
  He looked somewhat alarmed, sir,
Says he "By Jeff! the North's on fire,
  And every man is armed, sir!

"I heard," said he, "by telegraph,
  (The mail has just come on, sir)
That there are fifty thousand men
  Encamped in Washington, sir."
"Pshaw! weren't they stopped in Baltimore?"
  Said Barnwell, and he frowned, sir;
"Stopped!! a-hem, yes,"—"What then?"
  "Why then they traveled round, sir.

"They've come like locusts on the land,
  And ships upon the sea, sir,
Have brought Old Gunnybags himself,
  As quick as quick could be, sir.
And Wall Street, sir, has sent *the chest*,
  And now it's there quite handy;
With ne'er a Floyd to keep it safe
  For Yankee Doodle Dandy.

"New York has joined the hue and cry,
    Our friends have sunk like lead, sir,
The Union rage has run so high
    They dare not show their heads, sir.
Why, some who swore to stand by us
    Are innocent as babes, sir,
Now, when they 've led us in this muss,
    Turn round and shout for Abe, sir." [1]

"Tut, tut, my boy, that 's bogus news,
    Else were our plot imperiled ; "
"I swear 'tis true," says Pryor "look! here 's
    A copy of the *Herald !* "—
At this came in an orderly,
    " A telegraph dispatch,[2] sir ; "
"Bless me ! " said Jeff, " this Yankee trick,
    It will be hard to match, sir."

He read, and tore his hair in spite,
    " We are, in fact, invaded,
Pickens was reinforced last night,[3]
    And Charleston is blockaded."
They locked the door, they whispered low,
    They stayed all day and night, sir,
But what they did, no man doth know,
    It never came to light, sir.

But some suppose they took a vote
    And settled it by lot,
That Robinson [4] should go at once
    And buy off Gen. Scott.

[1] See Report of mass meeting in Union Square, April 20, 1861.

[2] Dispatches from Fort Slemmer, captured by the rebels, gave Davis the first intimation of his defeat ; no wonder the rebel chief was sick and went to bed.—*Evening Post.*   [3] April 12, 1861.

[4] Judge Robinson, of Virginia, who offered Gen. Scott a commission as commander-in-chief of rebel army.—*See N. Y. Times, April* 20, 1861.

But one thing sure is known to all,
   Jeff took an ague fit, sir,
And did a doctors' council call,
   Upon the case to sit, sir.

They found the symptoms very bad,
   His body politic,
Was broken out in angry spots,
   Internally was sick.
The doctors sighed, and shook their heads,
   And, " It is plain to see, sir,
A desperate case like this," they said,
   " Needs desperate remedy, sir."

Then Jeff, he rose in trembling haste,
   He saw his end was near, sir ;
Says he " If I must die,—at least
   I will not die of fear, sir.
Bring me my sword, and, Walker, stay,[1]
   Call all the boys together :
And send my pirates out to sea,[2]
   Before it 's stormy weather.

" There 's Houston,[3] if he sees us down,
   Most terribly will vex us,
Tell Twiggs [4] to tip the fellow's crown,
   Or drive him out of Texas.
And Hicks,[5] confound these crooked sticks,
   That never will fit in, sir,

---

[1] Walker, rebel Secretary of War.
[2] Jeff Davis offers to issue letters of marque.—*April* 17, 1861.
[3] Governor of Texas.
[4] Twiggs, by his treachery as a United States officer, purchased a commission in the rebel army.
[5] Hicks, Governor of Maryland, refused to call a convention to take Maryland out of the Union.

This one turns up in Maryland ;
  Our troubles to begin, sir.

" Send on in haste to Tennessee
  A hint of blood and arson,
Tell Harris[1] if he 'd favor *me*,
  He 'll burn that *printing parson.*[2]
And quick to Memphis a dispatch—
  Or stay, give me a quill, O,
A private hint about his ditch,
  I 'll write to General Pillow.

" Call out the mob along the shore,
  Straight up from New Orleans :
And ask McGoffin,[3] (stupid bore !)
  What Old Kentucky means.
Bid Bully Wise some plan devise
  To stop that brawling ' Andy,'
Or by the powers that be, we 're done
  By Yankee Doodle Dandy.

" Bid Mann and Yancey to set out,
  (Such news may thrones convulse, sir)
To see what Johnny Bull's about,
  And feel Napoleon's pulse, sir.
Since our own friends and brothers fail,
  We 're forced to this decision ;
We 'll fight the Yankees and prevail,
  With foreign recognition."

So said, King Jeff grew faint and ill,
  And sent for Mister Stephens,

---

[1] Gov. Harris, of Tennessee.   [2] Brownlow, of Tennessee.
                [3] Governor of Kentucky.

He didn't come, but seized a quill
  And wrote the best of reasons :
Says he, " King Jeff, I 'd like to please,
  And not to disappoint, sir,
But I am suffering from disease,
  My liver 's out of joint, sir.

" There 's lots of fellows, stout and trim,
  Up in Virginia waiting ;
Just change the venue, draft them in,
  They 'll snap at any baiting.
Take my advice, now, Jeff, for once,
  And keep the South in order,
And let Virginia (poor old dunce !)
  Meet Abram on the border."

Jeff takes the hint, a clever one,
  " Our way," said he, " is clear, sir,
We 'll pen old Abe in Washington,
  And strike him in the rear, sir.
You 're quick at figures, Toombs, just make
  A little calculation
How many chivalry 'twill take
  To smash this Yankee nation."

" Ahem," said Toombs, " a fraction, sir,
  And that a decimal,
Could hardly, sir, express a sum
  So infinitesimal.[1]
Don't enter into the details,
  Or the occasion 's lost, sir,
The Southron wills, his *dash* prevails,
  While Yankees count the cost, sir."

[1] See Southern bluster generally.

"Well then," says Jeff, "I'll make a draft,
　The people, they must pay, sir,
I'll date the note at—deuce take it—
　Where *is* the C. S. A. sir?"
"Richmond?"—"But then Virginia lags,
　The reason I divine, sir,
Her mettle's high! *I* know the tune
　Will wheel *her* into line, sir."

So said, Jeff took a scented sheet,
　A gilt-edged, tinted note,
And nibbed his quill, and fine, and neat,
　And carefully, he wrote :
"Mother of Presidents," said he,
　"Our fate is in your hand, O,
'Tis ours to *fight* for liberty,
　Virginia's to command, O."

Virginia blushed, and said 'twas sweet
　To be appreciated ;
And Jeff's proposal, it was meet,
　Should be at least debated.
She could not but reciprocate
　His well-bred courtes*ie*, sir ;
In fact, she nibbled at the bait
　And sent Jeff Mr. Lee,[1] sir.

Now Lee was bred in Washington,
　On governmental pap, sir ;
And lived with Scott, and made his punch,
　And now and then a map, sir.
'Tis said, one day he saw a plan
　Old Abe and Scott combined,

[1] Robert Lee commissioned Commander In-Chief of Confederate forces In Virginia on the 10th May, 1861.

Had made, without his (Lee's) advice,
    And in a miff resigned.

But others say, Lee *not* in spite,
    But rather more in sorrow,
Said fervently his prayers one night—
    Turned traitor on the morrow.
For conscience' sake, *not* for renown,
    He 'd Coriolanus be, sir;
And so march back against the town
    With all the chivalrie, sir.

Thus Jeff and Mr. Lee do meet,
    In mutual admiration;
And take together counsel sweet,
    To circumvent the nation:
"Down the Potomac's wooded bank
    Our batteries we 'll mask, sir,"
Says Lee; "to pen the mud-sills up
    Will be an easy task, sir.

"Letcher,[1] you know, has been at work;
    Virginia doth regard,
With favor, Jeff, what he hath done
    At Gosport navy yard.[2]
And Harper's Ferry[3] is redeemed,
    The forty knaves[4] are fled, sir;
We sent three thousand to the chase,
    They shot two 'blue coats' dead, sir."

"Oh, yes!" sighed Jeff, "that 's plain enough,
    So far as it does go,

---

[1] Governor of Virginia.   [2] April 15, 1861.
[3] Captured April 18, 1861.   [4] The United States garrison.

2*

But there 's some Massachusetts stuff
  Inside our Fort Monroe.[1]
But Lee, I 'm sure, that you will do
  To see these matters right, sir ;
I 'll pack my traps, and follow you
  To Richmond, by to-night, sir."[2]

[1] General Butler's head quarters at Fort Monroe, May 18, 1861.
[2] Jeff Davis arrives in Richmond, June 29, 1861.

CHAPTER V.

Wᴡɪʟᴇ Jefferson and Robert Lee
   Hold traitorous communion,
The Mayor,[1] out in Wheeling, struck
   A blow, sir, for the Union.
Knave Letcher wrote him of the fact
   (Embossed with rebel gildings)
Of Old Virginia's Traitor Act,[2]
   And said, the *public buildings*

He had in charge must be all seized,
   In Old Virginia's name, sir.
"I have," said Sweeney, "seized them all,
   And I shall hold the same, sir,
For Aʙʀᴀᴍ Lɪɴᴄᴏʟɴ, President
   Of these United States."
Thus Sweeney spoke his sentiments,
   And from his act there dates,

A split, which soon a chasm grew,
   And Old Virginia rent,
The western half struck out a new
   And separate government ;
The people liked the good old flag,
   'Twas just the one they needed ;
At Letcher's heels they would not drag—
   From Letcher they "seceded."

[1] Andrew Sweeney.   [2] Act of Secession, passed June 17, 1861.

In vain the Gov'nor would "coerce,"
 The patriots held their own,
Until, when Abe sent out a force,
 He found a State full grown;
Then skirmish there, and skirmish here,[1]
 For Rosecrans and Mac, sir,
With gallant Western volunteers,
 Got on the rebels' track, sir.

They pressed so hard, so valiantly,
 So full of righteous ire—
These Western boys—the rebs at length
 Concluded to retire.
They quite forgot to take their guns,
 Or e'en their dead to bury;
They vanished from Kanawha vale,[2]
 And so lost Harper's Ferry.

 * * * * * *

Out in Missouri strife was rife,
 Could anybody wonder
When loyal men and traitors met,
 They 'd rend the State asunder?
The Governor,[3] a traitor vile,
 Began to organize, sir,
State troops, but loyal men the while,
 To guard against surprise, sir,

---

[1] The rebels, 1,500 strong, were defeated at Phillipi on the 3d June, 1861, by the Union troops under Colonels Kelly and Lander. At Rich Mountain, on the 11th July, Rosecrans, with the 8th, 10th and 13th Indiana, and 19th Ohio, made a circuit of the rebel camp and attacked in the rear. Pegram surrendered on the 12th July at Beverly. The rebel General Garnett killed on the 18th at Carrick's Ford.

[2] General Cox announced, on the 20th July, that the Kanawha Valley was clear of rebel troops.

[3] Claiborn Jackson.

Began to drill right earnestly.[1]
  So when the Governor seized,
Their arsenal at Liberty,
  The *Home Guards* were displeased.
They drilled the more, till Captain Lyon,
  With Sigel and with Blair,
Led out the boys to rebel camp,[2]
  And had a skirmish there.

They captured all the traitor crew,
  They tore their tents all down;
But what should General Harney do,
  When he came into town,
But make a bargain with old Price[3]
  If he (Price) would preserve,
In *order* Old Missouri, why!
  His (Harney's) troops should serve.

As strictly ornamental; thus
  To rebel satisfaction,
He would repress the loyal tide,
  Then swelling into action.
Bold Lyon frowned, the Home Guards cheered!
  And Harney went away, sir,[4]
By Abe's command; then it appeared
  There 'd be some wilder play, sir.

Said rebel Governor and Price,
  To Lyon and to Blair,[5]
"If you will heed our kind advice,
  You 'll take especial care

[1] Home Guards.
[2] Camp Jackson, near St. Louis, on the 10th May, 1861.
[3] On the 21st May, 1861.
[4] Succeeded by Lyon on the 4th June, 1861.
[5] On the 4th January, 1861.

To move your troops *outside* and *wait*,
   And let us rebs alone, sir,
To keep the peace *inside* the State "—
   The Guards set up a *groan*, sir.

And Lyon said, his Government,
   So long as *he* had eyes
To see how things were being bent,
   Should never compromise,
Or bargain with a traitor clan
   The rights, sir, of the nation.
Then Jackson hurried up his plan,
   And wrote his Proclamation.[1]

He called for *fifty thousand*, then,
   To drive *invaders* home;
(He didn't mean McCullough's men,
   Who from the South had come,
With all the vagabonds at hand
   To "help Missouri out," sir;
But only Lyon's little band,
   Of patriots so stout, sir.[2])

They *didn't wait*, these Guards so bold,
   They started in the morn;
They headed for their capital—
   Their Governor was gone.[3]
They followed.   On a little bluff,[4]
   They met a battery, sir—

---

[1] Issued June 12, 1861.

[2] Four regiments of volunteers, a few recruits from neighboring States, and a few United States regulars.

[3] Lyon, on the 13th June, had possession of Jefferson city twenty-four hours after Jackson left.

[4] On the 17th June, eight miles below Booneville.

Four thousand rebs—as ugly stuff
   As one could wish to see, sir.

Some Union ball, some Union shell,
   And then a loyal charge!
The nest of traitors quickly fell,
   And Jackson, *now at large*,
With Price, so suddenly made sick,[1]
   Before them disappeared;
And then in Booneville, for their *Blair*
   And *Lyon*, how they cheered!

The rebels ran to concentrate,
   Grew stronger as they ran, sir,
And here and there, throughout the State,
   A bitter war began, sir.
The time was past with specious pleas
   The loyal to inveigle;
They pinned their faith to Uncle Sam,
   And went to fight with Sigel.[2]

[1] Price was too sick to command in person.

[2] Battle of Carthage on the 5th July. Sigel had 1,500 men; Price, 4,000.

CHAPTER VI.

In '61, the fourth of March,
　To Washington there came,
A prophet most infallible,
　And Seward was his name;
"This poison in the blood," he said,
　"Secession—thing accursed,
Has come at last unto a head—
　In sixty days 'twill burst."

Said Dr. Cameron, said he,
　"'Tis possible, by chance, it
May come too near a *vital* part—
　I'll sharpen up my lancet."
Says Betsey Jane,[1] "Which way you fix
　The thing, there'll be no stint, sir,　.
Of shedding blood; 'twill be for good
　To scrape a little lint, sir."

"Dear me," says Abe, "you take my breath,
　(He's sometimes pretty curt, sir,)
You'll fright the nation unto death,
　Why, *nobody is hurt*, sir."
"Not *hurt*," says Greeley, "more's the shame,
　Your cavalry are shod, sir;
Nobody hurt! then *where*'s the blame?
　Turn out and try the squad, sir.

[1] Jonathan's daughter.

(40)

"The rebels vile *must* bite the dust,
  'Tis cowardly to loiter."
"Well then," sighed Abe, "what must be *must*,
  Turn out and reconnoiter."
That night old Mansfield stroked his beard,
  And let his supper spoil
And ere the dawn had turned to morn,[1]
  Had trod the sacred soil.

And Ellsworth! Ah! what chilled the land
  And dimmed the sun that day?
With vengeful hearts his stricken band
  Their dead chief bore away ;
And Lincoln looked in silence sad,
  And mused upon his blindness,
Who dreamed last night,—the simple lad,
  "To kill the foe with kindness."[2]

   *   *   *   *   *

The tidings flew through Rebeldom,
  Jeff Davis laughed aloud,
And sent the gentle Beauregard,
  To tell it to the crowd ;
Now G. T. B. (like Washington,
  Who could not tell a lie, sir,)
Found stubborn facts were in his way,
  When he began to try, sir.

"But facts," said he, "to men like me,
  Are seldom worth the mention,
And for the rest, I think I'll test
  The merits of invention."

---

[1] May 24, 1861.

[2] "Show the enemy that you are men as well as soldiers, * * *
* * * * I want to kill them with kindness." (Ellsworth's last
speech to his Regiment before crossing the Potomac.)

" My Countrymen,"[1] said he, " the knave
  Called Lincoln, hath this day, sirs,
Your border crossed with his foul crew,
  To spoil, and burn, and slay, sirs.

" I, G. T. Beauregard am here,
  To lead you on to battle ;
By all Virginia holds most dear,
  Drive back these Northern cattle !
' Beauty and Booty ' is their cry[2]—
  To arms ! ye Southern braves,
Strike for your honor, and your homes,
  Strike for your wives-and—slaves !"

" Dear me !" said Satan to his imps,
  " This fellow does surpass us,
We 've followed hard this Beauregard
  From Charleston to Manassas.
Live and learn, imps ! here 's a skill
  That 's quite above *your* level—
Hats off ! a fiery bumper fill,
  To him who beats the Devil !"

   *   *   *   *   *

Virginians fired with frenzy, rushed
  Their services to proffer,
And answered gentle Beauregard,
  They 'd take him at his offer.
But while they *talked* death to the " Yanks,"
  And took their rout for granted,
The mud-sills stuck to sacred soil,
  In fact, got sort o' planted.

---

[1] See Beauregard Proclamation, dated Manassas, June 5, 1861.
[2] See the same.

They blossomed out at Arlington,
  And rooted in the West, sir,
And waxing fat and fearless, grew
  As boastful as the rest, sir!
'Twixt wrong and right wa' n't much to choose,
  If one could judge by bluster,—
I some suspect, it was a ruse
  To give us time to muster.

For just as some began to say
  We'd take it out in talking,
McDowell bade the drummers play,
  And set the squad a walking.[1]
Now Beauregard has longish ears,[2]
  That reach across the border,
And in McDowell's tent he hears
  Him give the forward order.

"My men," said he, "the news is good,
  The sheep come to the slaughter,
Go, mask your cannon in the wood;
  The Yanks are good as caught, sir;
They think to take *us* by surprise,"
  He laughed both long and loud, sir,
While swift the lightning message flies
  To bring Jo Johnston's crowd, sir.

Now Scott and Abe in Washington,
  Their fears essayed to smother,
When word was brought the squad had gone
  They looked at one another.—

[1] July 20, 1861.
[2] It is said a *lady* in Washington sent Beauregard intelligence of McDowell's movements.

Abe shook his head and Scott turned pale,
  "The troops are quite untrained, sir."
"They 're *brave*," said Abe ; "the *cause* is *just*,
  That's half the battle gained, sir."

" *The half won't do*,"—Scott glared around,
  And Abram tried to laugh, sir—
Click! click! they started at the sound,
  It was the telegraph, sir.
"The troops fight gallantly," it read,
  (At 4 o'clock 'twas dated),
"They drive the foe at every point,
  With ardor unabated."

"Now Scott," said Abe, "it 's going to clear,
  That message comes in handy ;
Turn out the band, I'd like to hear
  Old Yankee Doodle Dandy ;"
And all the people cheered and wept
  And grasped each other's hand, sir,
And tidings of the vict'ry swept,
  On lightning through the land, sir.

But somehow, as the music rolled
  'Twas followed by an echo,
And men to men in whispers told
  McDowell had a check, oh!
A rumor, born of rebel spite—
  A check! the thought was scouted,
But all the long and weary night
  Men dreamed, and hoped, and doubted.

That heavy night the skies were lead,
  The rain in torrents fell, sir,

Good Heavens!—that daylight when it broke
  Should such a story tell, sir;
For *Panic* seized upon the troops,
  Just as the field was won, sir,
And those who fought most valiantly
  Most valiantly did run, sir.

The men who fought nine hours so well,
  Could be no " coward crew," sir;
But whence their rout, 'tis hard to tell,
  For no one ever knew, sir.
Jeff Davis said, " The Lord had come,
  And fought upon *their* side," sir;
" If that be so," said General Jo,
  " The *honors* we 'll divide, sir."

So Jeff promoted Beauregard,
  Gave Jo a better living,
And to the " God of battles" gave
  A general Thanksgiving.[1]
The Devil walking o'er the field,
  And counting out his dead, sir,
Called to his imps, " A splendid yield,
  Nice Sunday's work," he said, sir.

Said General Scott, " Well, Abe my man.
  We 'll make another tack, sir;
This comes of trying Greeley's plan,
  I 'll send for little Mac, sir."[2]
" Don't start on Sunday," Abram said,
  " And Scott, how many fell, sir?

[1] Thanksgiving in Rebeldom July 28, 1861.
[2] McClellan arrived July 26, 1861.

Poor boys!"—he meekly bowed his head
    And learned his lesson well, sir.

Said *Jonathan,* " Tho' worst *is* worst,
    I *won't* be called a noodle,"
He lifts his banner from the dust,
    And whistles Yankee Doodle.
He wrote to Abe, "That Southern wind
    Blows hard against our shore, sir,
My boys will take the train to-night,
    Three hundred thousand more, sir."

*　　*　　*　　*　　*　　*

Before the echo of the guns
    At Bull Run died away, sir,
Fremont to Old Missouri went,[1]
    The tide of war to stay, sir,
'Twas surging high, the foe had pressed
    And Sigel had retreated.[2]
The rebs before they'd made the test
    Declared the Yanks " defeated."

Now Lyon smarted at the word,
    The twenty thousand foe
Were pushing on, so he had heard,
    His little band should throw
Themselves upon him in his camp,
    And ere the morning broke,[3]
To Wilson Creek, with steady tramp
    They went, and dealt their stroke.

---

[1] Up to this time the West had taken care of itself. Lyon had organized his little band himself. His entire force did not exceed 7,000. The rebel troops still increasing were about 30,000. In vain Lyon begged for aid from Washington.

[2] *After* the battle of Carthage.

[3] August 10, 1861.

A bold, brave stroke for Liberty,
  And in the sharp, quick strife,
He led the last decisive charge,
  And sacrificed his life ;
And not in vain the heroes fought,
  They stayed the rebel wave,
And won the thanks of this free land,
  That Lyon died to save.

McCullough slipped to Arkansas,
  Away from Yankee shooting ;
Fremont proclaimed his martial law,
  And both began recruiting.
The rebels did the best at this,
  There 's nothing could be stranger,
But then, you see, their capital
  Was not in any danger.

Abe needed all his troops out East,
  Where Mac was organizing ;
The need of men so much increased,
  It was in fact surprising
How long Fremont kept up a show,
  And held the rebs at bay, sir ;
What shifts they made to cheat the foe
  Brave Mulligan might say,[1] sir.

But somehow Abe was *not* well pleased,
  There must be something wrong
When traitors under Fremont's care,
  Had grown so very strong.

[1] At Lexington on the 20th September, 1861, an army of 25,000 rebels, after eight days' siege, and three days of hard fight, succeeded in capturing 2,700, under Mulligan, whose provisions, water and ammunition had entirely given out.

The fact was simply that the times
    Prolific, sir, of treason,
Had 'mongst a multitude of wants,
    A dreadful want of reason.

Thus, when Fremont went out at length,
    With his bold body guard,
An order came from Washington,
    That did his march retard;
And Hunter [1] nipped his brave campaign
    Right in the very bud, sir,
And marched his army back again
    To wait for winter's mud, sir. [2]

When looking back those times we see,
    We cannot help but wonder,
If rebels in so great degree
    Heaped blunder upon blunder.
Well, Halleck went to straighten things, [3]
    And put the traitors down,
Where we must leave him for a space,
    To look in Richmond town.

[1] Hunter superseded Fremont on November 3, 1861.

[2] "Months after an army under Curtis, pursuing the same plan, marched over the same ground to obtain Little Rock. It was mid-winter, and the troops toiled through mud and storm. They met the foe at Pea Ridge."—*Abbot's History, page* 20.

[3] Nov. 10, 1861, Halleck placed in command of department of the West.

CHAPTER VII.

IN Richmond there was blustering
  A fabulous amount, sir,
And Jeff & Co. in secret went
  To audit their account, sir.
They shut the door, else they might hear
  Outside the wounded groan;
The guard they placed as sentinel
  Was *whittling Yankee bone.*[1]

"Our plans," said Jeff, "begin at length
  In beauty to unfold, sir,
Manassas' field has proved our *strength,*
  How are we off for *gold,* sir?"
Said Memminger,[2] "I do infer,
  Our *banks* are somewhat rotten,
And in the end, we must depend
  For basis, sir, on cotton."

Said Robert Toombs, "There's something looms
  Up like an apparition,
All luminous with golden light,
  I mean our *Recognition.*"

---

[1] " The bones of the legs were taken for drum sticks; ear-rings and finger-rings were carved out of Yankee bones, to send as souvenirs to the female rebels. Yankee skulls were mounted for goblets and punch-bowls."—*See Senate Report, April* 30, 1862.

[2] Rebel Secretary of the Treasury

"Aha!" said Walker, "you may talk,
  'Tis but a film of fancy,
Or I divine we'd have a line
  From our commissioner Yancey."[1]

Said Jeff, "You know the foreign post
  Is now somewhat unhandy,
Since the blockade Old Abe has laid
  For Yankee Doodle Dandy.
Those diplomats have all been paid,
  Our envoys can't be idle,
Negotiations *must* be made,
  I'll Mason send, and Slidell."

E'en while he spoke, a voice outside
  His eloquence destroyed, sir,
A clatter, as when thieves do ride,
  And in rushed Mr. Floyd, sir.
"Give me," said he, all out of breath,
  "A little drop of brandy!
For oh! I'm whipped[2] well nigh to death
  By Yankee Doodle Dandy."

"Now Floyd," said Jeff, "no joking here,
  You disarrange our plans, sir,
You mean to say you've *stolen* a march
  From General Rosecrans, sir.
There! there! retire! go to the West,
  Where war is just begun, sir,
And bear in mind, however pressed,
  The *chivalry don't run,* sir."

[1] "Very soon after the establishment of the government at Montgomery, three commissioners were sent to Europe. The mission, we now fear, was premature."—*Charleston Mercury, Oct.* 26, 1861.

[2] September 10th, Carnifex Ferry; November 14th, McCoy's Mills; and November 20th, Gauley Bridge.

"Oh, yes, I know ! *we 'll never* fly
  Before the oppressor's might, sir,
But, zounds, who was it raised the lie
  That Yankees wouldn't fight, sir ? "
"In some respects," said Jeff, " are we
  Mistaken, I 'm afraid, sir,
These hirelings, they will fight or flee
  According *as they 're paid*, sir."

" When Twiggs surrendered his command
  No soldier in the lot, sir,
Would take *our* gold, but overland
  Reported to Old Scott, sir.[1]
I 'm told they came in, sir, on foot,
  Commanded by a sergeant,
The roll complete, *one* man o'ercome
  With too much of the ardent,—

" Dropped by the way,—they left him drunk
  'Twas somewhere down in Texas.
In two weeks time, with cursed spunk,
  (That specially doth vex us,
It 's so opposed to theory,)
  The fellow torn and dirtied,
Limped in, alarmed for fear Old Abe
  Would think he had deserted."

" But," added Floyd, " *we* have the *blood*,
  They 're *base born* and the *scum*, sir,
They 've got a fighting fever *now*,
  They 'll *in the end* succumb, sir ;
'Tis pity though, 'tis fallacy
  About our whipping ten

---

[1] The troops left in Texas, without a commander, by the treason of
Twiggs, arrived in New York April 11, 1861.

To one, O Jefferson! can we
   Supply the *drain* of men?"

Says Jeff, "One thing is hard to see
   Our soldiers, *how they eat*, sir,
Here's Lee already writes to me,
   He's short of bread and meat, sir."
"Why! didn't they capture at Bull Run
   Enough to last a year, sir?"
"Ahem,—'twas stated so, 'twas done
   To please the people's ear, sir."

Said Mallory, "A way *I* see,
   You spoke just now of gold, sir,
My pirates free will plough the sea,
   They are both brave and bold, sir.
The Sumter[1] is invincible,
   She'll lay, sir, an embargo,
Protected by the British flag,
   On every Yankee cargo.

"I've a despatch here in my hand,
   I've not had time to read, sirs,
The contents I'll examine now,
   If you are all agreed, sirs."
He broke the seal—the cypher scanned,
   Said he, "*The Yankee banner*
Is floating free, sir, from the mast
   Of privateer Savannah.[2]

"She met the Perry on her track,
   And felt herself quite cranky,

---

[1] Ran the blockade out of New Orleans harbor June 29, 1861.
[2] Captured June 15, 1861.

She caught a tartar, sir ; in fact,
  Was captured by the Yankee."
The Petrel too, that stout gunboat,
  As spunky as a ship, sir,
Of all her timbers that's afloat,
  You'd scarcely find a chip, sir."

" Whew ! " said Jeff, " and *that*'s your best !
  It is n't, sir, reliable ;
It can at least, sir, be suppressed,
  Our editors are buyable."
Said Mallory, " Don't bite your lips,
  But *half* the story's told, sir,
The *Sumter*'s taken seventy ships,
  And quite her weight in gold, sir."

" Ah ! that indeed will do *to tell*,
  The people must have fun, sir,
Just publish that, with what befell
  The Yankees at Bull Run, sir."
Said Benjamin, the Jew, said he,
  " 'Twill do, sir, by Gehenna,
To speak of Schenck and Butler, too,
  At Bethel [1] and Vienna." [2]

" Stay ! a postscript—' naval fight,'
  And ' Barron is checkmated.'
' Forts Hatteras and Clark last night [3]
  Were both *evacuated.*' "
" Oh, dear ! " said Memminger, " 't is clear,
  These cowardly invaders
Have laid a trap to catch, I fear,
  Our valuable blockaders."

[1] Big Bethel, June 10, 1861.   [2] Vienna, June 17, 1861.
        [3] August 29, 1861.

*   *   *   *   *   *

A knock upon the outer door,
  "A messenger from Polk, sir."
Jeff scanned the missive o'er and o'er,
  At last the seal he broke, sir:
"Dear Jeff,—*Missouri's lost*, at least,
  I take it, sir, for *Grant*ed;
Belmont [1] is captured, and our guns
  Are spiked, sir, or transplanted.

"And here's from Drayton,—here's a treat,
  It's something *emphasized*, sir,
Dupont and Sherman, with a fleet,
  Port Royal have surprised, sir." [2]
Jeff strove in vain to catch his breath,
  His hair he wildly tore, sir,
Then pale as "Bull Run Yank" in death,
  He fell upon the floor, sir.

They lifted him, the case was bad,
  All rebeldom did sigh, sir,
The doctors came, and said Jeff had
  "Neuralgia in the eye," sir.
They sent for Johnstone in a trice,
  He said the remedy, sir,
(If they would follow his advice,)
  Was Fabian Policy, sir.

"I differ from you quite," said Lee,
  (The wisest man extant, sir,)
"I would apply, if I were he,
  A counter irritant, sir."
"When doctors disagree," said Bragg,
  "Why, leave the case alone, sir,

[1] November 7, 1861, by Gen. Grant.   [2] December 8, 1861.

'Tis safe to wait to-morrow's news."
　　Jeff gave a feeble groan, sir.

To-morrow came.　Said Bragg, " I 've learned
　　Our plans are unfulfilled, sir,
As far as Old Kentuck's concerned,
　　For Zollicoffer 's killed,[1] sir."
King Jeff arose ;—said he, " 'Tis time,
　　My duty I 'll not shirk, sir,
Mere idleness is now a crime,
　　Let every man to work, sir."

" I own last night by press of news
　　My nerves did much disturb me ;
I owe this morn a perfect cure
　　Unto *the Earl of Derby.*
Read this my friend.—The London *Times*
　　(For us so interested)
Says Derby (who the Gov'ment primes,)
　　To Johnny Bull suggested,[2]

" That ships out bound should signals make
　　To those they met from home, sir,
That ' *War with Brother Jonathan*
　　Most probably would come, sir.'
" Those chaps at last begin to see
　　They 'll *profit by our winning,*
The tide will turn, 'tis clear to me
　　That *this* is the beginning.

" You see that lucky Trent affair
　　Has opened Johnny's eyes, sir,

----

[1] January 19, 1862, at Mill Spring, Kentucky.
[2] December 14, 1861.

We're all right now, 'tis glorious.
  Old Mason, if he tries, sir,
Can never do a better thing,
  So far as *we're* concerned, sir,
Than Wilkes did for him—by the by,
  To show how things *have* turned, sir,

"They're sending troops to Canada;
  I'm told the British band,
Just as the transports left the docks,
  Played out our 'Dixie's Land;'
His 'Yankee Doodle' Abe will find,
  Is left quite in the lurch, sir,
For Johnny Bull will *not* submit
  To *Yankee* Right of Search, sir.

" The South will ne'er be subjugated,
  What though her *sons* are killed?
With pride and scorn still unabated
  She'll have her *daughters* drilled;
And, if more yet of blood and life
  The insatiate Lincoln craves, sir,
We'll still defy him in the strife,
  For *then we'll arm our slaves, sir.*

"And after *that,*" (Jeff raised his voice
  To such an angry pitch, sir,
Said he;) "why then we'll go *ourselves*
  And die in the last ditch, sir.
Excuse me now, dear Captain Bragg,
  I hope I'm not uncivil,
But I *will* lower the Yankee flag
  If I enlist the Devil!!"[1]

[1] " Our people were greatly surprised on Saturday morning to see the
Black Flag waving over the Depot of the Va. and Tenn. R. R. We are

That night a stranger came to town
  Lank and long and wary,
He said that Jeff had sent him down
  To be a commissary
Of prisons, sir, for "*I know beans*,"
  (He used his tongue quite glibly),
"I 'm fertile, sir, in ways and means,
  And I 'll begin at Libby."

From this time on, till weary months
  Have grown to weary years, sir,
One long shrill wail of agony
  Doth fill the nation's ear, sir;
Though fierce the clangor of the field,
  And battle shrieks and groans,
From Anderson, and Belle Isle, still
  Comes up this undertone.

Said Jeff, "I don't sleep well at night,
  My dreams are much disturbed, sir,
The people can't see things aright,
  Their *growlings* must be curbed, sir.
'No wood,' 'no brooms,' 'no leather,' 'lead,'
  'No salt!'—have they forgotten,
How long ago it was they said
  They 'd every thing *in cotton?*

"Those *Tennesseeans* bother me,
  The fools are stiff as pokers,"
Says Polk,[1] "An easy remedy,
  Would be some hempen chokers."

for displaying that flag throughout the whole South."—*Lynchburg Republican.*
[1] Bishop Polk, General commanding in Tennessee.

3*

“ First catch your hare,” [1] said Jefferson,
 “ These rascally low scamps, sir,
In crowds across the hills have gone,
 Into the Yankee camps, sir.

“ The woods are full of fleeing men,
 All heading for Kentucky;
The loss of so much *muscle*, sir,
 Is deucedly unlucky.
I ’ll blood-hounds [2] send along the line,
 They ’ve dared to vex us thus, sir,
They ’ll see!—the hunting will be fine,
 I ’ll stop the exodus, sir.”

Says Cobb, “ We ’ve got the people’s *cash*,
 They ’ll hardly live on air, sir,
They may do something rather rash,
 Unless we speak them fair, sir ;
I would advise you to supply
 A circulating medium,
’Twill serve to hush that silly cry,
 And interrupt their tedium.”

So agents went throughout the land,
 And lots of cotton seized, sir,
Jeff gave for it his note of hand,
 And all the rebels pleased, sir ;
For principal and the increase
 It “ C. S. A.” did bind, sir,

---

[1] See Mrs. Glass’ Cookery.

[2] *Note.*—“ We the undersigned will pay five dollars per pair for fifty pairs of well bred hounds, and fifty dollars for one pair of thorough bred blood-hounds, that will take the track of a man. The purposes for which these dogs are wanted is to chase the infernal cowardly bush-whackers of East Tennessee and Kentucky to their dens and capture them. *Signed*, F. N. MC'NAIR. H. H. HARRIS.—*Bowling Green Courier.*

To pay in six months *after* peace [1]
  With Uncle Sam was signed, sir.

Jeff rubbed his hands, "We've sprung a mine,
  This cotton will be sold, sir,
To Johnny Bull, who, I divine
  Is ready with the gold, sir."
But Johnny Bull is sly and wise,
  He bargained for *free trade*, sir,
And sent his ships of merchandise
  To run Old Abe's blockade, sir.

Of shoes and blankets, he foresaw ·
  There'd be no intermission
Of wear and tear,—he said, "In war
  One must have ammunition.
I'll be consistent too," said he,
  "To principles of old, sir,
I hate this horrid slavery,
  I *always did love gold*, sir."

So Johnny Bull to Abraham wrote,
  In rather saucy tones.
It seems, in Charleston Harbor, Abe
  Had dumped a load of stones. [2]
The act, the like was ne'er before,
  Created a sensation,
It did, as Johnny loudly swore,
  Impede his navigation.

John said,—"Abe had no *right* to do
  So violent a deed, sir."—

---

[1] See Confederate Notes.
[2] Stone Fleet sunk 20th December 1861.

Abe read his little missive through,
  And smiled as he did read, sir.
Said he, "If pigs get in my field,
  Or if a burrowing mole, sir,
Gnaws at my trees, I shall not *yield*
  My right to stop his hole, sir.

"If Johnny Bull don't like the way
  Our house-keeping goes on, sir,
Just tell him, Seward, he can stay
  Where Englishmen are born, sir."
But Seward wrote,—" The stones are few,
  And scarcely worth the mention,
Since John had made the passage through
  Before his intervention." [1]

Then John, who always, sir, is great
  In small retaliation,
Proclaimed an order of the State
  Forbidding exportation
Of fire-arms and gunpowder,
  Of brimstone, lead, and nitre,
Then set to building rebel ships,
  With conscience made much lighter.

[1] See Correspondence on the Stone Fleet.

CHAPTER VIII.

. Now all this time, Abe sore amazed
　　The country tried to mend,
And dimly in the future gazed,
　　And sought, but found no end.
Said he, "Things are so jumbled up
　　It 's hard to find the clew, sir;
But Yankee Doodle has the job,
　　And we shall worry through, sir.

"There 's Butler down in Fort Monroe,[1]
　　I don't like *his* intrusion;
He 's lugging in our friend Sambo,
　　Just to increase confusion.
And Fremont's worse, he wants to lead,[2]
　　Sounds Freedom's trumpet tone;
I wish they 'd do their own hard work,
　　And let the LORD's alone.

" And Johnny Bull thinks we are *down,*
　　And slyly plans a gore;
.And shakes at us his horned head,
　　And gives a biggish roar.
And Wilkes has cut all our red tape,[3]
　　It should have served to bridle

---

[1] General Butler in May declared escaped slaves to be contraband of war and entitled to freedom. See his letter of May 27, 1861.

[2] See Fremont's proclamation of August freeing the slaves of Missouri.

[3] Captain Wilkes took Mason and Slidell from the " Trent," November 8, 1861.

His wrath at treason, in the shape
  Of Mason, sir, and Slidell."

"Why! what's the matter now?" said Scott,
  "It is that Slidell pack, sir?
"Well, hang the traitors, since they're caught."
  Says Abe, "*I*'ll send them *back*, sir.
One war's enough, Scott, at a time—
  It ain't that England's strong, sir—
She's got the law upon her side,
  We can't fight in the wrong, sir.

"And then there's *Sherman* in the West,
  His views are dreadful hazy;
My fears I haven't yet confessed—
  The *papers say* he's crazy.
I sent to him, the other day,
  To make some estimates, sir,
What troops he'd need to drive the rebs
  Out of the Western States, sir;

And Sherman actually said,
  He'd call them very lucky
If sixty thousand men could drive
  The rebels from Kentucky.
And as to putting matters through,
  And finishing the fight, sir,
The sixty thousand would *not* do,
  Two hundred thousand might, sir."

"I always knew," said General Scott,
  "The war was going to spread, sir;
I don't believe, as Seward thought,
  'Twill come to any head, sir.

The poison scatters through the land—
  North, South and West all o'er ;
If we *do* break our Union band,
  We 'll break it into four."

" It *shall not break*," said Abraham,
  " The rebs *can't* have their swing, sir ;
Old Jonathan will not submit
  To any such a thing, sir.
That Bull Run business, Scott, I fear,
  The rebs has greatly flattered ;
But when we 've fairly made a move,
  They 'll easily be scattered."

" Well, Abe," said Scott, " McClellan's here,
  In tactics he is skilled, sir ;
The city 's safe, the way is clear,
  The troops are now well drilled, sir.
I 'm old, and tired out with work,
  To vertigo inclined, sir ;
This war, I do not like to shirk,
  But, Abe, I have resigned, sir."[1]

*   *   *   *   *   *

Now little Mac all through the fall
  Had organized his army ;
'Twas nearly ready.   All at once,
  With something of alarm, he
Discovered that the mighty West
  Was almost unprotected ;
There was, in fact, a state of things
  He never had suspected.

[1] General Scott resigned 1st November, 1861.

'Twould never do for him to make
  Initiative movement
Until the West had undergone
  A radical improvement.
They had been fighting quite too soon—
  A terrible disorder,
In fact, a very chaos, reigned
  Along the Western border.

So Mac told Halleck what was wrong,[1]
  He was, indeed, quite sure
"Fremont had been indulged too long
  In rash expenditure.
His contracts must be overhauled,
  And it was to be shown, sir,
His troops had *legally been raised,*"
  So little had been known, sir,

About the Western volunteers,
  And their neglected plight,
One thing alone was very clear,
  That they knew how to fight.
'Tis true Fremont had gone to work
  And built a fleet of boats, sir,
For Uncle Sam at Cairo, where
  The iron-clads did float, sir.

The Western boys Mac rendezvoused
  With Foote and Grant at hand, sir;
And down at Louisville there stood
  Don Buell's brave command, sir.
Their skirmishes were very thick
  In Old Kentuck; the rattle

---

[1] Letter to Halleck, November 11, 1861.

Of musketry ere long was trained
  At Mill Spring to a battle ;[1]

Where Thomas led the willing boys
  Out to their *first* real fight, sir ;
And when the traitor host came on
  They shrank not at the sight, sir,
But veteran-like, stood to the foe—
  Stood brave and steadily ;
And from the chaos of the blow
  Worked out a victory.

The rebels mustered in their men—
  The Mississippi river
They closed at Island Number Ten—
  The West was in a quiver.
Fort Pillow sprang up, then they were
  No longer in the dark, sir,
When Beauregard, upon his map,
  At Vicksburg made a mark, sir.

And this while Mac in Washington
  Paraded in full feather,
And sat for his daguerreotype,
  And waited for bad weather,
Till JONATHAN in wrath did speak ;
  Said he, "A pretty sight, sir,
This dallying from week to week—
  My boys *came out to fight, sir.*

"Old Abe, I am ashamed of *you,*
  It 's like you were demented,
When all the country 's in a stew
  A-sitting down contented,

[1] January 19, 1862.

A-holding back the boys that fret
  Their span new guns to prove, sir,
Until your army 's grown so big,
  They say it *cannot move, sir.*

" The rebs have been all wide awake,
  While you and Mac have dosed, sir ;
They boast they can your city take,
  They *have* the river closed, sir.[1]
The sight is sad to contemplate—
  We 've sent our sons to chase
The rebel horde—you smile and wait,
  Ignoring the disgrace.

" What do *we* care for grand reviews,[2]
  And epaulets and feathers,
And patent tents and patent shoes[3]
  Impervious to all weathers ?
The West is roused to such a pitch,
  Delay it will not brook, sir,
If *you* don't move this general hitch
  We 'll fight on our own hook, sir."

Said Abe to Mac, " We 'd better try it ;
  What is your bulletin, sir ?"
" *On the Potomac all is quiet,*"
  The General did begin, sir.

[1] Flag-officer Craven reported the Potomac river effectually block-aded by rebel batteries, October 22, 1861.

[2] November 26, 1861. " The review was a grand display, nearly 100,000 men, a grand display of power ; but it passed away like the reviews which had preceded it, and quiet once more settled on the Potomac."—*Headley.*

[3] " McClellan is beset with all kinds of inventors, contractors, etc. He mostly indorses their suggestions, and on this authority the most extravagant orders are given to the War Department."—*Gaurawski's Diary,* 1861.

"Oh! yes, I know, but, sirs, the rebs
  You need not try to blind *them*,
They 'll never *come* when waited for,
  You 'd better go and find them.

"This *quietness* don't suit the boys,
  It looks too much like fear, sir,
They 'd rather have a little noise,
  When traitors are so near, sir."
McClellan stood with folded arms
  (He was a handsome man, sir,)
"I'm not quite ready yet," he said,
  Said he, "I have a plan, sir."

The blood flew up in Abram's face,
  He rose, pushed back his chair,
Took up his hat, with rapid pace
  Walked straight out down the stair.
That night Mac got a little note,
  "This is your troops to warn, sir,"
('Twas thus that Abram Lincoln wrote,) [1]
  "They 'll move to-morrow morn, sir."

Now little Mac twirled his moustache,
  And then began to scold,
Said he, "Old Abe is growing *rash*
  And difficult to hold ;
We 're all so comfortable here,
  I never would have thought, sirs,
He 'd have the heart to drive us clear
  Out of our winter quarters."

" Besides, I'm very far from well—
  To give me time to rally,

[1] President Lincoln's order No. 1, dated 27th January, 1862.

And write my speech, so it will tell,
   I'll send Banks down the valley."
So down the valley Banks did go,
   And left McClellan sick, sir ;
Right gallantly his troops went out,
   They came back double quick, sir.

    *   * . *   *   *

McClellan went to bed and sent
   For homœopathic doctors ;
While General Burnside sailing went
   To give the rebs a shock, sirs ;
Three weeks and more, his fleet storm tossed
   Found fighting was no joke,
Then just as Abe pronounced them lost,
   Turned up at Roanoke.

Now Henry Wise, of John Brown fame,
   At Roanoke commanded,
But lying ill when Burnside came
   And all his cannon landed,
He couldn't hang the General
   As he had hung John Brown, sir,
Nor could reb gunboats keep his fleet
   From taking Newbern town, sir.[1]

Thus Burnside went, to prove no boast
   What Abram did report, sir,
He sailed along the rebel coast
   And "*re-possessed the forts,*" sir.
Old Jonathan cried out, "Well done!"
   And Sambo shouted "*Glory!*"
Which in this place, as Abe would say,
   Reminds me of a story.

[1] March 14th, 1862.

CHAPTER IX.

When first the rebs began to shoot
  At Yankee Doodle Dandy,
They counted Sambo in "to boot,"
  They said "Hè 'd work in handy."
While master led the chivalry
  At home *he 'd* keep the pot on,
Would cure the bacon, grind the corn,
  And cultivate the cotton.

"The *mud-sills*, on the other hand,
  Unless ubiquitous, sir,
Would have no tillers of the land ;
  The Yanks iniquitous, sir,
Would reap destruction close at home,
  The while they sowed abroad—
Supported by no Patriarch's rule,
  And governed by no God.

"The servile race was trained so well,
  In case of a disaster
Why, Sam would hasten to the field,
  And *battle* for his master."
Well, Sambo toiled and Sambo dreamed,
  And nothing Sambo spoke, sir,
Till Yankee guns and bay'nets gleamed,
  And sleeping Sambo woke, sir.

"Ole Missus," rising in the morn,
    And very much belated,
Declared the house felt all forlorn—
    And strange ! no breakfast waited.
For Sambo Cook the night before,
    All suddenly inspired,
Had closed outside his cabin door,—
    In Sunday clothes attired—

With Dinah and the little ones,
    Had taken, in the damp,
And cold, and dark, the road that runs
    Into the Yankee camp.
Abe's generals saw the tide set in,
    It wasn't to their notion ;
Some did with their small brooms begin
    To sweep back, sir, the ocean.

Said they, "Our well digested plan,
    Our *duty* strict defines,
These *fugitives*, sirs, never can,
    Come thus within our lines." [1]
Ben Butler down in Fort Monroe
    Held Sambo out his hand, sir,
Said he, "You 're *free* to come or go,
    My worthy *Contraband*," sir.

And some cried out that Mac [2] was right,
    And some hurrahed for Ben, sir,

[1] See General Order No. 33, Department of Washington, July 17, 1861. Halleck's proclamation of February 23, 1862. General Buell's letter of March 6th, 1862, to Hon. J. R. Underwood. General Hooker's letter, March 26, 1862. General McClellan's letter to President Lincoln, July 7th, 1862.

[2] Extract from General McClellan's letter to President Lincoln, July 7th, 1862, Camp near Harrison's Landing: "Neither confiscation of

Some said that Sambo was a *fright*,
  That black folks were not men, sir,
But beasts of burden ; (it was clear
  As any point in law, sir,)
That Sambo shortly would appear
  The chief man in the war, sir.

Some did n't fight for Sambo's cause,
  But just to save the nation ;
The Constitution and the laws
  Had well defined *his* station.
Old Hunter swore the slaves had souls,
  And perfect right to freedom,
Were stretching out towards this goal,
  Would fight, and he would *lead them.*

And Lincoln, in a groping way,
  Surmised 'twould trouble save, sir,
If Congress would the rebels pay
  To liberate the slaves,[1] sir.
Then sent a Governor Stanley down
  The stubborn rebs to rule, sir,
Who ordered straight in Newbern town,
  To close the colored schools, sir.[2]

Old Jonathan pricked up his ear,
  Said he, "What is this clatter,
About the black man that I hear?
  It is a serious matter,
For us who happen to be white
  Our brother's skin to mark, sir ;

property, political executions of persons, territorial organization of states, nor forcible abolition of slavery, should be contemplated for a moment."

[1] See message of 6th March, 1862.
[2] 28th May, 1862.

The difference is in the light,
　　We're all black in the dark, sir.

"Suppose that Sambo *is n't wise,*
　　Admit him dull or duller,
Stupidity 's a charge that lies
　　Against no special color.
I 've known some *white* folks quite obtuse ;
　　If Sambo *is* a fool, sir,
We need n't such strange terror show
　　At sight of colored schools, sir."

So Jonathan in Congress made
　　A little resolution,
That is to say—a sort of trade
　　Within the Constitution ;
He bargained for a certain sum,
　　That Sambo in D. C. sir,
(Quoth he, "The rest will have to come,")
　　Hereafter should be free, sir.[1]

---

[1] Bill abolishing slavery in District of Columbia passed April 16th, 1862.

CHAPTER X.

'T_{WAS} late one February night,
  Beside a candle small,
Jeff Davis set him down to write
  His speech Inaugural.[1]
The streets were dark, black as his ink,
  (They 'd used up all their gas, sir,)
When suddenly, by his door chink
  He saw a lantern pass, sir.

"A light! 'tis news,—ho! there, outside,
  What tidings do you carry?"
"Hush, hush, from *Tilghman*, sir, I ride,
  He bade me ne'er to tarry
Until I came, as come you see,
  (I 've killed my horse to boot, sir,)
To tell King Jeff, in Fort Henry
  Old Abe has put his *Foote*,[1] sir.

"Another orderly 's behind,
  I heard his horse hoofs clatter ;
Ah! here he is, I fear you 'll find
  There's something *worse* the matter."
"Come in! come in! Put out the light,
  Or somebody will see, sir."
"O me! we 're in a sorry plight,"
  Cried out the orderly, sir.

---

[1] See Inaugural, February 22, 1862.
[1] Fort Henry taken February 6, 1862.

"You're faint," says Jeff, and poured him out
    Three finger widths of brandy,
"Now drink, my man, *A total rout,*
    To Yankee Doodle Dandy."
"King Jeff, I'd drink your pretty toast
    Until I were dead drunk, sir,
But Yankees fight while we do boast,
    They are choke full of spunk, sir.

"From Nashville, sir, I come direct,
    I left an awful panic,
Bull Run was play, sir, I suspect
    To this, this rout Satanic.
The city's sacked, our troops did throw
    Their whisky, corn and bacon
Upon the streets, to cheat the foe,
    For . . . . *Donaldson is taken.*"[1]

"'Tis false," said Jeff, "but yesterday
    A message came up here, sir,
Our boys were 'Driving Grant away
    And peppering his rear, sir.'
And Pillow said, 'The day was ours,'
    And after him did Floyd, sir,
Dispatch ('tis scarce a dozen hours)
    'The gun boats were destroyed,' sir."

"All that was true *till afternoon,*
    The Yankees did return, sir,
His cruel fate then all too soon
    Did General Buckner learn, sir."
"And Floyd, his name why do you miss?"
    "He did not like to stay, sir ;

---

[1] February 15, 1862.

While Buckner asked an armistice
 At dawn *he stole away*, sir.

"Twelve thousand men, and guns three-score,
 All to the Yankees lost, sir,
But paid, King Jeff, with Yankee gore,
 And at a fearful cost, sir."
"Enough!" said Jeff, "your tale is told—
 "Ho! guards, give him his ration,
But with the town let *him not hold*
 The least communication."

* * * * *

Jeff locked the door, and snuffed his light,
 And sighed, and took a dram, sir,
Sat down, and then began to write
 To all appearance calm, sir :
"My friends," wrote he, "the foe must *sink*
 Under *enormous debt*, sirs,
Through darkest clouds there is *this* blink ;
 We have no need to fret, sirs.[1]

"'Tis true we've had full many a trial,
 And loss in gold and blood, sir,
But they have taught us self denial
 And done us all much good, sir.
The people wiser too have grown,
 Their purposes are firmer ;
The gallant men to arms have flown,
 The women do not murmur ;

"But have their sons and daughters for
 Great deeds of valor trained, sirs.

---

[1] See Davis' Inaugural of February 22, 1862.

We're *self-supporting*, too; this war
    Alone we have maintained, sirs;
We've *asked no aid*, but when we've won,
    And our success complete, sirs,
All nations will cry out 'Well done!'
    And *for our trade compete, sirs.*"

So far King Jeff with ease did go,
    When, hist! his window rattles
Just as he writes, " All this we owe
    Unto the God of battles."
The beating of his pulses turns
    To distant booming guns,
The hot blood in his arteries burns—
    Like molten lava runs.

Exhausted nature can no more,
    She will have a respite, sir,
Jeff nods—his candle splutters o'er,
    And lo! it is daylight, sir.
Down dropped his pen, his nerves did fail,
    And sound asleep he fell, sir,
And dreamed, O horror! such a tale,
    Of Pea Ridge,[1] and of Hell, sir.

Of demons armed with tomahawks,
    Of dead men scalped in fight, sir,
Of desperate charge, and battle shocks,
    Of day thrice turned to night, sir,
In clouds of sickening sulphur smoke,
    Of horrid sights to see!
Of shrieking, till the dying choke
    With groans and blasphemy.
   *   *   *   *   *

[1] Fought on the 6th, 7th and 8th of March, 1862.

Jeff woke, but still the distant guns
  Were booming in his ear,
He called aloud. "Ho! orderly,
  What is this noise I hear?"
"That noise, King Jeff, the town has rent,
  And puzzled many men, sir,
Some say it is the bombardment
  Of Island Number Ten,[1] sir."

Jeff scowled, and frowned, and tried his best
  To look incredulous.
"Those Yanks," he said, "give one no rest,
  They keep a constant fuss.
The more we kill they more increase,
  And oh! so bold they've grown,
And all we asked was to have peace,
  And to be *let alone.*"

Thus, while Jeff scolded to himself,
  And boasted to his army
That things in Dixie, on the whole,
  Were working to a charm, he
Heard ever more the booming guns
  At Island Number Ten,[2] sir,
And read of strange and daring deeds,
  Of Pope and his brave men, sir.

[1] Bombardment commenced March 16, 1862.
[2] The bombardment was kept up twenty-three days.

CHAPTER XI.

"Now what do ye in Hampton Roads,[1]
  My gallant sailor boys?"
"Oh! sir, in Norfolk Navy Yard
  There is a wondrous noise,
They're plating our old Merrimack
  And giving her a 'snout,' sir;
We're here to drive the old ark back,
  If once she should come out, sir."

What's that black mass that's floating down
  Between two rebel steamers?
Both fore and aft defiantly
  She carries rebel streamers;
Straight out across the silent bay,
  The hearse-like monster glides, sir,
Silent as death she cleaves her way—
  Like Death, resistless rides, sir.

Now, clear for action Cumberland!
  Straight down on *you* she steers;
She speaks! Your gunners fearless stand
  And answer her with cheers!
A broadside give! Good God! her roof
  Turns off your shot like rain, sir,
Unchecked, unhurt, to cannon proof,
  She strikes the ship amain, sir.

[1] March 8, 1862.

Crash, through the plank and timbers riven
  She drives her iron snout,
Then rakes the deck with heavy guns,
  And still the heroes shout,
Nor flinch—those doomèd men, nor quail
  Before the horrid slaughter,
But man their guns defiantly,
  Till throttled by the water!

And so it sunk, brave Cumberland!
  Down with its dead and dying;
Down with its last dry gun still manned,[1]
  And with the flag still flying!
Unsatisfied the monster turns—
  Success the boast engenders,
"She'll sink the whole of Abram's fleet,"—
  The Congress soon surrenders.

The Minnesota runs aground,
  Right in the monster's track;
The rebel captain looks around,
  "'Tis late, we can come back
To-morrow morn—of this our prize
  The Devil can't us rob, sir;
We'll take a nap, and early rise,
  And finish up the job, sir."

So with the sun on Saturday,[2]
  The black ark hove in sight;
The stranded Minnesota lay
  All ready for the fight;

---

[1] "Standing knee-deep in water, Matthew Lenney fired the only gun that was still dry, and in another moment the Cumberland went down."—*Bonner's History.*

[2] March 9, 1862.

For Worden, with his Monitor,
    Was lying on her lee ;
"I 'll fight the monster," Worden said,
    "God speed the right," said he.

Said Buck,[1] the reb, "By Jeff, what 's that
    A-prowling round our prize, sir ?
It 's something bigger than a rat,
    The deuce confound my eyes, sir—
It is a cheese-box on a raft,
    Some stupid Yankee trick ;
Just send a ball into the craft,
    And sink her double quick."

'Twas easier said than done—the ball
    Don't *into* her just go, sir,
But glances, in the bay doth fall.
    And in return to show, sir,
That little things will have their day,
    The "cheese-box" does run out
Th' eleven-inch gun, and fires away
    Right at the rebel's snout.

And round and round the Merrimack
    The little "cheese-box" spun,
And then whene'er she spies a crack,
    Bang goes th' eleven-inch gun.
The monster tries to run her down,
    Ha, ha! she 's got her match, sir ;
She turns her nose up on the raft,
    And does n't leave a scratch, sir.

She only lifts to Worden's view
    A vulnerable side, sir,

[1] Franklin Buchanan, renegade naval officer.

When crash! the gallant gunners, too,
  The unarmed spot have spied, sir.
Right through the wooden hull, so true,
  That eleven-inch ball goes handy;
The splinters whistled as they flew—
  Old Yankee Doodle Dandy.

And thus the haughty Merrimack,
  And renegade commander,
While making haste to get safe back,
  Began to understand, sir,
That there's a Power above can foil
  The best hopes man can build, sir;
That plans the Devil cannot spoil,
  May still be unfulfilled, sir.

4*

CHAPTER XII

OLD JONATHAN took up his fife,
    He'd just heard from the West, sir,
About Forts Henry, Donelson,
    Columbus and the rest, sir.
"So much," said he to Abraham,
    "Has come of *one* brave move, sir;
Another stroke, and Dixie's might
    Will all a bubble prove, sir.

"We'll teach the traitors, Abe, my man,
    Their idle threats to bandy;"
And boastful Jonathan began
    His Yankee Doodle Dandy.
And while he played, Grant hurried up
    To find the enemy, sir;
And Abe sent valiant Andy down,
    To *bring back* Tennessee, sir.

And news from General Halleck came
    That out in Arkansaw, sir,
The flag was floating, and that Price
    Was cut up by the war, sir,
With Curtis hanging on his rear,
    His rapid flight delaying.
Then came a rumor of Pea Ridge!
    And Jonathan stopped playing.

He laid his fife aside in pain,
  He saw a red, red tide, sir,
Was setting in; his boasts were vain.
  O'er all the country wide, sir,
He knew the gathering waves of war
  Surged in a wild unrest;
He braced himself, and stood erect
  The coming storm to breast.

Abe did n't look so far ahead,
  He fixed his partial sight
On Gideon, and talked about
  The Monitor's brave fight.
Said he, "Fremont's idea of boats
  A lot of trouble saves, sir;
I think my fleets will ride upon
  Old Jonathan's war waves, sir."

Said Gideon, that very day,
  "I have a squadron handy,
And gallant tars to lead the way
  For Yankee Doodle Dandy.
The steam is up, the flag afloat,
  And Farragut on board, sir;
And Porter waits, with mortar fleet,
  For *you* to give the word, sir."

"The boys out West," said Abe, "do fret
  About their *shut up* river."[1]
"The very thing," said Wells; "I 'll let
  My tars the West deliver;
But there 's some forts, by rebels manned,
  And iron-clad gunboats, sir;

---

[1] The Mississippi.

And rebel rams, and heavy chains
   Across the river's throat, sir."

"Oh! yes," said Wells, "and big fire rafts;
   Perhaps we overrate them,
But if they sail such wicked craft,
   My Porter soon will mate them."
So down to New Orleans they sail,
   And slowly up the stream, sir;
The rebs had got the news by mail,
   And of a victory dream, sir.

Bold Porter slips along the shore,
   Half hidden by the trees;
Up to the two strong rebel forts,
   He works by slow degrees.
He wakes the traitors by his shell,
   Two thousand the first day, sir;
Growled Hollins, as they bursting fell,
   "There's two at that can play, sir."

Then out he towed into the tide,
   His fire-ship all ablaze, sir;
"Down to the fleet," said he, "'twill ride,
   Those skulking chaps amaze, sir."
Down, down! the frightful creature moved,
   The vessels stood for fight, sir;
It floated free, all harmless proved,
   And drifted out of sight, sir.

Said Porter, "There 'll be more anon,
   Put grapnels in your boats,
And ropes, and buckets, in the morn
   Be ready, what e'er floats.

"What's yonder light, with lurid gleam?"
  "A raft within a mile, sir."
She nears!   The Westfield, with a scream,
  Steers for the burning pile, sir.

'Mid crashing timbers, flying sparks,
  The staunch old vessel goes, sir,
And on the fearful mass of fire
  The Captain turns the hose, sir.
A moment more,—the fleet of boats
  Have grappled! "Now the oars, sirs."
And see! the baffled monster floats,
  Towed slowly to the shore, sirs.

*   *   *   *   *

Seven days they did bombard the forts,
  Seven days the forts replied,
And Porter would have banged away
  Till all his men had died ;
But Farragut looks on the lads,
  As faint and worn they lie, sir,[1]
Says he, "I'll slip my anchors, and
  These stubborn forts *run by*, sir."

'Twas two o'clock that April morn,[2]
  Beneath the star-lit sky
The forts sleep tranquil, and the ships
  And gunboats silent lie ;
Up from the Hartford's mizzen peak
  The signal lanterns shine, sir,

[1] "When relieved from their toil, the men instantly dropped down
upon the decks, and fell soundly asleep, in the midst of an uproar
well nigh sufficient to have waked the dead."—*Abbot's History*.
[2] 23rd April.

Ship after ship in answer speak,
  And fall quick into line, sir.

Now, up the stream!—The Hartford leads.
  Right in the gates of hell, sir,
She takes the flag!—Oh! bravest deed,
  To break the accursed spell, sir,
Of Treason and her vaunted skill ;
  And prodigies of might,
And rebel hate, and desperate will,
  Prove futile 'gainst the right.

Up! past the broken cable, up!
  Abreast the rebel forts,
"A broadside now!" cried Farragut,
  "Straight at their frowning ports."
Five hundred cannon, thundering,
  Unto the fleet replied, sir,
And shot and shell in torrents fling—
  Still, safe the vessels ride, sir.

Up! 'mid the drifting fire boats,
  Where hot shot crashing falls
Thro' wooden hulls,—the fleet still floats—
  One,[1] riddled quite with balls
Drops out of line, and one [2] in flames,
  The flag ship runs aground, sir,
Before a rebel ram ;[3] she backs,
  And fights, and comes off sound, sir.

Five gunboats Captain Boggs [4] sent down
  Beneath the turbid water,

---

[1] The Ithaca.   [2] The Hartford.   [3] The Manassas.
        [4] In command of the Varuna.

The rebels drive a famous ram
  To stop the wholesale slaughter—
The staunch Varuna reeled and broke
  Beneath the horrid blow, sir,
And carried in a wreath of smoke
  Her flying flag below, sir.

They passed the forts, the fleet's brave crew
  Have crushed the rebel power,
And Farragut's church pennant flew
  Within the very hour.
" Give not the glory of the deed
  To living or to dead, sirs,
Let every heart its duty read,
  Give thanks to God," [1] he said, sirs.

[1] See General Order of April 26th, 1862.

CHAPTER XIII.

In New Orleans, the rebs amazed
  Declared it was a pity,
'Twas infamous—in short, quite crazed,
  They vowed they 'd burn the city;
They swore, these rebs of noble birth
  Of chivalry begotten,
They 'd ne'er submit, they 'd strew the earth
  With ashes of—their cotton.

So, while the fleet lay off the town,
  They raved on without stint, sir;
Grim Farragut a flag sent down
  To hoist upon the mint, sir;
The Mayor[1] whined about "their rights,"
  And said such open dealings
Would not be pleasant in their sight,
  In fact, would hurt their feelings.

And when the sailors went on board
  One, Mumford, took the flag, sir,
Tore out the Stars with ruthless hand
  And in the mud did drag, sir.
Now Farragut, the records say,
  Did not retaliate, sirs.
Quoth he, "Ben Butler's on the way,
  We can afford to wait, sirs."

[1] Mayor Munroe.

Ben's army came the first of May,
  The chivalry subsided,
The women in their own sweet way
  Ben's soldiery derided,
They pouted, sneered, and venom spit,
  Turned up their pretty noses,
The troops, well disciplined, submit
  Until Ben interposes.

Said he, " Politeness is all lost
  Upon a worthless jade, sirs,
As you have learned here to your cost,
  They think you are afraid, sirs.
Hereafter, let no soldier bear
  Such unprovoked abuse, sirs,
Take every such insulting fair
  Straight to the calaboose, sirs."

The rebels raised a hue and cry,
  Which as it rolled increased,
From rebeldom abroad did fly,
  And Butler was a 'beast,'
A 'brute,' a 'knave,' a 'base born fool!'
  A 'thief, come down to steal,' sir,
And Beauregard, the ready tool,
  Wrote out a new 'appeal,' sir.

Said Ben, "They're skilled in throwing dirt
  O me! it is a pity
To waste such talent, when we need
  It here to clean the city ;
'Tis foul almost as rebel tongues,
  Such garbage as one meets—
Ugh! Boys, bring out the malcontents
  And make them sweep the streets."

Now *Mumford* still did walk the street
  And led a swaggering crew, sir,
Who swore Ben should not justice mete,
  Or dreadful things *they'd* do, sir.
Ben sent a sergeant from his camp,
  And being always partial
To law and order, took the scamp
  Before a full Court Martial.

The court decreed death was too good,
  But hanging recommended ;
Ben made a gallows of stout wood
  And Mumford was suspended.
Jeff Davis howled and talked about
  The usages of war, sirs,
And martyred Mumford hung without
  The shadow of a law, sirs ;

Said, "Ben was outlawed," held him up
  To general execration,
As an excrescence hideous
  Of a besotted nation.
Ben took the compliment and kept
  A hearty appetite, sir,
And under Jeff's outlawry slept
  Quite soundly every night, sir.

The *Consuls* next took up the theme
  And quoted rules of war,
And bullied Ben, until they found
  He knew somewhat of law.
They held "Their Governments at home,"
  Right up to Butler's view, sir,
Ben cocked his eye, said he, "You're good,
  My friends, at crying Boo !" sir.

Jeff's Cabinet in Richmond met
  Affrighted by the shock,
Said one, "This does my temper fret,
  We must the Yankees block."
Said Benjamin, "My noble state,
  My Crescent City dear
Has fallen—but has met her fate
  With her escutcheon clear.

"No tame submission on *her* brow,
  She still defies Abe's power,
Brute force alone hath laid her low,
  And only for the hour."
Said Mallory, (the while he wrote,)
  "You sentimental ranters,
Just sign this little business note
  I'm writing to the planters.

"I have advised them, as a friend,
  To burn each cotton bale, sir,
That when the Yankee traders send
  They'll find not one for sale, sir;
You see that Seward's advertised
  At New Orleans a port, sir,[1]
And all the diplomats advised
  From every foreign Court, sir.

"Now let the conquest barren be
  When vessels come to trade,
Why let them only *ashes* see,
  Or our enslavement's made.[2]
Let Europe grumble at the waste
  The barbarous North hath wrought, sir,

The Port of New Orleans opened for trade May 2, 1862.
Charleston Mercury May 14, 1862.

The market will not suit her taste,
  She 'll feel that she is caught, sir."

" She 'll be, or I am very green,"
  (I quote now, sir, from Slidell,)
"No tame spectator of the scene,
  She will not long be idle."
'Twas ever thus in each mishap
  To their Confederation,
The rebels turned to Johnny Bull
  In hope of consolation.

CHAPTER XIV.

Mᴀᴄ read aloud his little speech[1]
  And all his men did cheer, sir,
He said he'd held them back to teach
  (As shortly would appear, sir,)
How best to deal the sharp death blow
  To this gigantic treason ;
And if he *had been rather slow*
  'Twas with sufficient reason.

Said he, "The hour is now at hand,
  In you my trust I place, sirs,
And with the rebels (if they stand,)
  I 'll bring you *face to face*, sirs ;
Then to Manassas, with a shout,
  The army went with Mac, sir,
They found the rebels just stepped out,
  So turned them *back to back*, sir.

Says Mac, "That Johnston is a fox,
  My *will*, sir, does not falter,
But *mud* my transportation blocks,
  It 's best my *plans* to alter.
To float on the Potomac's breast
  Is easier than to walk down,
My heavy guns, and all the rest,
  I 'll ship forthwith to Yorktown."

[1] See McClellan's address to his Army, March 14, 1862.

Then followed.   On the sorry sight
  It will not do to brood, sir ;
One hundred thousand went to fight
  Five thousand with Magruder.
When Mac was ready to begin
  Upon the thirtieth day, sir,
The rebels with a wicked grin
  Walked quietly away, sir.[1]

"Now up, my children, brave and true,"
  Said Mac, "I do intend, sir,
These craven traitors to pursue,
  Unto the bitter end, sir."
Oh! patriots, wrestling with the wrong ;
  Oh! heroes, all sublime ;
Oh! General, valorous and strong,
  Not *now* the appointed time.

What boots your willing sacrifice,
  Your heart's blood flowing free ?—
Alas! ye cannot pay the price
  God asks for victory.
From Williamsburg to Richmond town
  Ye drove the stubborn foe ;
Then all unwillingly sat down,
  Ye could "no farther go."

The fiat had gone forth, but oh!
  Old Jonathan at home, sir,
Did sound afar the glad huzza !
  He thought the end had come, sir ;
And Jeff and crew looked very blue
  And cursed their hapless fate, sir,

---

[1] Yorktown evacuated May 3rd, 1862.

And sent their wives and children to
  A distant rebel State, sir.[1]

Through bolts and bars the tidings wing;
  In Libby, patriots grim, sir,
Spring to their feet, as one they sing
  Aloud their battle hymn,[1] sir.
In Belle Isle too, imprisoned men,·
  Half starved, with hope elated,
Grew patient in their noisome den,
  And for McClellan waited.

They wait till blighted hopes all go,
  They wait McClellan's plan;
They wait till hearts beat faint and low,
  Until their cheeks are wan;
Until their ghastly skeletons,
  The boon no longer crave,
And find their freedom while they wait
  Down in a nameless grave.

[1] See Pollard, I. 322–325; II. 28–31. The panic in Richmond was excessive. Congress adjourned on the 21st April. The rebel officials packed their archives for transportation to Columbia, and sent their families South.

[2] " Glory Hallelujah !" The soul stirring battle-hymn of the Republic, written by Mrs. Dr. Howes.

CHAPTER XV.

Where Mac was carrying out his plan
  On the Peninsula, sir,
And Farragut his cruise began
  There came up from afar sir,
A sound that filled the nation's ear,
  It came from Shiloh's field, sir,
Where Grant surprised, (so rebels say,)
  To furious onslaught yields, sir.[1]

For Beauregard had sworn that night,
  That in the Tennessee, sir,
His horse should drink;—the stream in sight,
  His oath fulfilled may be, sir;
Grant's men are huddled up behind,
  His guns are still before,
If Beauregard don't change his mind
  They 'll die upon the shore.

But, somehow, Grant did never know
  When he was fairly beaten;
When morning broke, and Buell came
  They both rose up to meet, then,
The foe, who flushed with victory,
  The desperate conflict led, sir,
And fought,—till rebels ran away
  And left three thousand dead, sir.

[1] April 6, 1862.

That very day New Madrid Isle [1]
  Succumbed to Captain Foote, sir,
And Pope cut off the rebs' retreat
  And took their guns to boot, sir.
For Bissel's wonderful canal
  That morning navigated,
Revealed to stubborn Island Ten
  How Yankees had checkmated.

Then Foote steamed down the muddy stream,
  To fight the rebel rams,
All plated o'er above, below,
  Just like some iron clams,
Or terrapins with steel clad snouts;
  But Foote has iron walls, sir,
The rebel craft he quickly routs,
  And sinks the monsters all, sir.

And on the day that Mumford swings [2]
  By Butler's stern command, sir,
Our army Yankee Doodle sings
  And down at Memphis lands, sir;
With battles here and battles there,
  War through the land was flying,
And maimed and wounded everywhere,
  And everywhere the dying.

*   *   *   *   *   *

Said Jonathan to Betsey Jane,
  " Go put your bonnet on,
And be all ready for the train,
  That goes to Washington;
Our boys are crippled, bruised, in pain
  They draw their weary breath,

[1] April 7.   [2] April 7, 1862.

Go, nurse them back to hope again,
  Or comfort them in death.

" Tell them their gallant deeds are known
  To all the neighbors round ;
That every battle field has grown
  To be familiar ground ;
That little ones leave off their play
  To hear the thrilling story,
The old men bow themselves to pray
  And give to God the glory."

" Now Jonathan," said Betsey Jane,
  " Our Uncle Sam is kind, sir,
Nor do the gallant boys complain,
  But oh ! it 's in my mind, sir,
That wounded men can hardly take
  Their rations as they come, sir,
We 'd better some small parcels make
  Of ' *something good from home, sir.*' "

Said Jonathan, " For ready wit,
  Give me the womankind, sir ; "
He fumbled in the bureau drawer,
  It was his purse to find, sir ;
" To think," said he, " it 's lying here
  Just like a miser's gold,
When in the field these boys, so dear,
  Are hungry or are cold."

So bag and bundle, box and bales,
  Went lumbering to the front, sir,
Till ready transportation fails.
  Says Jonathan, " I won't, sir,

Submit to this; the remedy
  Is easier than it seems, sir."
He sent to market speedily,
  And bought himself the teams, sir.

Where'er the cannon ploughed the ground,
  Or soldier bore the flag on,
Old Jonathan's "Commissions"[1] found
  A place to dump his wagon.
Where'er one sank in agony,
  Oft 'neath the leaden rain,
Came Betsey Jane, with gentle hand
  To soothe away the pain.

As to and fro the Devil runs,
  He hot displeasure feels,
When at the side of dying ones
  A good man praying kneels.
"That ever I should live to see
  On battle-fields such sights, sir;
These grasping Yankees interfere
  E'en with the Devil's rights, sir."

[1] Sanitary Commission, organized June, 1861. Christian Commission, organized January, 1862.

CHAPTER XVI

THE Scripture saith, "Offence must come,
  But wo to the offender!"
Of spades and mud the boys wrote home,
  The subject soon grew tender.
'Twas getting on towards harvest time,
  The farmers with a shrug, sir,
Did hint, if *digging* was the rhyme,
  Potatoes could be dug, sir.

Old Jonathan is worried out,
  And growls in his displeasure;
And Mac's sound wit begins to doubt:
  He says, that life and treasure
Are wasted by his strategy;
  That *somebody*'s to blame, sir;
He 'll talk to Abe; and speedily
  To Washington he came, sir.

He finds old Abe is sore perplexed,
  And Stanton in a rage;
For Stonewall had been up and vexed
  Our Banks.   He tried to cage
His little army, but it seems
  There 's two ways to defeat, sir;
And Banks brought off his men and teams
  In masterly retreat, sir.

Mac had been crying out for help—
    McDowell must come down, sir,
By steam, the rebs were "*awful*" *strong*,
    'Twixt him and Richmond town, sir.
"Of course I 'll fight," said Little Mac,
    " *Without* McDowell's force ;
I 'll close right here my sad career,
    Or vindicate my course."[1]

Abe sent McDowell down by land,
    But just before he started
Bold Stonewall moved out *his* command,
    And Mac's bright hopes departed.
He got another note from Abe,
    Before the day was ended ;[2]
The order for McDowell's move
    Had been, Abe said, suspended.

Banks was at Strasburg with his troops,
    Six thousand men all told, sir ;
Fremont at Franklin o'er the ridge,[3]
    Then Stonewall Jackson bold, sir,
A bird's-eye view took of the case,
    "At Fredericksburg," quoth he,
"McDowell plans a southward race,
    Mac wants his company.

"I think I 'll veto that device,"
    He gathered up his ranks ;

---

[1] "But in any event, I shall fight with all the skill, caution and determination which I possess, and I trust that the result may either obtain for me the permanent confidence of my Government, or that it may close my career."—*McClellan's Dispatch, May* 21, 1862.

[2] May 24, 1862.

[3] Shenandoah mountains, seventy miles from Banks.

And from New Market, in a trice,
   Went out to settle Banks.
He swept off Kenly,[1] hastened on,
   To get on Banks' rear, sir,
And cut him off from Winchester ;—
   'Twas growing very clear, sir,

That Banks was in a dangerous place ;
   But Banks was far from blind, sir ;
He started at a rapid pace,
   And Stonewall soon did find, sir,
There was n't much to gain from him
   Who could so quickly rally,
And chase, and race, and fight his way
   Straight down the fatal valley.

Banks with his brave six thousand men,
   Brings off his guns and teams
In spite of twenty thousand rebs
   And interposing streams.
He crosses the Potomac,[2] and
   Bold Stonewall says his prayer
On t 'other side, quite satisfied
   With glory for his share.

McDowell's force and Fremont's troops
   His stroke has neutralized, sir ;
And he 's advised in Washington
   Old Abe is paralyzed, sir.
'Tis true, he has hot work at best,
   In beating *his* retreat ;
He trembles, as he hurries, lest[3]
   Fremont and Shields should meet

[1] At Front Royal.　　[2] On the 26th May, 1862, at Williamsport, Md.
[3] He rested but a single day, and had divine service performed in his camp, and started back the 29th May.

And fall upon him.   But they don't—
  It 's too late to complain, sir ;
But, oh ! the many mysteries
  Of that ill-starred campaign, sir ;
Abe Lincoln said, "Though it might read
  As glorious in the books,
That Banks should make such wondrous speed,
  He didn't like the looks."

Said Stanton, "I shall telegraph
  The capital 's in danger,
We have n't troops enough, by half,
  To check that Jackson ranger."
Said Jonathan, "The troops will come,
  There is no doubt of *that*, sir ;
Although *you can't use what you have*,   .
  And that 's the truth out flat, sir.

"You 've quite too many heads, Old Abe,
  Too many politicians ;
Among them all you 're but a babe.
  I have my strong suspicions
You 're being used for party ends."
  Says Lincoln, "How is that, sir ?"
Says Jonathan, "When mice abound,
  It 's wise to keep a cat, sir.

"There 's mice and rats a-gnawing at
  The vitals of this nation ;
Upon her blood they 're growing fat.
  This scum of God's creation
Would dance and grin, though any day
  A battle should come off, in
The country's death, so 'it would pay'
  In *contract* for the coffin.

"And Lincoln, other rats are they
  Who 'rally round the flag,' sir,
And let our treasures slip away,
  And guard the *empty bag*, sir;
And some who stand quite *at the head*
  And talk of Revolution,
And would put treason snug to bed
  Within the CONSTITUTION.

"And Abe, *you're* trying to keep in
  . Beneath that coverlid, sir,
With stretching it is worn *so thin*
  It's long now since it hid, sir,
The country's sore; the gaping rent
  The rebels made with ball, sir,
You cannot mend, although you've sent
  Old Hunter to the wall, sir." [1]

"What can I do?" said Honest Abe,
  "You're drifting fast to leeward."
Said Jonathan,—"Your pilots wise
  (I don't refer to Seward,)
Are letting drift the ship of state
  In sight of Bunker's steeple;
Drift, Abraham, as sure as fate,
  Away behind the people!

"You've got to march, sir, at the head
  Of this determined nation,
Or you had better far be dead
  Down at Manassas Station."
"I'd give my life, if that would do,"
  Said Abram, with a glance, sir,

---

[1] Hunter's proclamation of emancipation, repudiated by the President May 19, 1862.

So sorrowful—" but still I 'll tend
　　The rebs a final chance, sir.[1]

" The nation's crazed with wars alarms,
　　I 'd sound a *parley* now, sir,
Perhaps the rebs will ground their arms
　　If I can show them how, sir;
As things now stand 'tis best for all
　　To arbitrate by law, sir.
To pay for slaves, dear Jonathan,
　　Is cheaper much than war, sir."

Growled Jonathan, "I wonder if
　　Old Abe and sense have parted?"
Then choking down his little miff,
　　He said, " He 's chicken hearted;
I 'll go back home, and nudge the folks,
　　We 'll keep it in the dark, sir,
'Twill take an awful sight of steam
　　To tow Abe to the mark, sir."

[1] See Lincoln's message to Congress, March 6, 1862.

5*

CHAPTER XVII.

Meantime the rain came down and mado
  A river of the plain, sir,
Destroyed the bridges, and so cut
  Mac's army into twain, sir;
The rebs who never have "a plan,"
  And never, sir, are lazy,
Caught up their guns, in columns ran
  Right down upon Old Casey.[1]

Mac sound asleep on 'tother side
  Hears something of a rattle,
And his balloon sends up to get
  The tidings of the battle.
"'Twas clear," he said, "that Casey had
  Made most disgraceful fight, sir,[2]
And well nigh caused *my* ruin,"—ho
  To Washington did write, sir.

Next day ho rodo upon the field
  His generals had won, sir;
Ten thousand dead and wounded lay
  Beneath that Sabbath sun, sir.
And foremost in the battle-ground
  And trampled in the dust, sir,
Were General Casey's soldiers found
  Dead, with the bayonet thrust, sir!

[1] Fair Oaks, May 31, 1862.   [2] See McClellan's dispatches.

Mac didn't follow up the foe,
  And fight him man to man, sir,
He could not then to Richmond go,[1]
  For why? he had "*a plan,*" sir.
His troops were tired, and besides,
  Not half were o'er the streams,
He'll move them when the flood subsides,
  And liberates his teams.

Day after day the army lies
  Right in the broiling heat,
Day after day a hundred dies,
  'Twas worse than a defeat,
They say Mac's plans were very deep,
  They're deep enough in blood, sir,
And one would think just now they sleep
  Deep in a bed of mud, sir.

The "troops were where he wanted them,"
  Mac said in his dispatch,
But recently he *counted* them
  He thought they were no match,
In numbers for secesh; he said,
  His plans he would *mature,*
If Abe would send him ten brigades,
  To make the victory sure.

Now Abe between two fires exposed,
  Sat still and vacillated:

---

[1] "When the enemy had retreated after the battle of Fair Oaks, what military reason was there for not immediately following them to Richmond?"—"I know of none." * * * "I do believe that if the General had crossed the Chickahominy with the residue of the army, and made a general attack with his whole force, we could have carried Richmond."—*Testimony of General Sumner.*

To Peter pay by robbing Paul
    He couldn't choose, so waited.
"I'd send to Mac, but then," thought he,
    "The capital might fall, sir,
Then Jonathan is pushing me—
    I'll send Mac down McCall,"[1] sir.

But while Mac sowed his men in mud,
    Expecting them to grow;
Jeb Stuart took a little turn[2]
    His cavalry to show.
All round about McClellan's camp
    He rode a Gilpin race, sir;
Said Mac, "I find this ground is damp,
    I think I'll change my base, sir."

He Casey sent to pack his trunks,[3]
    All ready for the move,
Poor Mac! the rebs won't give him time,
    But most harassing prove;
Bold Stonewall hurls his columns down,
    And Lee from Richmond rides, sir,
To end the war and victory crown,
    With humbled Yankee pride, sir.

Seven days of onslaught and of rout,
    Seven days of untold slaughter,
Seven dreadful days of death, dealt out
    By bay'net, gun, and mortar.
Each morn the rebels massed their troops,
    Each morn McClellan stood,

---

[1] McCall's division of 11,000 men. McClellan's army was then over 100,900 men.

[2] On the 15th of June, 1862,

[3] Gen. Casey appointed 23d June to superintend the removal of stores, etc., from White House, prior to McClellan's change of base.

Fought manfully until the night,
    Then fell back through the wood.

On! wearied men, the James is nigh,
    Where Abram's boats are lying;
Their guns all shotted, and on high
    An untrailed flag is flying;
Oh! patriots, why *from* victory
    Should ye be falling back, sirs?
An echo comes responsively
    " Three cheers for Little Mac, sirs."

Mac placed his cannon on a hill
    And went away to wait,[1].
Then Lee came up with ready will;
    Magruder was not late,
He only stopped to deal his men
    Out whisky and gunpowder,
Then up the hill with horrid yell
    To meet a roar still louder.

For Mac's great guns roared out like fiends
    And mowed the rebs in rows,
Magruder staggers,—rallies, and
    Straight up the hill he goes.
Not far,—Old Sumner[2] is at bay,
    His cannon cut down deep
And merciless, as wears the day
    The hill grows slippery steep.

---

[1] " Gen. McClellan had deemed it necessary to go down to Harrison's Landing to determine on the point to which the troops were to retire."

[2] " I therefore found myself, by virtue of my seniority of rank, in command of the army, without having been invested formally with that command or having received any instructions in relation to it."—*Testimony of Gen. Sumner before Congressional Committee.*

“ 'Tis madness sheer,” at last cries Lee,
 “ 'Tis folly to attack;
Hell might be stormed as easily
 Go, call Magruder back.”
Back rolled the seething sullen tide
 Of that great human sea,
And left its dead strewn far and wide
 And,—Little Mac breathed free.

Breathed free! why not? his troops had won
 Another hard fought fight.[1]
And he was safe once more, but still
 Before he slept that night,
To make quite sure, he bade his troops
 To fall some seven miles back,
Then on his gunboat, duty done,
 To bed went Little Mac.

His worn out men dispirited
 To Harrison's retreated;
They hardly knew if they had been
 Triumphant or defeated;
One thing pressed home with certainty,
 Their toil it scarcely lightened,
They'd learned these last few bloody days
 Their General was frightened.[2]

  * * * * * *

'Twas here Count This and Baron That,
 And Prince the other thing,

---

[1] See McClellan's dispatches of that date.

[2] Gen. McClellan posted the troops in the morning, and then went off to his headquarters and we did not see anything more of him.”— *Testimony of Gen. Heintzelman before Committee on Conduct of the War.*

Slipped from McClellan's staff in haste,
  And for the North took wing.
They 'd come to learn the art of war
  From our immortal chief;
They 'd read him through—but *Abe* had still
  To turn another leaf.

CHAPTER XVIII.

OLD Jonathan had waited long,
   His *boys* he still could trust, sir,
Thought he, Old Abe is getting strong,
   And Mac is more than bluster.
He 's worked up close to Richmond's walls,
   What if he has been slow, sir?
He 's *sure*, hurrah! for Mac, he 's got
   But five miles more to go, sir.

I 'll send to town,—next week 's the Fourth;[1]
   We 'll joyful celebrate, sir,
The Stars and Stripes ere that, will float
   In every rebel State, sir;
So Jonathan sent up to town,
   And ordered lots of rockets
And fireworks to be sent straight down—
   He didn't spare his pockets.

The rockets came, but Jonathan
   Had somehow lost his spirit,
There was a sudden lull of news,—
   Said Jonathan, "I fear it
Portends a storm,—'tis very strange,
   The telegraph's unbroken.
'Good news flies fast,' this silence doth
   No victory betoken."

[1] July 4, 1862.

(112)

Hour after hour they watched the wires,
    At last the message came,
Old Jonathan's strong faith ne'er tires,
    They heard him but exclaim,
"*Just God!*" "*Just God!*" then turning straight,
    " Good folks," said he, " don't weep, sirs ;
God's time ain't come ;—be still and wait,
    The fireworks—they will keep, sirs."

But Jonathan to Abram wrote :
    " 'Tis hard not to complain, sir,
The news such wantonness denote ;
    My boys ! dead all in vain, sir ;
Dismay and doubt are gathering fast,
    And hope almost departed,
The future will be like the past,
    I own I am down hearted."

Said Abraham, " We 'll live and learn,
    And every error mend, sir ;
To-morrow a new leaf I 'll turn,
    I 'll straight for Halleck send, sir ;[1]
Dear Jonathan, 'twill never do
    To give up to depression ;
Just send me down a quota new
    To crush out this secession."

Stout Jonathan called on his boys,
    He found them *not* so willing ;
For some held back, and made a noise
    About the wholesale killing ;
Some swore at Stanton, and hurrahed
    With the McClellan party,

[1] Halleck appointed General-in-Chief on July 11, 1862.

And some cried shame, and while they sparred
  The rebs were waxing hearty.

And British sympathizers were
  All barking in accord, sir;[1]
For in perverted garbled guise
  The news had gone abroad, sir;
And hints that looked like threats came back
  Across the briny water,
That Johnny Bull his brains did rack
  To "stop the horrid slaughter."

And Jonathan had some bad boys,
  Unfriendly to the cause, sir;
They rallied now, and raised a cry
  Of "Union as it was," sir.[2]
They said the war perverted was
  If Sambo lost his collar;
They would n't "give another man,
  And not another dollar."

Said Jonathan, "My lads, look here,
  You set of wretched shirks!
Your miserable rebel souls
  You 'd bolster with such quirks.
'Tis such as you more mischief do
  Than Stonewall on the border.
To block your, game, you coward crew,
  A speedy *draft* I 'll order."

[1] 9th July, 1862. Public meetings in England called on the Government to mediate, and, if necessary, to acknowledge the independence of the South.

[2] At New York a meeting was held at Cooper Institute, responsive to a call addressed to those who desired the *Union as it was*. Speeches by J. Brooks, Fernando Wood, Wickliff, of Ky., and others.

Then Congress, just to show the rebs
  This spunky Yankee nation
Ain't scared at trifles, made by law
  An Act of Confiscation.[1]
The very day the Bill was passed,
  (I don't know that he waited,)
Three thousand slaves, at Vicksburg held,
  Ben Butler confiscated.[2]

And volunteers sprang into life,
  The quota far above, sir;
Said Jonathan, "We'll end this strife
  If Abe takes off his gloves, sir."
He sent a message then to Abe,
  That *all means* coming handy
To throttle treason, must be used
  By Yankee Doodle Dandy.

So Abraham sits down and dreams—
  Said he, "Thus far I *can* go—
When Jonathan tells me of means,
  He must refer to Sambo.
Well, if my generals like the plan,
  One thing is pretty clear, sir,
If Sambo *wants* to be a man
  I shall not interfere, sir.

"With what I want, and what I feel,
  I must not hold communion,
The object paramount to me,
  Is to restore the Union.[3]

---

[1] Passed the Senate 12th July, 1862.
[2] General Butler confiscated 3,000 slaves employed on the Vicksburg Canal.
[3] See President Lincoln's reply to Horace Greeley, August 22, 1861.

If I can compass best the end
  By freeing all the slaves, sir,
I 'll free them *all ;* if slavery
  Will help the cause to save, sir,

" I 'll save the cause *with* slavery ;
  Or if by war's coercion
A *part* be freed, and Union saved,
  Why, then, I 'll free a portion.
Poor Sambo's fate doth trouble me,
  It 's heavy on my soul, sir,
But just as far as I can see,
  It 's out of *my* control, sir."

Meanwhile Mac's army on the James
  So worn and decimated,
Sat down to wonder who to blame,
  And reinforcements waited.
"I've fifty thousand men," Mac said,
  "I've counted them all o'er, sir;"
Abe figured up the lists, and made
  Out thirty thousand *more*, sir.

*   *   *   *   *   *

Jeff quickly counted up *his* cost;
  Said he, "I well divine, sir,
The Yanks have played their trump and lost;
  Now Lee call out in line, sir,
Your invalids—those skulking ones
  Into the ranks must go, sir;
Each man who can support a gun,
  Whether he will or no, sir.

"If ever we're to strike a blow,
  'Tis now when Abe's surprised, sir,
By Mac's defeat; his army lies
  So much demoralized, sir,
That Mac must spend a month or two
  In getting it in order.
Besides, we'll strike beyond *his* reach,
  I mean, we'll cross the border.

"The war, so far on our own soil,
  A dreadful price is costing;
The drain, in fact, as all can see,
  Is perfectly exhausting.
Kentucky lies beneath the heel
  Of despot Abe, now quaking;
Her garners bursting full of grain,
  Are ready for our taking.

"I'll change my programme, Mr. Lee,
  Since you the change advise, sir;
We'll take the *war to Africa,*
  Take Abram by surprise, sir."
The rebs with Jeff do sympathize,
  His army soon quadruples;
For wrong will always energize—
  The Devil has no scruples.

*   *   *   *   *   *

Now Halleck straight from Corinth come,
  Soon finds out Lee's intention.
To meet the case he sent for Pope,
  Then ordered a suspension
Of Mac's great plan. "Your men we need
  To keep the rebels down, sir,"
He wrote to Mac; "so make all speed
  And bring your troops to town, sir."[1]

Now Mac could fight or run away—
  Could talk with any man;
But when it came *just to obey,*
  It was n't in his plan.
To Halleck's order much opposed
  He still *his* plan advised, sir;

---

[1] Halleck ordered the evacuation of the Peninsula, August 3, 1862.

And wrote for reinforcements, or
    He would be sacrificed,[1] sir.

"Good Heavens!" roared Stanton, in a rage,
    "With Lee upon our border
With full one hundred thousand men,
    Mac disobeys this order!
Pope's forty thousand men are all
    Between Lee and the town, sir?"
"Tut, tut!" said Abe, "he'll surely come,
    The transports have gone down, sir.

"It's but ten days since Halleck wrote,[2]
    He'll start now by and by, sir.
Do keep the peace, or his key-note
    Old Jonathan will cry, sir;
Pope's active, and he will hold out
    And keep himself from harm, sir,
'Till Mac comes up,—for pity's sake
    Don't Jonathan alarm, sir."

Out rode Pope headlong, *on* his head,
    ("Headquarters in the saddle,")
His novel horsemanship soon led
    Him into a skedaddle.
Lee's tattered veterans, like a blast,
    Sweep everything aside,
They cross the Rapidan.   In vain
    Pope tries to stem the tide.

He struggles, and with longing eye
    Looks out for Little Mac, sir.[3]

[1] On the 4th August McClellan protested against the withdrawal of his army from the Peninsula, as a fatal measure.

[2] Evacuation of Harrison's Landing completed August 16, 1862.

[3] Gen. McClellan's army commenced arriving at Alexandria, Va., August 22, 1862.

He spies at length Old Heintzelman
  And Porter at his back, sir.[1]
Then over sanguine, Pope cries out,
  "They 're coming all! I see, sir,
We 've got the rebs," he telegraphs
  To Abe, "*a victory, sir.*"

The telegram came quick to town,
  But Pope came most as fast.
The Second Bull Run battle turned
  Out very like the last ;
Pope left his cannon and his dead
  Upon the battle field,
And back to Centreville he led
  His troops all scorched and peeled.[2]

Said Jonathan to Betsey Jane,
  "There is a dreadful stint
Of things they need in hospital—
  They 're sending out for lint.[3]
Just call the children in from play
  And lay aside your sewing,
We 've been asleep until to-day,
  And treason has been growing.

"Whatever hand can find to do,
  Or tongue can find to say,
To help the cause—the task anew
  Commences from to day ;

---

[1] Heintzelman and Porter reinforced Pope at Warrenton Junction
on August 26, 1862.

[2] On August 30, 1862.

[3] Surgeon-General Hammond telegraphed to Governor Andrew for
lint and bandages. It is calculated that enough of the latter was sent
to swathe the whole army, *à la* mummy.

Henceforth we falter not, we swear
  By those we love that bleed, sirs,
To crush this hellish treason out
  In spite of our poor leaders."

'Tis said McClellan's officers,
  His wounded pride to plaster,
Their prophesies of evil found
  Fulfilled in Pope's disaster.
Some would n't serve except with Mac,
  One wrote—('twas strange he dared, sir,)
Pope might get out of his own scrape,
  For anything he cared, sir.[1]

Pope came out of his scrape (long since
  His blunders were retrieved, sir;)
Of his command, what there was left,
  He asked to be relieved, sir.[2]
And Abraham—what could he do,
  On all sides thus check-mated?
To Mac the army would be true,
  So Mac he reinstated.[3]

Old Stanton growled and Halleck winced,
  And some said a court-martial
Was Mac's desert; but Abraham flinched
  And thought himself impartial.
Said he, "The greatest general
  Mac *may* be or may *not*, sir,
At all events, the army thinks
  He is the best I 've got, sir."

[1] Bonner's History, page 157.
[2] September 3, 1862.
[3] Gen. McClellan took the field, Sept. 7, 1862.

6

Mac's troops were scattered far and wide,
  He got them well in hand, sir.
While Lee upon the other side
  One anxious moment stands, sir;
"To cross, or not to cross," said he,
  "That is the mooted query,—
I'll dare! my men are full of pluck,
  But then they're dreadful weary.

"There are no soldiers on the route,
  The big militia rabble
That Abraham has trotted out
  Will make a homeward scrabble
At sight of our brave boys in grey;
  Their unprotected cattle
We'll gather up and drive away,
  And with the land do battle.

"Each blade of grass that fire can touch
  Is ripe for the occasion,
We'll teach the Pennsylvania Dutch
  The beauties of invasion;
They have no negroes in the State,
  Their grain can all be spilled, sir,
There's many ways to confiscate,
  Their cattle can be killed, sir.

"The Central Railroad can be cut,
  And bridges can be dropped,
And Washington left in the cold,
  With reinforcements stopped;
With fire in front and fire in rear,
  As can be in a trice, sir,
We'd have, as surely would appear,
  The Yankees in a vice, sir."

So Lee rode out in bold array
   Across Potomac's river,
He told his men he went to stay,
   The wretched to deliver;
That Maryland was crushed to earth,
   Although the truth to grant, he
Of pigs and poultry saw no dearth,
   But then her rights were scanty.

He wrote and printed as he went
   A proclamation grand, sir;
He said his army had been sent
   To succor Maryland, sir;[1]
He told the people they were bound,
   Degraded and oppressed,
That he had travelled that way round
   To see their wrongs redressed.

"My Maryland," most strange to say,
   Responded to Lee's call, sir,
In rather a cool sort of way.
   She wa'n't oppressed at all, sir,
She didn't like this sort of talk;
   That he was quite mistaken;
And from the State he 'd better walk,
   And let alone her bacon.

Militia men were out to ride,
   They didn't like secession,
Their bread wa'n't buttered on *that* side;
   In fact, Abe had possession
Of all their hearts, and they woould fight
   The Union to maintain, sir,

[1] Issued 8th September, from Frederick, Maryland.

That now they had set Lee aright
  He might ride back again, sir.

But Lee went on; they closed behind
  Militia volunteers, sir,
And veterans with Bull Run begrimed,
  Till Lee begins to fear, sir,
Some interference may take place
  With his communication,
He turns about—Good heavens! to face
  Th' entire Yankee nation.

Down on the rebs McClellan swoops,
  Lee fights him at Antietam;[1]
His troops were brave, but then you see,
  The *boys* were there to meet them.
Brave men! the country cries, huzza!
  Lee's troopers homeward go, sir,
And Abram asks of Stanton, if
  He thinks McClellan *slow*, sir.

*   *   *   *   *   *

The rebs went sad from Maryland,
  But made themselves quite merry
With what Stonewall, and his bold band
  Took out of Harper's Ferry.[2]
Old Jonathan " begrudged " the loss,
  'Twas anything but small, sir;
'Twas " shiftless," traitorous, a crime,
  That such a place should fall, sir.

---

[1] September 17, 1862.

[2] Harper's Ferry surrendered to rebel Gen. Jackson, Sept. 15, 1862. 10,500 men surrendered with forty-seven pieces of artillery and a vast amount of stores.

CHAPTER XX

As Lee crossed into Maryland
  Bragg, equally as lucky,
Did start to lead his ragged band
  Across oppressed Kentucky.[1]
His plan,—to strike Ohio's line,
  And grab at Cincinnati,
Enticed by smell of well-cured swine
  And other things as fatty—

Was just as good a plan as Lee's,
  Both founded on delusion,
For Old Kentuck, who'd learned to see,
  Resented the intrusion.
When Bragg proclaimed that he had come[2]
  According to their wish, he
Found out they cheered for Abraham,
  And brought out their militia.

Bragg, not so mild a man as Lee,
  At this grew desperate, sir,
He couldn't rule, "Well then," said he,
  "I'll *plunder* the old State, sir."
His men rob here, and they rob there,
  All unopposed the while, sir,

[1] Mumfordsville, Ky., surrendered to Bragg September 17, 1862.
[2] General Bragg issued his proclamation September 18, 1862.

And gather up a plunder train
    Extending forty miles, sir.

Bragg starts in haste for Louisville
    To get a-head of Buell,
A day too late, the scamp has met
    A disappointment cruel,
Militia swarm about the place,
    With regulars to lead them ;
The rebs begin a backward race
    With Buell now to speed them.

They have a brush at Perryville[1]
    With Buell's cavalry, sir,
And both sides claimed, and do claim still,
    A splendid victory, sir ;
One thing is certain, Bragg got off[2]
    With all his plunder train, sir,
And Abram gave a nervous cough—
    It went against his grain, sir,

To have two Generals at once
    Protested as *too slow*, sir ;
And Rosecrans some ready wit
    At Corinth once did show, sir,[3]
So Rosecrans took Buell's troops[4]
    Which somebody had drilled, sir,
With promises we soon shall see
    How well they were fulfilled, sir.

[1] October 8, 1862.

[2] Bragg entered Tennessee without opposition on November 22, 1862.

[3] Battle of Corinth commenced October 3, 1862; rebels numbered 38,000, Rosecrans's forces not over 20,000. The rebs were defeated and pursued forty miles in force and sixty miles with cavalry.

[4] November 30, 1862.

CHAPTER XXI.

While Mac sits down, as sit he will,
   Exhausted by exertion,
And Uncle Sam foots up the bill,
   We'll, just for our diversion,
Run guard across the picket line,
   And where Mac will not come, sir—
We'll go across the battle field
   And chase the rebels home, sir.

Jeff Davis sits upon his throne
   In a splint-bottomed chair, sir,
His eyes have dim and hollow grown
   And streaked is his hair, sir;
Around him group the rebels wise
   Who make his Cabinet,
The men who ways and means devise
   In solemn conclave met.

"The news at home is all we wish,
   That is to say, it's better,"
Said Jeff, "and as to things abroad
   I've got a foreign letter.
It seems that our affairs have made
   A palpable sensation,
In fact, I think the train is laid
   To *recognise* our nation."

"But things go slow on t' other side,
   We run while they but walk, sir ;
In Parliament, the other day,
   They had a little talk, sir,
Our side, Old Gregory, and such,
   Have stakes upon the winning ;
The talk did not amount to much,
   'Twas good for a beginning.

"Lord Brougham got up and made a speech,[1]
   He said 'There was no law, sir,
In all the land, that he could reach,
   To meddle with our war, sir ;
Most dreadful crimes were perpetrated,
   The conflict ought to cease,
The state of things he deprecated,
   And would do much for peace.

"'That slavery was horrid, he
   Had long ago confessed, sir ;
But still the Northern remedy
   He thought was not the best, sir ;
The whites would suffer by the war
   More than the negroes had, sir ;
The strife was very mischievous,
   In every phase was bad, sir.'

"Then Mr. Lindsley[2] rose and said,
   'That it was his intention,
By most unselfish motive led,
   To urge an intervention ;
He thought the States Confederate
   Deserved his approbation,

[1] In the House of Lords, June, 1862.
[2] July 18, 1862.

'Twas difficult to overrate
  Their grim determination.

" 'Their independence (*great applause*)
  So far they had maintained ;
And he considered that their cause
  Was just as good as gained.'
Said Mr. Gregory, 'The South
  On her side is for right ;
The North, moved only by revenge,
  Has nothing else in sight.'

"Quoth Palmerston, 'I hope the House
  Will vote itself content
To leave the subject in dispute
  Unto the Government.'
So Gregory deferred the task,
  'Twas useless, he foresaw, sir ;
And Lindsley did permission ask
  His motion to *withdraw*, sir."

*   *   *   *   *

Said Jeff, "Why don't Old Mason try
  The dodge so pop'lar here,—
Get up mass meetings, raise a cry,
  And *pay* the crowd to cheer ?"
"They tried that, Jeff, in Manchester,
  The craven-hearted crowd there,
Starving for lack of cotton, sir,
  Roared out for Abe so loud there—

"That little Vic in London heard,
  And wiped her weeping eyes,
And bade her Lords (a thing absurd)
  A little plan devise ;
        6*

A plan that never could have sprung
  In any other head, sir :
It was to stop their foolish mouths
  By filling them with bread, sir."

Said Regan, "What Floyd prophesied
  Has happened true, indeed ;
As well depend on England as
  Upon a broken reed.
Her forfeiting our confidence
  Is not so much through knavery ;
Her hands are tied, to all intents,
  She daren't support our slavery.

"How would it do if Mason should,
  In short, insinuate, sir,
That things were ripe (an idea good)
  For a Protectorate, sir?
Republics (on that point agreed)
  Have proved to be but failures ;
A Monarchy (by her own creed)
  Would cure our chronic ailures.

" Well that might have a little weight
  With England ; but there 's France, sir ;
Her power to help us is too great
  To risk upon that chance, sir.
Besides, we dar'n't in good faith yet
  Propose this wise solution ;
The people still have strength to fret
  And foment revolution."

Said Jeff, "What can be Nap's intent,
  Old 'Thouvenal was dry ?"[1]

[1] A letter to the *Mobile Register*, of 13th March, says " The Southern

So Slidell wrote, the day he went,
  His sentiments to try.
'Tis very strange, events turn out
  For this Confederation,
So different in all respects
  From wisest calculation."

Said Benjamin, " These foreign powers
  Are watching General Lee, sir ;
Their blood is not so hot as ours,
  They wait a victory, sir.
To make them sure our cause is just
  We must make Abram bleed, sir ;
They don't take principles on trust,
  We 're right if we succeed, sir.

" Napoleon has eagle eyes,
  He looks for our resources ;
And I 'll be bound he 's weighing now
  Both ours and Abram's forces.
Whichever way the things may turn,
  His plan will cost much labor ;
He still has many things to learn
  If he 's to be our neighbor.

Munroe's old doctrine troubles him ;
  In case our cause is lost, sir,
Why, Mexico 's a Tartar grim ;
  He 'll find out to his cost, sir,
That Jonathan, if he whips us,
  No idle words will bandy ;
O'er all this continent he 'll play
  His Yankee Doodle Dandy."

Commissioners are greatly dispirited at the reception which M. Thou.
venal gave Mr. Slidell.''

"Good heavens! one would think," cried Jeff,
    You were a Union man, sir—
WE WHIPPED! and *our cause* LOST. Why zounds!
    There is no power that *can*, sir,
Subdue the South. Our cause is *won!*
    The enemy at bay, sir,
With grave dissensions in his camp,
    Grows weaker every day, sir."

Said Walker, "Drafts are very close,
    And rations *very* small, sir,
And fever raging, and no dose
    Of quinine, none at all, sir."
Said Mallory, "And the blockade
    Is growing very tight, sir;
It's dreadful risk, I've heard it said,
    To run it day or night, sir.

"The Florida[1] has just got in
    By dint of desperate zeal, sir,
And lies all bruised and battered in
    The harbor of Mobile, sir.
Our privateers do well enough,
    They've cleared th' Atlantic route, sir;
And captured lots of Yankee stuff,
    But then it's all *kept out*, sir."

"Well, well," said Jeff, "our friends abroad
    At every foreign court,
(I won't include the Czar's,) you know,
    Will never grudge a *port.*
John Bull has more at stake than we,
    He'll help us in this scrape, sir;

[1] September 4, 1862.

Look at the splendid ships he sends
  All fitted in fine shape, sir,

" With guns and ammunition, manned
  By British sailors bold, sir ;
He 's something new upon the stocks ;
  Whenever we 've the gold, sir,
He 'll send us navies, fleets of rams,
  (But this is not to mention,)
My information comes direct
  That this is his intention.

" Earl Russell did a clever thing,[1]
  The Yankees have their master,
And Seward will have need of skill
  To make a soothing plaster
For Abraham's sensibility,
  And Jonathan's back bone, sir,
When Semmes the Alabama sails
  A privateer full grown, sir."

Said Memminger, " In my strong box
  Our money safe doth lie, sir ;
Nice printed notes, a mine of wealth,
  If there was aught to buy, sir.
I need a coat, and so do you,
  And Jeff I 'm *not* in fun, sir,
What Benjamin has said is true,
  And something must be done, sir.

" Our friends up North are rising now,"
  Said Jeff, " there 's help at hand, sir,

---

[1] When minister Adams complained of the building of the Florida at
Liverpool Lord Russel said that she was being built for the Italians.

There 's many a foe in Abram's camp,
    And many a secret band, sir,
At work for us,—to undermine
    The sanguine Yankee nation,
We 'll make, when all our plans combine,
    A startling demonstration.

" They don't just like to show their hand
    Until they have good hold, sir,
They hesitate to take a stand,
    Success will make them bold, sir ;
This negro question soon will give
    A chance for an attack, sir,
They 'll use to purpose for our cause
    Abe's Habeas Corpus Act, sir."

Said Memminger, "I read last night
    That Foote—sly as a mouse, sir,
Had made, if I have read aright,
    And pressed it on the House, sir,
A motion, it comes in so well
    If you are so agreed, sir,
'Tis printed in the *Daily Whig,*
    I 'll from the paper read, sir.

" 'Resolved, that Providence Divine
    Continuing to bless
Our arms, for several months now past
    With eminent success ;
That the Confederate Government
    With strength on the increase, sir,
Would be most fully justified
    In fixing terms of peace, sir.'"

"That's good!" in chorus roared the whole
  Of this vile traitorous clan, sir.
"*So true!*" cried Reagan (postmaster);
  "Foote is a useful man, sir;
But *we* all know there's much to do
  Before our troubles end, sir;
Contingencies to struggle through,
  And broken plans to mend, sir.

"There's still one other thing to try
  Our desperate cause to save, sir,
'Twill golden commendations buy—
  Emancipate the slave, sir."
"EMANCIPATE!" roared out King Jeff,
  "Knock out our corner stone!"
"EMANCIPATE!" cried Memminger,
  In a lugubrious tone.

"*Emancipate!* why that's the cause
  Of all our tribulation,
The ground of our secession was
  The ghost emancipation."
"Well, well, the ghost will be a fact,
  Or I'm not wise at all, sir,
'Tis policy for us to act,
  And *Yankee Abe forestall*, sir.

"We can't make other people's eyes;
  The eyes, Jeff, of the masses,
Don't see things of a proper size—
  We must provide them glasses;
They don't like slavery 'tis clear,
  There's something in a name, sir,
Just change it, Jeff, the thing itself
  Will always be the same, sir.

Whoever in this mortal strife
  First writes the one word 'FREE'
Upon their flag,—of Johnny Bull
  Will have the sympathy.
Old Abe stands in the Yankees' light ;
  The phantom Constitution
Will soon be laid—another fight
  Will banish that illusion."

"If I thought *that*," said Jeff, "I'd play
  My card upon the instant,
But, bless my soul! what could I say
  To make it seem consistent?"
"Why, you forget, we always said
  That England might rely
Upon our honor, that the slave
  We'd free, sir, by and by.

"That 't wa'n't expedient at first,
  The thought to entertain;
But deference to England's views
  Our people does constrain,
To sacrifice the right divine.
  And Jeff, look, here's a pen, sir,—
To see how such a thing would read,
  Just write a specimen, sir."

Jeff half in earnest, in a trice
  Took up a brownish sheet,
And wrote according to advice,
  And logically neat ;
The while his fellow traitors sat
  In mocking speculation,
Of how Old Abe would look upon
  Jeff's Freedom Proclamation.

Jeff finished and threw down his quill,
  He looked somewhat excited;
Said he, "How feeble is man's will;
  We mortals how short-sighted!
What none could guess one year ago
  This paper doth reveal,
Our desperate shift,—here, Benjamin,
  Put on the official seal."

[The seal was something just got up
  In "Congress," lately met, sir;
A grey-back in the foreground stood
  A-charging bayonet, sir;
Behind, a woman and a child
  Just coming out of church,
With hands upraised, as if the reb
  Had left them in the lurch.

The background was a sun rampant
  Just over a plantation;
A wreath around the whole, composed
  Of products of the nation;
Of sugar-cane, tobacco, rice
  And cotton in profusion;
The margin bore the gay device—
" *Our Homes and Constitution.*]

As Benjamin took up the wax
  And lit a tallow candle,
There was a movement at the door,
  A turning of the handle.
A voice called, "Jeff, do let me in,
  My entrance do not hinder;
With none to send, I came myself;
  It's I, sir—General Winder."[1]

   [1] Commandant of Department of Richmond.

"Come in," said Jeff, "what is the news?
  Is 't something from the front, sir?"
Old Winder turns the quid he chews,
  And gives an awkward grunt, sir.
Said he, "King Jeff, the slaves in town
  Have got some news, I swear, sir;
In groups they 're walking up and down
  With most mysterious air, sir.

"They look exactly as they did
  Sometime in April last ;
They got before us *then* the news
  The District Bill was passed.
I cannot, for the life of me,
  Get hold of any clue, sir;
But here 's a note from Ould, just come,
  I 've brought, King Jeff, for you, sir."

Jeff tore it open, quickly scanned,
  And passed it to another ;
Dead silence fell upon the band
  As each essayed to smother
His deep emotion, as he reads
  The "Clownish Yankee nation
Has made, once more, the better speed,
  And *won*—'The proclamation.'"

Ould wrote "The truce-boat had come in
  With papers which he reckoned
King Jeff might like to see ; they were
  All dated *twenty-second.*"[1]
He called attention to the fact
  There was a proclamation

---

[1] September 22, a preliminary Proclamation of Emancipation was issued.

Just issued by the despot Abe,
  Of full emancipation.

Jeff raised *his* luckless document,
  The candle still was lighted ;
He put the paper in the blaze,
  And one more scheme was blighted.
He watched the blackened ashes fall,
  The puffing smoke ascend, sir ;
Said he, " So Abe's bright hopes will fall,
  His proclamation end, sir."

" What 's to be done, King Jeff," said one,
  (Despairingly he spoke, sir,)
" To burst Old Abraham's big gun
  And *make* it end in smoke, sir ?"
" We 'll think of that anon ; meanwhile
  I'll send the papers *out*, sirs ;
'Twill be diversion to the crowd,
  A thing to talk about, sirs."

The rebel press[1] in spasms went
  And spread the hot infection ;
Declared " Abe's pen had made a bid
  For servile insurrection ;
That Butler was a holy saint
  Compared with his vile master ;
But such a fiendish programme would
  Bring Abraham disaster."

[1] Richmond *Whig*, October 1, 1862.

CHAPTER XXII.

But Abe, unterrified, at home
    Was busy calculating
The cost, with Jonathan, and both
    Were quietly debating
The ways and means, for both agreed
    The war was just begun, sir;
So steadily they set to work
    To do what must be done, sir.

Said Jonathan, "The foe at home,
    Right in the family, sir,
Must be attended to, Old Abe,
    And that, too, speedily, sir.
Some foreigners who 've come ashore
    Among our honest folks,
Make awful discord; John Bull roars,
    And Johnnie Crapeau croaks.

"They claim protection from our laws,
    And act as rebel spies;
Discourage those who go to fight,
    And send abroad vile lies.
These cunning copperheads can dodge
    The law; it is a fact, sir.
You 'll have to set aside for them
    The Habeas Corpus Act,[1] sir."

---

[1] Set aside October 24, in cases of those who aid and abet rebellion and discourage enlistments.

"One thing," said Abe, "this Government
  (And I must make *that* clear, sir,)
Will not allow a traitorous crew
  With it to interfere, sir.
The only place for *them* to stand
  (There's surely no delusion)
Is with the rebs, with Lee, and *not*
  Upon the Constitution."

At this the copperheads hissed well,
  And talked of *despotism ;*
And prophesied in Abram's camp
  A speedy, dreadful schism.
"With traitors North, and traitors South,"
  Said Abe, "I am surrounded ;
New York and Richmond, in my mind,
  Get terribly confounded.

"A big job, Jonathan, this war,
  Is plainly bound to be ;
And what would be our wisest plan
  I'm sure I cannot see ;
I only know with hand and brain
  We 'll toil day after day, sir ;
And at the Union you and I
  With faith will peg away, sir."

So Abram sent to Mac to know
  If he was almost rested.
"Large bodies, Abe," said Mac, "move slow ;
  But I have just requested
Some extra rations, when they come,
  With shoes, and guns, from town, sir,
I 'll make a move, some horses first
  Will have to be sent down, sir."

Abe sent the horses, guns and shoes,
    McClellan still was idle ;
Old Jonathan did patience lose,
    His wrath was hard to bridle.
He wrote to Lincoln just to say
    That "Mac had got the cramp ;"
So Abe one bright October day[1]
    Stepped over to the camp.

Said he, "I've happened in to see
    If you have any news, sir,
Of Lee this morning ; by-the-by,
    Your men have got their shoes, sir,
I s'pose they'll start at once, now, Mac ;
    It's rather late I know, sir,
To catch Lee's army, for his track
    Was washed out long ago, sir.

"They say his transportation was
    Impeded by the rains,
And that you *might* have hurried up,[2]
    And captured all his trains."
"I'd like to know," cried Mac, "when Lee's
    Light wagons heavy run, sir,
How you could well expect of me
    To move my heavy guns, sir ?"

"Oh, well," said Abe, "I didn't know,
    Of course, you must be right.
But, seems to me, your cavalry
    Might keep the foe in sight.

---

[1] October 2, 1862, Mr. Lincoln visited the Army of the Potomac at Harper's Ferry.

[2] After the battle of Antietam, September 17, 1862.

There's Stanton in another rage,
  He says you let them go, sir,
And Jonathan wrote me a page
  About your being slow, sir.

"His patience's almost at an end ;
  You'll save yourself much sorrow,
'Tis my advice, as I'm your friend, •
  You'd better start to morrow."
Said Mac, "'Tis not at all my fault,
  We sadly need some pegs, sir,
For tents, I telegraphed for them,
  A week ago, to Meigs, sir.

"I don't know how it is—the fact
  I hardly like to mention,
But seems to me, they're all agreed
  To pay but slight attention ;
To what *I* need." "Tut, tut," said Abe,
  (He felt his choler rising,)
"What I, alone, have sent you makes
  An aggregate surprising."

Then Abe went home, and sent for Meigs,
  And to his satisfaction,
Found Little Mac had no excuse
  At all for his inaction,
Then took his pen and in a word,
  He *ordered* Mac to move ;
Now orders sometimes are absurd
  And ineffective prove.

Mac did n't budge—he lay so still,
  That Lee, as rebels said,

Sent out Jeb Stuart on a raid,[1]
  To see if Mac was dead.
Jeb rode and plundered far and wide,
  And made a little map, sir,
Of Mac's position, as he lay
  A-taking of his nap, sir.

He burned the depots, tore up rails,
  And lots of horses stole;
And guns and clothing, stopped the mails,
  Went back and called his roll.
Said he, "I've traversed Maryland,
  And all our pockets filled;
Destroyed a half a million's worth,
  And not a man is killed.

*   *   *   *   *

The best of sleepers must awake;
  The end, sir, of October,
Mac rubbed his eyes, and then he spoke,
  His words were few and sober;
He gave his orders for a move,
  With wonderful precision,
And crossed the river,[2] just as Abe
  Had come to a decision.

When Mac had reached the other side,
  And skirmishing began,
Up Burnside came and made a bow,
  And said *he* was the man,
Sent down to lead the "Army Grand."
  Now, Mac perhaps, was grieved,

[1] October 10, 1862.

[2] Army of the Potomac entered Virginia east of the Blue Ridge 25th of October, 1862.

But I've no doubt of his command,
  He felt himself relieved.[1]

*   *   *   *   *

Said General Lee to Jefferson,
  "This *new* man may be prying,
We'd better some precautions take
  In case he comes a-spying;
Just send me in, sir, from the West,[2]
  Where they're not worth, I'm told, sir,
The salt they're spoiling, some brigades—
  This Burnside *may* be bold, sir."

So Lee lay ready waiting, till
  He quite began to wonder,
Of course he did n't know—(who did?)—
  About the pontoon blunder.
Said he, "With nothing else to do,
  While Sumner makes pretenses,[3]
I'll beautify this tiresome view,
  By building some defences.

The pontoons came up just as Lee
  Had manned his rifle-pits, sir;
Each rifleman has steady aim,
  And every bullet hits, sir.
The pontoons lay upon the shore,
  To launch them Burnside, tried;
The storm of bullets dashing o'er
  His bravery defied.

[1] November 5, 1862.

[2] West Virginia, where the rebels were destroying salt works.

[3] General Sumner threatened to burn Fredericksburg, November 20, 1862.

"Now who will cross that stream of death,
　　The rifle-pits to try, sir ?"
Cried Hendershott, the drummer-boy,
　　"*I'm ready*, though I die, sir."
Then leaped into a boat.—"My lad,
　　Give way to older hands, sir."
The boy hung on behind the boat,
　　And was the *first* to land, sir.

    *　　　*　　　*　　　*　　　*

Slow, dreadful work; at last the stream
　　Is crossed,[1] the foe in sight, sir,
Secure beyond the sullen town,[2]
　　Entrenched upon the heights, sir.
Now, up the slopes, where cannon deal
　　Out canister and grape,
Good heavens ! from such a storm of fire
　　Can anything escape?

They stagger back, they charge again,
　　They waver, reel and fall—
Recharge, until the carnage might
　　The stoutest heart appal.
All day they press, as if their death
　　Were emulous to meet;
But never foe at Malvern Hill
　　Won such a dread defeat.

Night fell, the battered army lay,
　　Some sunk in dreamless sleep;
But eyes there were that o'er that day
　　Hot bitter tears did weep.

---

[1] Union troops crossed the river 11th of December, 1862.
[2] Fredericksburg, Va.

Twelve thousand men, who in the morn,
  Were glad in buoyant life,
Now "missing"—lying mangled—torn,
  Or martyred in the strife.

How sped the hours on yonder slopes?
  Did any dream of home,
To flickering, fluttering, fainting hearts,
  Did any succor come?
Drop down the curtain, let our gaze
  Be clouded by the night;
Ah me! but there are those who live
  Who saw and bore the sight.

The army lay two days in camp
  Expecting General Lee, sir;
Lee didn't come, he was content
  With Fabian policy, sir.
Then Burnside wrote to Abraham,
  "We couldn't stand the fire;
Lee won't come out and fight us fair,
  And—so—we must retire."

Abe read the note, and with a groan,
  He handed it to Chase.[1]
Said he, "This will not help your *Loan*,"
  Then—tried the worst to face;
And wondered how Old Jonathan
  Would bear the chilling news;
"If *I* were gone," thought he, "they might
  A better leader choose.

"But then things do not go by chance
  In this strange world of ours;

[1] Chase, Secretary of the Treasury

And Right will not be crushed by Wrong—
   There *is* a Ruling Power.
I'm but a way through which to work
   God's plan : I cannot alter ;
I can be patient.   He is wise,
   His purpose will not falter."

But Abram's Cabinet declared
   They felt aggrieved ; in fine,
Old Jonathan was finding fault,
   They'd better all resign ;[1]
Things didn't please *him*—as for that
   Nobody *could* be pleased, sir ;
The odium would fall on *them*,
   They'd like to be released, sir.

"Why, as to *blame*," said honest Abe,
   " *That* isn't hard to bear, sir ;
Old Jonathan *is* bowed to earth
   With sorrow and with care, sir.
If he can have the heart to blame,
   Perhaps 'twill do him good, sir ;
And I don't mind, it's all the same,
   He'll quickly change his mood, sir."

Just here a note from Jonathan
   Was put in Abram's hand :
"I write in haste, dear Abe," it ran,
   "That you may understand
A Nor'-west storm is setting in,
   You may rough weather find, sir ;

---

[1] Secretaries Seward and Chase tendered their resignations December 18th, in consequence of the action of some Republican senator concerning the fight on the Rappahannock. They were subsequently withdrawn.

But just stand steady at the helm,
  And scud before the wind, sir.

"Nail to the mast the starry flag,
  Look out each rotten plank, sir;
Don't touch at any foreign port,
  And never drop an anchor.
Don't swerve a hair's breadth from your course,
  Whatever blasts may come, sir;
You 've got the *chart* now safe aboard,
  Let drive the vessel home, sir."

"Ah! that reminds me now," said Abe,
  "Here, Seward, take a chair, sir;
Pull out that lower table-drawer,
  The chart is lying there, sir."
Abe tried his hand (he was to do
  What never could be altered)—
"It must not tremble," Abram said,
  "Or men may say I faltered.

"They had fair warning I would strike,
  The *rebs would have it so*, sir;
Now come what will, I keep my word
  Alike with friend and foe, sir.
Because the South *wants* to be blind,
  Shall we hold back the sun?"
Abe took his pen, sat down and signed
  His Order No. ONE.[1]

"Now that will do," said Abraham,
  "And we shall know anon, sir,

____

[1] Emancipation Proclamation, issued January 1, 1863, in the form of Order No. 1.

How it will *work;* at any rate,
   Our harpoon 's in the monster.
We must take care, that we *steer* straight—
   What would this stroke avail, sir,
If he should swamp our ship of state
   With one flop of his tail, sir."

CHAPTER XXIII.

Says Rosecrans to his brave men,
   "Unfurl the starry flag,
For Abe is watching how we play
   Our little game of Bragg."
Up rose a hundred thousand men,[1]
   "*All ready*, now are we," sir;
The rebs to Murfreesboro run,
   In Western Tennessee, sir.

Down in the cedar glades they lurk
   "Lie low, till they are near,"
Said Bragg, "then up and deal them out
   A gift for the New Year."[2]
They fought that drear December day,
   That day with blood so red, sir,
That day our boys at Vicksburg spent
    In burying their dead, sir.[3]

That night the awful closing year,
   Bore upward to their God
Seven thousand souls, whose bodies lay
   All broken on the sod.
Seven thousand men, that Rosecrans
   Led gaily in the morn;

[1] Left Nashville on December 26, 1862.

[2] Battle of Murfreesboro commenced December 31, 1862.

[3] Sherman attacked the works at Vicksburg on the 27th, 28th, and 29th. Was repulsed with a loss of between 4,000 and 5,000.

The rest were driven slowly back[1]
  With banners stained and torn.

Cried Rosecrans, "What shall we do?"
  " Alas! we must make speed
To Nashville," said his officers;
  " And so you are agreed,"
Old Rosey said, "to make retreat?"
  " Oh yes, sir, to our sorrow."
" Well, *first*, my lads, we'll up and meet
  The rebs again to morrow."

    *   *   *   *   *

McCook went out at early dawn,[2]
  Took back the ground they'd lost, sir,
Then Bragg awoke, and furious on
  He lead the rebel host, sir;
Now Rosecrans upon a hill
  Had placed his guns in rows,
And plunging down through rebel ranks
  The shot deep ploughing goes.

'Twas fearful din, the shock of arms,
  The shout, the groan, the cheer,
Pierce through and through the cedar groves
  Till little birds in fear,
Flutter and fall all paralyzed,
  And timid hares confounded
Grow tame, run in upon the field
  And nestle 'mong the wounded.

'T was fiercely hot, Old Rosey's will
  They cannot hope to alter;

[1] Nearly four miles, with the loss of 28 pieces of Artillery.
[2] January 2, 1863.

His cannon belch out fire until
  The rebels pause and falter;
They turn, surge back, and turn again,
  And down the hill they flee, sir,
And Rosey sends to speed them quick
  Across the Tennessee, sir.

Then, while he waited there to watch
  The raiders and guerrillas,
Old Rosey turned his swords to ploughs,
  His army into tillers;
Quoth he, "We'll have, our next campaign,
  A vegetable diet;
This soil should good potatoes grow,
  At any rate I'll try it."

Meanwhile, Sir Beauregard he makes
  Another proclamation,[1]
(The usual form his terror takes,)
  That he has information
The brutal foe ere long will come,
  The attack will soon be made, sirs,
And to protect their wives and homes
  He calls for men and spades, sirs.

Now Gideon Welles and Abraham
  Their monitors had sent,
To Charleston Harbor, for to try
  A wise experiment,
The fleet had thirty-four great guns,
  Three hundred in the forts, sir,
To silence these Dupont went out[2]—
  It was n't pleasant sport, sir.

[1] February 18, 1863.
[2] Attack made April 7, 1863. The action lasted 30 minutes.

7*

Dupont was worsted and the rebs
   Thereby were so elated
They would have burst, but they were used
   To being so inflated.
But while they crowed in ecstacy,
   Bold Grierson hot haste made, sir,[1]
And swept clean through their Dixie Land
   Upon his famous raid, sir.

And Morgan's troopers rob and slay
   Like other chivalrie, sir,
While Jeff sends up his imps to play
   In Eastern Tennessee, sir.
They pinch the children—fathers kill,
   And flog the grey-haired mother,
And loose their hounds among the hills,
   To hunt the fleeing brother.

Theft, murder, aye, and crimes too foul
   To breathe in mortal ear
They perpetrate, and Jeff will howl
   In agony of fear,
When in the retribution land,
   He hears the devil say, sir,
"Here comes the prince of our brave band
   Of chivalry in grey, sir."

[1] Left La Grange April 17, 1863.

CHAPTER XXIV.

In Richmond one bright April day
   Jeff gave a dinner party
To Orr and Wigfall, Foote and Clay,
   And Pryor (just as hearty
As when he went with flag of truce
   And drank the Major's brandy [1]
Way down in Sumter, to the tune
   Of Yankee Doodle Dandy.)

And Stephens came, but could n't stay
   He said he felt quite sick, sir.
At sight of food, his liver lay
   As heavy as a brick, sir.
He took his hat, and went away
   With a decided shiver,
He did n't know, I 'm free to say,
   His conscience from his liver.

"Now, gentlemen," said Jeff, " you 'll find
   This is a splendid roast
Of Yankee beef, caught on a raid,
   Let 's give old Jeb a toast ;
Says Wigfall, " This is better fare,
   Than dining on mule meat, sirs,

[1] Pryor acting on the staff of Beauregard, went to propose conditions to Major Anderson. During the interview Pryor helped himself to a glass of *something* which he mistook for brandy. The doctor and a dose of ipecac (and some say a stomach pump,) were summoned to enable Pryor to survive the effects of the dram, which the doctor pronounced poison."—*See Tribune, April* 19, 1861.

They say Port Hudson garrison,
  Think mice and rats a treat, sirs."

"Ah, well!" said Jeff, "our soldiers dine
  On glory every day,
But taste this sparkling champagne wine,"—
  "Oh! yes," said Clement Clay;
"This wine has run Old Abe's blockade."
  "Not so," said Jeff, "it came, sir,
From *New York friends*, a present made,
  By—well! we'll call no names, sir.

"They wish us well, and by the by,
  Peace movements are begun;
Our friends have found their voice at last,
  And Abram's course is run.
The mighty rabble of New York,
  Has caught the infectious cry, sir,
Raised by the Hoosiers of the West,
  Ere long they will *defy*, sir,

"The dungeons which had been their doom
  But one short year ago;
Vallandigham in Congress *now*,
  The white flag dares to show.
This party new will not consent
  The South to subjugate, sir,
We've but in one more shock of arms,
  Our course to vindicate, sir."

Said Mr. Foote, "I'll introduce [1]
  In Congress resolutions,

---

[1] On January 28, 1863, Henry S. Foote introduced resolutions, offering an alliance offensive and defensive with such of the Northwest States as would lay down their arms, etc., etc.

That this confederation deems,
  It would be no intrusion
If these *North Western States* lay down
  Their arms, and ask admission,·
We'd grant them Mississippi trade,
  On only one condition.

"That they unite with us in war,
  In fierce undying hate, sir,
Of everything, that ever saw
  The curs'd New England States, sir."
"I'd die in peace," said Jeff, "if I
  Could only once behold,
The South and West in one firm tie,
  The North 'out in the cold.'"

"Our organ, Jeff," said Mr. Orr,
  "I mean the *Daily News,*
Is coming out a *little strong,*
  I'm fearful we shall lose
What we have gained, if Jonathan
  Our intercourse should guess, sir;
He's fit for any deed; he might
  The *Daily News* suppress, sir."

"No fears," said Jeff, "Old Jonathan
  Is busy with the negroes,
Fernando Wood's a Union man,
  For anything that *he* knows;
He has enough to do, to feed
  His mercenary Hessians,
And furnish powder to his Grant,
  At least that's *my* impression."

Said Wigfall, "What *is* Grant about?"
  (Now Wigfall in the Senate,
Was apt to let grave secrets out,
  Somewhat as Gordon Bennett
Among the paper folks,) said he,
  "That Grant I know of old, sirs,
The bull dog's got us by the throat,
  He'll never lose his hold, sirs."

"Oh, Grant," said Jeff, "doth exercise,
  The muscles of his men, sirs,
He'll find canals will not surprise
  Another Island Ten, sirs;
But gentlemen, give me an ear,
  There's Hunter in Car'lina, [1]
That he means mischief is quite clear,
  Or I am no diviner."

"He's arming slaves."   "Well, Jeff," said Orr,
  "You know they'll never *fight*, sir,
Just tell our boys to carry *whips*,
  They'll run quick at the sight, sir—
Skedaddle like Old Abram's fleet
  At Charleston, on blockade,
When Beauregard in handsome style
  That proclamation made." [2]

Said Clay, "I see that an exchange
  Of pris'ners is effected;
The thing will work well for our cause,
  If skillfully directed;

[1] Hunter orders negroes to be drafted March 6th, 1863.

[2] The rebel gunboats attacked the fleet,—the inner line of blockaders were dispersed for a few hours. Beauregard and Ingraham issued proclamations that the blockade was legally raised January 31st, 1863.

I noticed as I came along
  Some soldiers just come in, sir:
We have not got their match, King Jeff,
  So sleek, and fat, and trim, sir."

"I 've given orders, sir," said Jeff,
  "To Ould, who has approved,
The plan to send off all the sick
  That can be safely moved ;
You see, I have a tender heart,
  And so the thought did come, sir,
That these poor fellows at Belle Isle
  Would rather die at home, sir.

"I hear from Memminger, the Yanks
  Do counterfeit our notes,"
Said Orr, "That spurious currency
  Quite undetected floats
All through the States Confederate ;"
  And Memminger, he said, "It,
 Unless soon stopped, ere many days
  Would undermine our credit."

"I 'll introduce," said Foote, "a bill,
  The evil is immense, sir,
The bill must make it once for all,
  A capital offence, sir.[1]
To have, to hold, to circulate,
  To look at such a note,
I 'll draft the bill this very night
  And press it to a vote."

---

[1] Rebel Congress passed a bill making it a death penalty for Union soldiers to have in their possession counterfeit rebel notes.

Said Wigfall, "There 's a scarcity,
  We feel it little here, sir,
(I 'll take a glass of that old port,
  It does one's spirit cheer, sir,)
The soldiers' wives and families
  Most bitterly complain,
You know, our commissariat
  Has taken all their grain."

Said Jeff, "We pay for what we take,
  If the supply doth fail, sir,
Why let them plant a greater crop,
  I 'm sick of idle tales, sir ;
They growl at this and growl at that,
  No matter what you do,
And all this talk of scarcity
  I tell you is *not* true.

"There 's plenty in the land, I know,
  Within the reach of all,
Hark! don't you hear outside a noise,
  Did any body call?"
A tramp of feet rushed past the door,
  A noise of women's tongues, sir,
And fierce, loud cries, in shrillest tones,
  In through the window rung, sir.

" Good Heavens!" cried Wigfall, "here's a riot[1]
  Of women at the stores,
They 're smashing in the windows, Jeff,
  And breaking down the doors ;
They 've got the bacon and the corn,
  They 're crying out for salt, sir ;

[1] April 5, 1863.

Ah! here's the soldiers charging down
    There now! they make a halt, sir,

"Right opposite! the Mayor's out,
    He's got the Riot Act!
My goodness, Jeff,—it is no use,
    The city will be sacked.
They're armed with hatchets and with knives,
    They're crying out for bread;"
Jeff rose and called his orderly,
    "Send Letcher here," he said.

Jeff's company slipped out in haste,
    And quickly disappeared,
And as by magic, Jeff's full board
    Immediately was cleared.
When Letcher came,—the clever twain—
    (The riot had subsided,)
Sat down and wrote a "true account,"
    And to the Press confided.

Next day, the *Whig*[1] declared the row
    As every body guesses,
Was groundless,—that the female mob
    Were hunting for silk dresses!
And not for food; that they were fat,
    Well fed, and that their pranks, sir,
Were instigated, as was proved,
    Directly by the Yanks, sir.

[1] Richmond *Whig*, April 6th, 1863.

CHAPTER XXV

While Roscy plants in Tennessee,
   And fights, and scouts, and raids, sir,
The army in Virginia
   Has caught, I am afraid, sir,
The old disease of strife and mud.
   At any rate it lies
In winter quarters, till the sun
   Shines out in April skies.

The troops were worn with useless toil,
   Some said demoralized ;
I only know that they were men,
   And who could be surprised,
If sad experience had taught
   A lesson of despair, sir ;
" We 're cut and slaughtered by brigades,"
   Said they, " and who does care, sir ?"

But Burnside cared, and so did Abe ;
   " To run the big machine,"
By pouring oil upon the springs
   They tried, but soon 'twas seen
That General this, and General that,
   Were dreadfully out of joint, sir,
And here and there, the colonels spat—
   Said Burnside, " I 'll appoint, sir,

Some officers, who 'll keep their fight
    To spend upon the foe."
It would n't do, the ghost of Mac
    Went stalking to and fro
All through the camp,—it won't be laid ;
    Quoth Burnside, " I divine, sir,
This sort of work is not my trade,
    So, Abe, I shall resign, sir !" [1]

Said Fighting Joe, "I 'm not afraid
    Of ghosts, or living men,
Or roaring rebs."—"Then go," Abe said,
    " And fall upon their den."
He crossed the Rappahannock,[2] thence
    Marched to the Wilderness,
Said Jonathan, " In Fighting Joe
    Lee 'll find his match, I guess."

Jo made a splendid fight,[3] for he
    Did nothing else so well ;
" He whipped the rebs," so much is clear,
    Then happened what befell
So oft in former victories
    To those who won a fight,
And *kept a way for a retreat*—
    Jo crossed back in the night.

If any grumbled, 't was n't the boys
    Who lay among the slain,
In yonder burning woods,[4] until
    The fire did ease their pain.

[1] Burnside superseded by Hooker, January 26th, 1863.

[2] Army of the Potomac commenced crossing the Rappahannock, April 29th, 1863.

[3] Battle of Chancellorsville, May 2nd, 1863.

[4] A number of wounded were consumed by the burning of the woods, in the rear of Charlottesville,—the fire was caused by shells.

It wa' n't the dead, that piled in heaps
  Lay festering in the sun.
Perhaps 't was Lee ; they say he weeps,
  That Stonewall's[1] course is run.

*　　*　　*　　*　　*　　*

Abe told Old Jonathan the news,
  And all about the *plan*,
That Stoneman went in back of Lee
  Before the fight began,
To cut the rebels from their base,
  If Hooker *could* have known, sir,
Communication had been cut,
  "I wish he 'd cut his own, sir."

Growled Jonathan ; "I do n't like raids,
  They 're well enough for rebs."
"We want to show them we can match,"
  Said Abe, " that one of Jeb's."
"Well, well," said Jonathan, "there 's Straight[2]
  He 's made a pretty trail, sir,
Fetched up at last in Georgia State,
  Inside a rebel jail, sir."

"But Grierson[3] did a handsome thing ;"
  Said Abe, "that little trip, he
Did dreadful damage to the rebs,
  Way down in Mississippi."
"I 'm thinking, sir," said Jonathan,
  "Indeed, I 'm much afraid, sir,
Lee 's been so still for two whole weeks,
  He 'll hatch another raid, sir."

[1] General Jackson wounded May 2nd. Died on 10th of May, 1863.
[2] Colonel Straight and whole command captured near Rome, Georgia, on the 3rd May, 1863.
[3] Left La Grange, Tennessee, 17th April, 1863.

And Jonathan was right, for Lee
  Impatiently had waited,
And moved his troops the very day
  Ohio nominated,
For Governor, Vallandigham,
  It was the eleventh of June, sir,
Lee's troopers ride with guidons gay,
  His band plays Dixie tune, sir.

Straight out across "My Maryland,"
  They ride to Pennsylvania,
The Yankee Dutch a second time
  Take the militia mania.
And quick as Lee his charger goads,
  So quickly do they muster,
And all along the turnpike roads,
  Rise heavy clouds of dust, sir.

Tramp! tramp! from Jersey and New York,
  And gallant old Ohio,
Came regiments and whole brigades,
  The rebels to defy, O;
For Abraham had "called" again,
  And Jonathan was ready,
And solid masses of new men
  Tramped on, determined, steady.

Till Lee, who came to bring the war
  Into the Northern States, sir,
Astonished—listens from afar,
  And thinks the earth doth quake, sir;
He's brought the war to Northern soil,
  He shrinks now from the test,
The very ground seems to recoil
  And spurn him from its breast.

With troops behind and troops before,
    And gathering on all sides,
Lee halts, and stands at Gettysburg,
    The issue there abides.
Now, if he wins—alack! who knows,
    Perhaps on Bunker Hill, sir,
He 'll call his roll, at any rate,
    We know he has the will, sir.

But if he fails to crush in fight
    The Yankees now at hand, he
May once for all take up his flight
    From Yankee Doodle Dandy.
No more invasion of the North,
    No more of rebel brag, sir,
For bow he must, however loth,
    To Jonathan's old flag, sir.

*   *   *   *   *   *

And where is fighting Jo? asleep?
    Across Potomac's river?
To think what might have been, doth creep
    Upon us till we shiver.
Jo moved at last, and placed his men
    'Twixt Washington and Lee,
Then gave them up to General Meade,[1]
    The *why*, no one could see.

Now for a ride to Hagerstown,
    To Frederick a race,
(Where Barbara Freitchie waved the flag
    In Stonewall Jackson's face.)

[1] General Hooker superseded by General Meade, June 28th, 1863.

A dash at Carlisle, where the Dutch
  Sigh after Little Mac, sir,
Then down in famous Gettysburg[1]
  The rebs their muskets stack, sir.

Meade hurries up the loyal host,
  And skirmishing begins,
The rebs are checked, they charge again
  And neither party wins,
For night-fall halts the advancing foe,
  The armies sink to rest,
Lee in the shelter of the wood,
  Meade posted on the crest

Of Cemetery Hill. The bluffs
  All bristling on each side,
With guns, down pointing to the town,
  The morning sun abide.
The cold white marble o'er the graves,
  Doth catch a glimpse of dawn,
Bright bayonets throw back the first
  Faint blush of coming morn.

The light grows stronger, and the sun
  Looks out upon the tombs,
The birds have now their song begun,
  When flash! a cannon booms!
The rebels send a greeting up,
  Meade throws an answer back,
And all along the line, his troops
  Stand waiting the attack.

At length, a heavy cannonade,
  Foretells the coming strife ;

[1] Battle of Gettysburg commenced July 1, 1863, and lasted three days.

Then comes a momentary pause,
　When groans and shrieks are rife.
Then from the woods, three columns deep
　Sweep forty thousand men,
Determined, desperate, is their aught
　Of help in mortal ken?

They wrestle, sway, advance, and reel,
　Surge up against a rock,
Foe pressed to foe, steel clashing steel,
　Shock answering to shock;
Brave Sickles falls and Hancock's down,
　But Sedgwick's in the breach;
The rebel line ebbs slowly back
　Beyond the cannon's reach.

Another night upon the field,
　Another sunlit morn,
Breaks peacefully upon the earth,
　By war all gashed and torn;
With day the strife swells up anew,
　Again the cannon's roar,
Again the fierce grey tide is dashed
　On adamantine shore.

*　　*　　*　　*　　*

The devil rides astride a gun,
　A Whitworth, British make, sir,
"I never had," cried he, "such fun,
　My sides do fairly ache, sir."
He cheers, at every desperate charge
　His imps the music swell;
And far above the cannonade
　Rolls up the rebel yell!

They charge, and grapple, hand to hand,
  And death for death they mete,
Till dead men thick as autumn leaves
  Are trampled 'neath their feet.
In vain bold Ewell hounds them on,
  They wrestle all in vain,
No single inch disputed ground
  The rebel columns gain.

Fresh patriots rally to the strife
  And enfilade the foe.
They hurl them back,—Hurra! Hurra!!
  They stagger 'neath the blow.
Flash! crash! shell, shrapnel, shot, and grape
  Their murderous journey speed,
And all along the line of fire
  The enemy recede.

Then silence on the field of death,
  If silence we can call
The horrid lull, war's bated breath,
  Whose utterances fall
More heavily on heart and brain
  Than clang of clashing steel,
For he's unmanned among the slain
  Who has the time to feel.

Three heavy hours of silence dread—
  A pall upon all hearts—
Meade watches ; with defeat, Lee stung
  To desperation starts
In one last struggle of despair ;
  His guns against the hill,
One hundred strong he brings to bear,
  And instantly they fill

The air with missiles,—as a storm
　Of hail from summer sky,
So unexpectedly they fall
　Upon the sward, where lie
Meade's wearied officers, and death
　Springs on them unawares—
Right on, through graves and living men
　The shot relentless tears.

The driving storm sweeps bare the hill,
　It does n't frighten Meade ;
His batteries, with deafening roar,
　An answering challenge speed.
Said General Lee, " The Yankee fire
　It seems to me is slack,
Now up, my men, the foe doth tire,
　He 'll yield at our attack."

On ! on ! they rush—those men in grey,
　In bravery and folly,
They near the patriots' rifle pits,
　When, flash ! a dreadful volley—
They falter, close their ranks, and press
　Right up to meet their doom ;
They sweep swift through the rifle pits—
　But hark ! the deafening boom

Of Meade's great guns sounds out their knell,
　And crash ! a storm of grape,
And that intrepid charge of grey
　Is crushed all out of shape.
The wretched men swept by the blast
　Are blinded and confounded,
They turn, and so does Lee, at last,
　And leaves his dead and wounded.

Meade didn't push him very hard,
  And Abe had grown so used, sir,
To *half* done work he didn't stop
  To feel himself abused, sir.
"It might have been so much the worse,
  And 'half a loaf,'" said he,
"Will stay one's hunger, till we win
  A lasting victory."

Lee didn't stop till he was safe
  On sacred soil again ;
Said he, "The chivalry may chafe,
  One thing is very plain,
I'll never more the North invade
  As I'm a precious noodle ;
I wish to goodness I had stayed
  Away from Yankee Doodle."

CHAPTER XXVI.

When Farragut had done his part,
   It wa'n't his way to loiter ;
So after taking New Orleans
   He sent to reconnoitre.
Far up the stream Commander Lee
   For days steamed unmolested,
Past Baton Rouge, past Natchez, up
   The unknown way he tested.

At length before a little town,
  .His squadron boldly came,[1]
 Where rebels had their guns put down,
   And Vicksburg was its name.
The rebs were not disposed to yield
   To Yankee Lee's demand,
So back to New Orleans he sent
   For Farragut's command.

Then up steamed Porter's mortar fleet,
   With Farragut's gun boats,
And Foote came *down* the fleet to meet ;
   And Uncle Sam's blue coats[1]
Began to dig a nice canal
   Across the river's bend.

[1] On 18th May, 1862.
[2] Four Regiments under General F. Williams.

They would cut off the saucy fort
  And put a speedy end

To such obstructions of their route ;
  But, ah ! for seventy days, sir,
The fleet upon the stubborn rebs
  Its storm of iron plays, sir.
Still Vicksburg stands,—at length comes out
  A ram from the Yazoo,
And Farragut and Porter leave,
  And Foote,—he steams off, too.

The grand canal had brought no good,
  The blue coats backward wended
Their way,—and Vicksburg frowning stood,
  Its first great seige well ended.
Said Jeff, "The Yanks may save their shot,
  And Abe may keep his spite, sir,
For Vicksburg stands, and we shall hold
  The Mississippi tight, sir."

Now Abraham had in the West
  A man of open eye,
Who looking out for rebel nest,
  Did stronghold Vicksburg spy
Three hundred miles away.   Van Dorn
  And Price stood firm between,
And swamps, and bayous, and forlorn
  Dull streams did intervene.

"I 'll force the rebels from the road
  To Vicksburg," said grim Grant ;
"Then on their ramparts, his old flag
  For Uncle Sam I 'll plant."

He sent his cavalry around—
    They never did work harder ;
They cut the railroads ; Pemberton
    Fell back upon Grenada.[1]

Grant pushed ahead through Holly Springs,
    A leap of fifty miles, sir ;
But Pemberton, the wily reb,
    Looks out and grimly smiles, sir.
He thinks 'twill be an easy task
    From his Grenada station
To make a quick, effective dash
    At Grant's communication.

But Grant has thought of that himself,
    And also what he 'll do ;
He Sherman sends to make a base[2]
    By way of the Yazoo.
They 'll meet at Jackson, and then strike
    At Vicksburg in the rear, sir ;
And his supplies can come by steam—
    The plan was very clear, sir.

But, ah! Van Dorn, he made a swoop,
    Grant's depot of supplies
At Holly Springs he boldly struck[3]
    And took it by surprise.
Grant hurried back, and Sherman had
    A dreadful work to do
That drear December, when he lands
    At Chickasaw bayou.

[1] December 1, 1862.
[2] On the 21st December, left Helena for Vicksburg.
[3] On the 20th December, 1862, Van Dorn captured Holly Springs.

For when he disembarked his troops
   · He stood right face to face
With Pemberton and his whole force,
   Who occupied the place.
Interminable swamps spread out,
   And fierce abattas frowned
A fort to right, a fort to left—
   He looked o'er all the ground

To force his way; then Sherman felt
   He never would be able;
But still he doesn't like to yield
   To the inevitable.
He pushes up to meet his fate;
   The rebs their fire deliver;
And Sherman, horribly repulsed,[1]
   Drops down the Yazoo river.

He meets McClernand, and the two
   To Milliken's go back,.
Where Grant has fixed the rendezvous
   To make a new attack.
And while he plans a new campaign,
   McClernand takes the war, sir,
Still up the stream, to Hindman Fort,[2]
   Upon the Arkansas, sir.

Now Grant sits down and smokes awhile
   With many an anxious thought;
His boys for many a weary mile
   Had worked, and all for nought.
Said he, "I 'll try the old canal,
   And Vicksburg isolate, sir."

[1] On the 29th December Sherman attacked and was repulsed.
[2] Captured June 11, 1863.

The volunteers then with their spades
  Worked early and worked late, sir.

Week after week they toiled away,
  Their hearts were growing light,
When lo! upon the eighth of May
  They saw a dreadful sight.
The river *rose*, their dam broke through,
  And woeful to relate,
The water rushed in like a flood
  Their camps to inundate.

The rebels jeered, Grant's boys hurrahed—
  (They were amphibious, sir,)
They scrambled out, but Jonathan
  He scolded at the muss, sir.
Said Grant, "I 'll open up a route,
  My transports from the Bend,
Down by the bayou Roundabout
  To Carthage I shall send."

The dredge-boats cleared a passage through,
  The boys they got up steam ;
The water fell and put an end
  To that nice little scheme.
Then Grant tried many other ways,
  Lake Providence was one, sir,
Which he gave up, as quite too hard,
  When it was scarce begun, sir.

And then by pass and by bayous,
  Though horribly impeded,
He dug and wormed a channel through,
  And *almost* had succeeded ;

When all at once his trusty scouts,
  Made the discovery, sir,
The *other ends* were fortified—
  Closed by the enemy, sir!

Then Grant smoked harder than before :
  Said he, "The thing I 've planned ;
My boats shall *run the batteries*,
  And we 'll *march down by land.*"
But how they marched, the painful task,
  I 've no heart here to tell, sir ;
The hardy boys, they took the job,
  Of course, they did it well, sir.

Nor how the daring volunteers
  Got all the transports ready,
And ran them by the batteries[1]
  So cool, sir, and so steady,
Beneath the storm of fire that made
  The gazer hold his breath
And watch, as when a friend goes down
  Upon the stream of death.

At length they halt—"Hard Times" 'twas called,
  Grand Gulf was just across,
And Porter shells[2] while Grant decides
  He will not risk the loss
Of storming up the beetling bluff.
  The rebels grow quite merry,
As he moves off—until he makes
  At Bruinsburg a ferry.[3]

[1] April 16, 1863, and April 23.
[2] On 29th of April, a fleet attacked Grand Gulf.
[3] April 30th.

And while he crossed—a little feint
  By Sherman's wise direction,
Was carried out at Haynes' Bluff
  For Pemberton's inspection.
With transports, iron-clads and boats,
  Up the Yazoo he lay,
At evening disembarked, as if
  He came this time to stay.

The rebels gathered for a fight,
  Their strength began to vaunt, sir,
But Sherman starts late in the night,
  And steams away to Grant, sir.
Meanwhile McClernand gains the height,
  With Logan strikes a blow,
That takes Port Gibson from the rebs,[1]
  And does quite plainly show

To Pemberton—"The bull-dog's" teeth,
  He feels the grinders craunch, sir,
He squirms away, and General Grant
  At Grand Gulf takes his lunch, sir ;
And Pemberton, who wants more men,
  Sends off to General Jo,
Who gives this very good advice—
  "Unite, and beat the foe."

Jeff Davis said, the while he smiled,
  "Vicksburg could not be shaken,
That Grant, old Jonathan beguiled,
  It *never would* be taken."
Some weak-kneed rebs began to wince
  And breathe a little hard,

---

[1] Battle of Port Gibson, May 1, 1863.

And said, Jeff should the Yanks convince
  By sending Beauregard.

Grant paused a moment, should he go,
  Thought he, to General Banks,
And take Port Hudson, Bank's troops
  Would reinforce his ranks.
The Mississippi governor howled,
  And wrote a proclamation,
Which like a blister on the rebs,
  Drew out an inflammation.

Said Grant, " I can't afford to *wait*,
  The case is very clear,
I must make haste and operate
  On Vicksburg in the rear."
He draws his plans.   His corps go out,
  McPherson finds the foe, sir,
At Raymond'—makes him face about,
  Which so distresses Jo, sir.

He sallies out from Jackson—*he*[2]
  Will meet Grant's bold advance,
His military eye takes in
  McPherson at a glance;
He squints at Sherman, who sends out
  To spy the ground in front, sir;
Then pushes up—Jo doesn't wait
  To bear the battle's brunt, sir.

He takes a northward flight, nor stops
  Till some time after dark,
Then Grant he faces to the rear,
  With Vicksburg for his mark;

[1] Battle of Raymond, May 12, 1863.   [2] May 14th, Battle of Jackson.

He leaves a squad to burn reb mills,
  And off in haste doth start, sir,
He 's bound to keep the cunning Jo
  And Pemberton apart, sir.

Jo writes to Pemberton, " To fight,
  Grant must not concentrate ;
His bold detachment must be met
  Before it is too late."
But, Pemberton was short of sight,
  To Vicksburg he was tied,
He dare n't uncover that to fight—
  A better plan, he tried.

He moved with seventeen thousand men,
  Southeast from Edward's station,
To make a quick decisive stroke
  At Grant's communication.
Now, Grant in pressing Vicksburg-ward,
  Meets Pemberton *en-route.*
(It 's in this very sort of scrape
  He *likes* to put his foot.)

Now, Pemberton caught in the act,
  Looks foolish, thinks of Jo,
And counter-marches, and, in fact,
  Grant being rather slow
In *crossing* rebel tracks, he fights,
  But half against his will—
And strikes a feeble sort of blow,
  And fails at Champion's Hill.[1]

He formed his line of battle well,
  He turned the first attack

[1] May 16, 1863.

That Hovey made, but Logan, he
  Was reconnoitering *back;*
He worked upon the rebel flank,
  Indeed got on his rear, sir.
Said he to Grant, "*You* dash in front
  And *I* will finish *here,* sir."

Poor Pemberton, he sees at last,
  At last begins to yield;
Pressed front and rear, the die is cast,
  And from the fatal field
His troops pursued, one part to Jo,
  The other with himself, sir;
Dash towards Vicksburg, and are laid
  Ere long upon a shelf, sir.

At Big Black River,[1] Pemberton
  Essayed to make a stand,
But terror seized his troops, they ran
  A panic-stricken band;
They never stopped, they ran all day,
  It was a Bull Run sight, sir,
When they swarmed into Vicksburg town,
  At ten o'clock that night, sir.

"Get out of Vicksburg," Johnston said,
  When Pemberton fell back,
"Give up the *place,* and keep the *men.*"
  While Pemberton did rack
His brains to hit a better plan,
  He got a dreadful shock, sir;
Outside, from Grant, that fearful man,
  There came an awful knock, sir.

From bank to bank in splendid style,
  Grant's gallant boys deployed,

[1] May 17, 1863.

And Vicksburg doomed, cursed Pemberton,
    Who had its hopes destroyed.
Shut up at last, with all his boasts,
    And thirty days of ration ;
Outside, in tireless, countless hosts,
    The hated Yankee nation !

*   *   *   *   *

Bold Porter, on the river hears,
    A noise like Yankee guns,
He gets up steam, across he steers,
    And up the Yazoo runs,
His gallant tars haul up the flag,
    With shouts of approbation,
On Haynes' Bluff, and so give Grant
    A new communication.

Says Grant, "If rebel Jo comes up,
    Our task will then be double ;
I think if we can strike at once,
    'Twill save us lots of trouble."
He makes assault,[1] he gains not much,
    He tries another day,[2] sir.
A fearful blow, his loss is such,
    He tries another way, sir.

He uses spades, sits down and waits,
    According to reports,
The rebs, ere long, will find he has
    An ally in their forts ;
For hunger stalks through Vicksburg town ;
    In vain Jo sends a scout
To cheer the garrison, and bid
    Poor Pemberton "hold out."

[1] May 19, 1863.   [2] May 22d.

Grant mines—the rebels countermine,
  I cannot tell the story,
Nor when such dread explosions come,
  Do I see any glory.
Grant plans a last and grand assault,
  But Pemberton has eaten
His last starved " cow, hog, horse, and dog,"
  And feels that he is beaten.

A flag of truce droops in the sun,
  Then short negotiation,
And thus was stronghold Vicksburg won ;
  The hateful Yankee nation,
Paroled the rebels ; who'll deny
  Grant has a right to brag, sir,
When on that scorching fourth July,
  He hoists the Union Flag, sir.

The shout that rose that afternoon
  From his devoted band, sir,
Was caught at Gettysburg, and rolled
  O'er all this mighty land, sir ;
From California through the West,
  To Maine so bleak and sandy,
The cheer resounded from the breast
  Of Yankee Doodle Dandy.

In five days more, Port Hudson fell,
  And then down to the strand,
The Mississippi, wrested from
  The grasp of traitor hand,
And groaning in its liberty,
  Its troubled waters sped,
And carried to the moaning sea
  The blood of heroes dead.

CHAPTER XXVII.

WHEN Lee went back and told King Jeff
  The upshot of his battle,
And how his gallant chivalry
  Had run from " Northern cattle ;"
King Jeff was seized with ague chills,
  And sent across the park,
For Mr. Seddon,[1] who gave him
  A dreadful dose of *bark*.

Said he, "*I told you so*, you 've done
  Some very foolish things, sir,
You 've strengthened fainting Jonathan,
  And then you 've clipped the wings, sir,
Of our peace friends, and all for what?
  To please a fretful rabble."
Said Jeff, "I swear, I ne'er again
  Will listen to their babble."

"But Seddon,—Lee once reinforced "—
  " With *what*, I 'd like to know, sir,"
Growled Seddon, "if the men we 've sowed
  Should take a start and grow, sir,
It might de done,—if you can 't raise
  The soldiers from their graves,
Why, in the name of common sense,
  Why don't you arm the slaves?"

[1] Rebel Secretary of War.

Said Jeff, "You know as well as I,
   That is with danger fraught, sir,
In fact, ahem!—unsafe to try,
   You see Sambo has fought, sir,
On t'other side,[1] and got a taste
   Of Abraham's liberty, sir,
We *dare* not put him in the field,
   Beside the chivalrie, sir.

"I own, I apprehend no end
   Of evils and disaster,
The phantom, sir, of Sambo armed
   Against his lord and master,
Pursues me even in my dreams."
   "The accursed Yankee nation,"
Said Seddon, "*must* be balked in this,
   We'll try retaliation."

"We'll take no negro prisoners,
   We'll shoot them on the spot, sir."
"And then," said Jeff, "*our property*
   Oh, Seddon, *you'll have shot, sir.*"
Brave Seddon scratched his witless head,
   Said he, "These Yankee curs, sir,
Will send *white* men to *lead* the blacks,
   We'll shoot the *officers*, sir."

"I have an idea now," said Jeff,
   "There's Stephens, he's a fool, sir,
Not spunk enough to kill a fly
   But useful as a tool, sir ;
He has a reputation North,
   As quasi-Union man,

[1] The 2d Louisiana Regiment, (Colored,) at Port Hudson, on the 27th
of May, 1863, lost 600 out of 900 men.

If he could only get at Abe,
  The two might make a plan.

" (Old Abe is soft about the heart,)
  To mitigate the wo,
The horrors of this dreadful war,
  (Abe's pitiful) and so,
If Stephens choose he might depict
  A servile insurrection,
And plead *humanity*, and gain
  His point without detection."

Jeff sent for Stephens and he came ;
  At once advised a peace,
Said he, " King Jeff, the more we wait,
  The more our ills increase ;
We 're whipped, that is the solemn fact,
  We wouldn't like to show it,
We needn't, if we 've any tact—
  Let Abraham, sir, know it."

" Well, Stephens, *I* can 't make a move
  In any such direction,
I 've done my best, and owe defeat
  To unforeseen defection ;
Our friends were going to rise with Lee,
  The plan has got a balk, sir,
There's no dependence—zounds ! I wish
  The Devil had New York, sir."

Just here, a fellow long and lean,
  Put in a shaven head ;
" I want, King Jeff, a week or two
  Of absence now," it said.

“Who 's that ?” said Stephens. “Oh, a scout,
  A secrct service man, sir,
A trusty fellow, always out
  A-working up some plan, sir.”

“Well, Jeff, I 'll try, I 'll go with Ould,
  And with a flag of truce,
Steam up, and have a talk with Abe ;
  It might be of some use,
To hint Napoleon's latest views
  Upon the situation,
That France and England might unite,
  And make an arbitration.”

So Ould and Stephens took a boat,
  And steamed to Fort Munroe,
Thence sent to Abraham a note[1]
  That they would like to go,
“A little farther, if he pleased ;”
  Quoth Abram, waxing hot, sir,
“They want to talk with me, a-hem—
  Well, I should rather *not*, sir.”

So round about the truce-boat turned,
  And headed for the South,
And Stephens back to Dixie steamed,
  His finger in his mouth,
They called a council, Jeff and he,
  And had a long debate,
Discussing how to keep concealed
  The secrets of the State.

All out of blankets, out of shoes,
  And short of corn and bacon ;

[1] July 4, 1863.

Their *rights* of course, they would n't lose,
  Their courage was n't shaken ;
But then their wives and families—
  Ah ! here was no illusion,
The fact so patent to them all
  Was dreadful destitution.

Jeff Davis groaned ; at last he said,
  "Our families can go, sir,
Across the lines, Old Abraham
  Will treat them well, I know, sir."
(Now this reminds me of a fact,
  Pray pardon the digression,
It happened just about the time
  John Bull winked at secession.

A letter came to Abe one day,
  'Twas dated Manchester,
It seems Abe's proclamation had
  Abroad, made quite a stir ;
This letter from " the suffering poor "
  Of sympathy for him,
Did Abram read, but I am sure,
  His spectacles were dim.

He took them off and rubbed them clean
  And winked and rubbed his eyes,
And winked again.   Here Jonathan
  Takes Abram by surprise ;
He walks right in, and sees Old Abe
  A-sitting in his chair ;
The letter open in his hand,
  All blotted here and there.

"Now, Jonathan," said Abe, "look here!
    Here comes the gasping breath
Of want, to speak good words of cheer
    To *us.*   Why, man, 'tis death
That in their wretched faces stares,
    And this the word they send, sir,
That *though their death be in our war,*
    To fight it to the end, sir."

Said Jonathan, "I have enough,
    And something yet to spare, sir,
If Johnny Bull won't take a huff,
    I'll send a cargo there, sir."
So Jonathan the Griswold sent[1]
    All full of yellow corn, sir;
The pirate rebs on mischief bent,
    As sure as you are born, sir,

To capture her a ship dispatch,
    The Griswold made the slip
As she went out, but pirates catch
    Her on the homeward trip.
While Jonathan, whose hand is in,
    Sends off a lot of beans
And pork, to feed the starving rebs
    Way down in New Orleans.)

Quoth Stephens, who in great degree
    Possessed that virtue rare,
That *Southern trait, consistency—*
    "Now Jeff, I would n't care,
Although our hopes are quite forlorn,
    Our plans all out of joint,

---

[1] The Griswold left New York January 9, 1863.

To have it known we counted on
  Old Abraham's weak point."

Said Memminger, " Gold 's out of sight,[1]
  It is n't safe to wait,
We 'd better put in foreign stocks
  Our personal estate."
" That 's very true," responded Jeff, ·
  " If there 's to be a smash, sirs,
'T won't better things for *us* to be
  Included in the crash, sirs."

An orderly, with terror pale,
  Came in here with the news
Of Vicksburg ;—'twas a startling tale,
  Jeff did his temper lose ;
He raved at Pemberton and Jo,
  And in a piteous state,
He ground his teeth in helpless wo,
  And cursed his dreadful fate.

In vain his Cabinet declared
  They had not been deluded,
That *this* must come to pass, in fact,
  They had long since concluded,
And it was better *as it was*,
  Their *lines* were quite too long ;
And in proportion as they shrank,
  Their government was strong.

Jeff could not be consoled, not he—
  Why should he toil and toil
When any stupid General
  His wisest plans could spoil ?

[1] Gold in Richmond 1,600.   Greenbacks 1,200, in August, 1863.

What would come next, no one could tell,
    He 'd half a mind to pitch, sir,
The South, and North, at once, pell mell,
    Into the last great ditch, sir.

Just here in rushed a General—
    'Twas Winder (Provost Marshal);
Said he, "Good news! we are in luck!
    As I 'm a judge impartial!
New York has risen! from the Park
    To Trinity's famed steeple,
One great, resistless, desperate, armed
    'Procession of the people.'[1]

"The negro and Vallandigham,
    The Habeas Corpus Act, sir,
The draft—whate'er the cause may be,
    It is a patent fact, sir,
The mob at last has grasped the reins,
    Our peace friends didn't talk, sir,
In vain; they 've raised against Old Abe
    The Devil in New York, sir.

"I 've brought some papers for a treat,
    A *News* is in the lot;"
The rebels gathered round the sheet
    And aid and comfort got.[2]
Jeff stiffened up; said he, "The news
    Gives solid satisfaction;

---

[1] Draft riot in New York commenced 12th July, 1863.

[2] "All the embarrassments with which that party [peace party] can surround Mr. Lincoln, and all the difficulties that it can throw in the way of the war party in the North, operate directly as so much aid and comfort to the South."—*Letter of M. F. Maury, dated August 17, 1863, to the London "Times."*

It 's worth the forty thousand men
    Lee lost in his late action."

King Jeff dismissed his Cabinet,
    Each took a glass of brandy,
And vowed they never *would* submit
    To Yankee Doodle Dandy.
Then Jeff sat down and wrote a speech ;[1]
    Recovered from alarm, he
Applied his renovated spunk
    To stiffen up his army.

He told his soldiers that the foe
    By partial victory lured
Were massing troops, and so they hoped
    Success might be insured.
"You know too well," said Jefferson,
    "What *they* mean by success—
Exterminate yourselves, your wives,
    Your children—nothing less.

"What they can't plunder, to destroy
    In infamous debauch, sirs ;
To carry ruin to your fields
    And to your homes a torch, sirs.
Soldiers ! with triumph in your reach,
    Save the Confederation !
There 's only one alternative,
    Victory or subjugation."

Jeff signed the paper, (so, indeed,
    Did Benjamin, the Jew, sir,)

---

[1] See Mr. Davis' "Address to the Soldiers of the Confederate States," dated August 1, 1863.

Then set him down in peace to read
  Of deeds Quantrell did do, sir,
In Kansas,[1] such nice genteel play
  Suited to chivalry, sir ;
And quite unlike, Jeff well may say,
  To Yankee deviltry, sir.

[1] Quantrell's raid in Lawrence, Ks., 21st August, 1863.

9

CHAPTER XXVIII

"Oh, Jonathan," said Betsey Jane,
  "When will this fighting cease?
Is there no way to bring again
  The blessed days of peace?"
"You, too, are tired, Betsey Jane,
  Of battling for the right,"
Said Jonathan.   "It seems so vain,"
  Said Betsey, "in our sight;

"With raiding here, and skirmish there,
  And fights upon the seas;
Death all abroad, strife everywhere,
  'Till e'en the gentlest breeze
Comes laden with a wailing cry—
  Our eyes are dim with weeping;
Each waking breath is but a sigh,
  We sob while we are sleeping.

"And when you wake, you miss the boys."
  Said Jonathan, "I know it;
And sometimes when the grief wells up,
  I cannot help but show it.
But Betsey Jane, this much is plain,
  Our day's work we must do;
And when we think upon the end,
  What *is* a life or two?"
(194)

Cried Betsey Jane, "There *must* be news,
  Look at the garden gate!
The neighbors beckon! now they call!
  Oh, Jonathan, don't wait.
'Hurrah! hurrah!' the town is out,
  And now the bells are ringing.
Oh, Jonathan, hear how they shout,
  And there's the children singing."

Said Jonathan, "It is the fourth!'
  The schools are out a-playing.
A battle, eh! oh, Betsey Jane,
  What *is* it you are saying?"
"A *victory* at *Gettysburg!*
  And *Vicksburg*, too, is taken!
Hark! how the guns at Bunker Hill,
  The answering echoes waken."

Cried Jonathan, "Its come at last,
  Send up into the garret;
But first lay out my Sunday coat,
  To-day I mean to wear it.
Bring down the old flint locks once more,
  They always spoke so true;
I want to hear their voice to-day—
  The fire-works, bring them, too."

Then Jonathan he nailed his flag
  Beside his weather-cock;
Of Chinese crackers to the boys
  He gave a double stock.
Then rolled his cider barrels out,
  And left them lying handy;

¹ 4th July, 1863.

And all the live-long day the band
    Played Yankee Doodle Dandy.

When Betsey Jane that evening train
    For Gettysburg departed;
Said Jonathan, "I wonder if
    Old Abe is chipper hearted.
I guess I'll go to Washington,
    He may have need of me, sir;
Perhaps his money is all gone,
    'Twill do no harm to see, sir."

He finds Abe sitting all alone,
    A thinking out a plan, sir,
To make the rebels *Sambo* treat
    Like any other man, sir.
"Now, Jonathan," says he, "you've come
    Just in the nick of time, sir."
"What is the matter Abraham?"
    Says Abe, "It is the crime sir,

" Of putting Sambo in the field
    To fight for our salvation;
Unless we can *protection* yield
    By stern retaliation."
" *That* must be done," said Jonathan,
    " The rebs the way have paved, sir:
For every captured soldier, Abe,
    By Jeff's decree enslaved, sir,

" You must at hardest labor put
    One of the chivalry, sir,
And keep him there, whate'er befalls,
    Till Sambo is set free, sir."

"That's not the worst," says Abe, "I know
  Port Hudson, 't other day, sir,
Poor Sambo did such valor show,
  That, as the rebels say, sir,

"He got no quarter in the fight
  So desperate and hot,
If Sambo wounded fell, the rebs
  Dispatched him on the spot."
Says Jonathan, "If *prisoners*
  Or white, or black, they *kill*, sir,
Why, we can then retaliate,
  By—Uncle Sam—we *will*, sir. [1]

"'Twill work out right, sir, in the end
  The rebs learn by degrees ;
Be steady, Abe, till Jefferson
  His wicked folly sees.
Its hard to manage desperate rebs,
  The *copperheads* are worse,
What's to be done to rid the earth
  Of this increasing curse ?"

"I can't tell, Jonathan," said Abe,
  For every thing I 've tried, sir,
I do my best, with all I do
  They are dissatisfied, sir ;
They cry for peace—*hound* me, as if
  For war *I* was to blame, sir ;
I tell them peace is what *I* want,
  They grumble all the same, sir.

"They don't like *my* way Jonathan
  Of getting at a peace ;

[1] See President Lincoln's Order, No. 252, July 30, 1863.

They talk about a compromise ;
  Perhaps the war would cease
If I should send for Jefferson,
  And very humbly say, sir,
' Now, Jeff, *do* stop—we 're fairly whipped,
  Take everything *your* way, sir.' "

Here Jonathan stood up enraged—
  (I am afraid he swore, sir,)
He struck the table with his fist,
  He knocked Abe's inkstand o'er, sir.
"Sit down," says Abe, " the *Union*, sir,
  Is not *their* point *we* know ;
These disaffected would swap *that*
  To keep enslaved the negro.

" And here again we disagree—
  That is the tender spot,—
I 'd like to have *all men* go free,
  The copperheads would not.
When I suggested *buying* slaves,
  Their scowl did not relax, sir ;
' Buy niggers !' was the hue and cry,
  They wouldn't pay the tax, sir.

"They hate my order Number One,
  They say I 've wrongly acted ;
It is n't constitutional,[1]
  They want it all retracted.
I don't agree ! I have the right,
  By military law, sir,
The property of enemies
  To seize in time of war, sir.

[1] See President's letter to Illinois Convention, August 26, 1863.

"The proclamation valid is,
   Or valid it is not, sir;
If valid it must stand, for death
   Cannot to life be brought, sir.
They will not fight to free the slave—
   Well, Sambo, sir, is willing
To fight for *them*, for us and ours
   His blood he's freely spilling.[1]

"And shall he do for us, and we
   Do nought for him, except, sir,
Make specious promise. No, oh, no!
   My promise *must* be kept, sir."
"It *shall* be kept," said Jonathan,
   "Cheer up, now, Abe, my man;
Look how much God for truth hath wrought
   Since first the strife began.

"The river Mississippi goes
   Unvexed now to the sea."
Said Abraham, "To the North-west
   Our grateful thanks must be ;
Nor wholly yet to them they met,
   As up their way they cleft, sir;
New England and the Middle States
   Down hewing right and left, sir.

"Nor is that all, 't is hard to say
   Aught has been better done,
Than at Anteitam, Gettysburg,
   And Murfreesboro won.
Then, too, for 'Uncle Sam's web-feet,'[2]
   Our praise must not be slack;

---

[1] "There have been men base enough to propose to me to return to slavery the black warriors of Port Hudson and Olustee, and *thus win the respect* of the masters they fought."—*Mr. Lincoln to Governor Randall.*   [2] The Navy.

Wherever, sir, the ground was damp,
  They 've been and left their track.

"Peace doesn't seem so distant now,
  'Twill come, I hope, to stay, sir;
There 'll be some black men who can well
  Remember on that day, sir,
With silent tongue, and steady eye,
  And brave determination;
With well poised bayonets they helped
  To bring this consummation.

"And there 'll be some white men, I fear,
  Unable to forget
That with malignant heart and speech
  They 've striven·to upset[1]
God's plans."   Said Jonathan,
  "We must apply the means, sir;
We 've got this treason to sweep out,
  And we will sweep it clean, sir.

"It 's got into the corners, Abe;
  It 's hid behind the doors;
It 's spread across the briny pond,
  To European shores."
"Ah! that reminds me, Jonathan,
  There is some *recent* news;
You haven't heard it? Well," said Abe,
  "It 's much too good to lose.

"Quite lately rumors had been brought
  To gentle Seward's ear,
That Johnny Bull, in truth, was not
  As tamed as would appear;

See Pres. Lincoln's letter to the Hon. Jas. Conkling, Aug. 16, 1863.

That rebel rams were being built
    Right under Johnny's nose, sir;
So Seward pokes up Mr. Bull,
    And pristine valor shows, sir.

"Says he, 'You're building rebel rams!'
    Growled Bull, 'Your no diviner;
These little rams, I hear, are for
    The Emperor of China.'
Said Seward, 'Will you *stop* these rams?'
    'That is no easy task, sir,'
Said John; 'perhaps it can't be done,
    I will my lawyer ask, sir.'

"Now Seward had just then in mind
    The pirate Alabama;
And her career was fitted ill
    To make his temper calmer.
Said he, 'These rams *must* be detained,
    Whatever be the law, sir;
If not, your Bullship may prepare,
    I take it—this is *war*, sir.'

"At this Bull held his head quite stiff,
    He was but illy pleased;
But Adams wrote, that very night,
    The rebel rams were seized.[1]
And Johnny looked about to find
    Some other way more handy,
From off the sea to drive the ships
    Of Yankee Doodle Dandy."

[1] Two iron-plated rams, built on the Mersey, England, by the Messrs. Laird, for the use of the rebels, were seized by order of the British Government upon a charge of an intention to evade the neutrality laws, October 9, 1863.

CHAPTER XXIX

"Now Abe," said Jonathan, "the cries
   From Eastern Tennessee
Ring in my ears; you must devise
   A way that land to free.
Lee 's whipped so badly, he must wait
   Till reinforcements come, sir;
I wish to goodness Grant had brought
   His Vicksburg prisoners home, sir.

"They 'll all be up in one short week
   To join Lee on the border,
He 'll have them properly exchanged
   With *skeletons* to order!"[1]
Here Jonathan stamped angrily,
   And Abram seemed to chafe, sir;
As if the thing, right in his mind,
   To speak out—was n't safe, sir.

At last, he said, "Well, Jonathan,
   The fighting will not stop,
Now Rosecrans in Tennessee
   Has gathered in his crop
And started, pressing Bragg along
   Till he has made a halt

---

[1] The Vicksburg prisoners were declared exchanged, and immediately put into the field by the rebels.

At Chattanooga.   They will meet,
   Or 't won't be Rosey's fault.

"And Burnside 's well upon his way,
   At Knoxville, Buckner waits ;
The war will have a wicked sway,
   Within the Border States."
Said Jonathan, "We 'll fight it through,
   Press hard now, Abe, don't falter ;
By all our dead boys, brave and true,
   King Jeff must wear his halter."

So Burnside o'er the mountains rode,
   Full thirty miles a day, sir ;
Growled Buckner, "I 've surrendered *once*,
   I think I 'll run away, sir."
Then all the people cheered in glee,[1]
   Tore down the rebel rags,
And hoisted right triumphantly
   Their hidden Union flags.

And on brave Rosey's soldiers went,
   The rebels made no show
At Chattanooga[2]— what that meant,
   Old Rosey did n't know.
'Twas rumored, Bragg declined a fight,
   Was reinforcing Lee ;
How far that rumor was from right,
   We very soon shall see.

On Rosey pushed, the mountain o'er,
   He pushes to his goal ;

---

[1] General Burnside occupied Knoxville, Tenn., September 4, 1863.
[2] General Rosecrans crossed the Tennessee and invested Chattanooga, August 31, 1863.

Jeff sends up Longstreet's army corps,
　With prisoners on parole ;
The Vicksburg and Port Hudson men,
　To Grant and Banks surrendered ;
Declared exchanged, they marched to Bragg
　And bloody service tendered.

The nineteenth of September breaks
　On Chickamauga stream,
And on the left of Rosecrans
　The rebel bayonets gleam ;
Bragg's troops are massed—he 'll turn the left,
　But Rosecrans has tact, sir,
And Thomas from the centre comes,
　The move to counteract, sir.

Alas ! for Rosey, he has met
　His more than match to-day,
The rebels press so sorely up,
　His gallant men give way ;
They rally, charge—along the front
　Is one consuming fire,
And from the ground the rebs had gained
　They sullenly retire.

All night on the disputed ground,
　Old Rosey's soldiers stay ;
The morn breaks, with no warlike sound,
　It is the Sabbath-day ;[1]
There 'll be no fight—the rebels sleep.
　Was *that* the musket rattle ?
To arms ! the foe upon the left
　Is opening the battle.

[1] The 20th of September, 1863.

The rattle of the musket turns
  To deafening cannon roar ;
And Rosey to his sorrow learns,
  As Bragg's great columns pour
Right down upon him, that the foe
  From every quarter come,
Is pressing with resistless weight,
  To drive the Yankees home.

His men fall back, they turn and flee,
  Force Rosey from the field.
But Thomas—like the mount behind—
  Stands firm, he will not yield ;
He stands, to breast the rebel tide
  That surges at his feet,
There "like a lion, when at bay,"
  Fierce onsets firm to meet.

Wave after wave rolls up and breaks,
  Upon that crescent line ;
The rebels spy a mountain gap,
  Said Bragg, "The day is mine,
If I can get my columns through ;
  Go, Longstreet, strike the rear, sir."
The rebels rush into the gap,
  When suddenly appear, sir,

Bold Granger and his brave reserves,
  Of victory the token ;
Their "charge was terrible and swift,"
  The enemy was broken.
They fight till cartridges are out,
  And daylight well nigh o'er,
Then with the bayonet they rout
  The rebs, who come no more.

Next day—when Thomas thought it best
    To hunt up Rosecrans, sir,
And left the field.—the rebs at rest
    Waked up and quickly ran, sir,
And *squatted on the little plat,*
    And cheered, and called it *theirs,* sir;
For such a victory as that,
    Jeff doth forget his cares, sir.

He smiled and praised the rebel troops
    For Chickamauga won, sir,
But hinted, there was heavy work
    Remaining to be done, sir.
And Abram, when *he* heard the news,
    Said, "Stanton, now I can't, sir,
Run any risk—I 'd rather choose
    To send down *General Grant,* sir."

So Grant to Chattanooga went,[1]
    Found Rosey out of bread,
His men and horses almost spent—
    Bragg knows it too, he said;
Now, Bragg had sent a message up,
    All civilly to state, sir,
Non-combatants should now forthwith,
    The town evacuate, sir.

Said Grant, "That means he 'll run away,
    The fact I 'll ascertain, sir;
Go, Thomas, drive his pickets in,
    And make his meaning plain, sir."
They found Bragg felt himself so strong,
    He 'd sent up Longstreet's corps

[1] General Grant assumed command of the military division of the
Mississippi, comprising the Departments of the Ohio, Cumberland,
and Tennessee, on the 15th of October, 1863.

To sweep off Burnside—but ere long,
  Brave Sherman's columns pour

In Longstreet's rear.   Burnside besieged[1]
  At Knoxville stubborn fights, sir,
Day after day, though well we know,
  His was a sorry plight, sir.
He won't abandon Tennessee,
  He never will retreat,
But though his men fight cheerfully,
  They 've little left to eat.

Day after day, brave Burnside waits
  While Grant is whipping Bragg ;
The twentieth day of siege is come,
  Still waves the Union flag—
Waves free, as if in confidence,
  It takes it fully granted,
By rebel rag it never more
  Again shall be supplanted.

At last a horse pants into town,
  " Good news !" the rider said ;
The cavalry are bearing down,
  And Sherman, too, has led
His men from Chattanooga field,
  And Longstreet from the meeting,
Falls back in haste, the victory yields
  By everywhere retreating.[2]

Then Sherman walked about the place,
  And looked at the redoubt

---

[1] Knoxville besieged, November 17, 1863.
[2] Longstreet raises the siege December 4th.

Named Saunders—where on Sunday last,[1]
  So many lives went out.
Then traveled down to General Grant,[2]
  Lest Bragg might make attack;
"I would not like a fight," thought he,
  "Before I can get back."

But Bragg of fight had had his fill,
  The reason was conclusive;
Said he, "I'm driven off the hill,[3]
  'Twould be a dream illusive,
Now Grant is posted safe and high,
  And strongly fortified, sir,
For me to think of getting back,
  'Twon't do—my best *I've* tried, sir."

He tells King Jeff his desperate case,
  King Jeff is quite surprised,
And sends up Johnston to the place—
  The rebs demoralized,
Make dreadful speed; in Dalton town
  Their horses foam and pant, sir,
Just anything to get away,
  Out of the sight of Grant, sir.

[1] The 29th of November, 1863.
[2] Left Knoxville, Tenn., December 8, 1863.
[3] Lookout Mountain stormed the 26th of November. Mission Ridge captured the 25th.

CHAPTER XXX.

THE rebels grumbled awfully,
   And said 'twas very plain,
Bragg could n't lead the chivalry,
   He need n't try again ;
And Mr. Foote, he made a speech,[1]
   Said Jeff was all to blame—
"*He* spoiled the fight.   At Gettysburg
   He did the very same.

"If he kept on his present course,
   'Twould end in ruination.
He," Mr. Foote, "could but condemn
   The project—by starvation
To thin the Yankee prisoners out,
   As Jefferson was doing."[2]
Quoth Davis, when he read the speech,
   "Another storm is brewing."

He sent for Ould, to ask him if
   He could n't move the hitch
In the Exchange—but Ould said, "No!
   Abe's roused to such a pitch

---

[1] In rebel Congress, December 8, 1863.

[2] "It is true that many of our officers felt the injustice of the treatment inflicted upon the prisoners, but what could they do?   Orders came from headquarters, and they were bound to obey them, for the first duty of a soldier is obedience."—Page 170 of Notes from War Pictures, by B. Estvan, Colonel of cavalry in Confederate army.

About the 'niggers,' but I 've sent
 A note will fret him some, sir;
I wrote that no more loads of food
 Could to the prisoners come, sir."[1]

"You acted hastily," said Jeff;
 "I have," said Ould, " 'tis true,
Cut off from Turner,[2] and his set,
 A source of revenue."
"Well, well," said Jeff, "these perquisites
 Do no one any hurt, sir,
I don't see where your order hits,
 For Winder doth assert, sir,

"This matter of Old Abe's supplies
 Is neither here nor there,
Trust *him*, the Yankees will not get
 Much comfort from their share."
"The point is this," said Ould, "you see
 I 'm shooting at long range, sir,
For while the Yanks can feed their men,
 We 'll never get exchange, sir.

"This sending food 's a safety-valve,
 The injured Yankee nation
Without it, sir, would scald Old Abe
 In boiling indignation.
And so, I 've put a stopper, Jeff,
 On Abram's cunning measure,
He 's read my note by this, and can
 Digest it at his leisure.

"So Yankee knaves must learn to live
 Upon the soldiers 'ration;'"

[1] See Ould's official letter of December 11, 1863.
[2] Maj. Turner (and bro.) Commander and Inspector of Libby Prison.

And Ould's decision, from the rebs
   Met general approbation.
'Tis true, a few, like Mr. Foote,
   Who had no sort of tact, sir,
Declared that Ould's fair promises
   Were better than the fact, sir.

'Twas said, that even Winder came
   From Anderson direct,
To beg King Jeff, for his own sake,
   Their larder to inspect.[1]
But Jeff was out of sorts that day,
   · And was not very civil,
And in a rage was heard to say,
   "Go, Winder—to the Devil !"

If Winder to the Devil went,
   It did not much avail, sir ; -
The Devil could no wo invent
   But was already stale, sir.
At Anderson and Saulsbury,
   If Winder *had* depicted
Their scenes, the Devil would have stood
   Of *jealousy* convicted.

His imps but lately had been scared
   Out of those same stockades,
Such sights, they in accord declared,
   Since e'er the world was made,
They never saw ; they 'd like to know
   The *author* of the plan,

[1] "Two surgeons were at one time sent by Davis to inspect the camp, but a walk through a small section gave them all the information they desired, and we never saw them again."—Deposition of Prescott Tracy, 82d Regt. N. Y. V.

So comprehensive, they would show
   Great honor to the man.

But, if the Devil would consent,
   They 'd rather not go back, sir.
The things that Winder did invent,
   Their *tender souls* did rack, sir.
They 'd go again with Keith to play
   In Eastern Tennessee,
With Quantrell on his Kansas raids
   They would keep company.

They 'd go out West to Albert Pike,
   And paint their faces red.
"Good Devil! anything you like
   But Southern jails," they said.
The Devil smiled—said he, "My dears,
   Right well your cause you 've pleaded,
It ain't my way to send my imps
   Except where they are needed."

"They 'll do without you in the South,
   Smooth off those little scowls,
Draw down the corners of your mouth,
   And look as wise as owls.
Be off to *Indiana* State,
   Be 'Golden Circle Knights,' sirs,
On 'Despot Abraham' dilate,
   And 'Constitutional Rights,' sirs.

"Now, don't forget the side your 're on,
   There 'll be a great confusion;
Jeff pays the best—and slavery
   Is my pet institution;

Keep this in mind, whate'er you do,
  However you disguise it,
Save *slavery*—IT IS DIVINE!
  Whatever man denies it.

"A few of you had better go
  To Canada, by land, sirs,
There 'll be a blaze at Buffalo,
  As I do understand, sirs ;
A plot's on foot to free the rebs,
  At Johnson's Island Camp, sirs,[1]
There 'll be rare sport, I 'd like to go,
  But I 'm just off a tramp, sirs,

"From stirring up New York allies,
  I 've no more time to roam, sirs,
Jeff looks to me for his supplies,
  And I must stay at home, sirs.
If you can take it in your way,
  Just make a small detail,
To help our soldiers at Camp Chase[2]
  And Morgan out of jail."

'Twas so the Devil had advised,
  His imps in last October,
Since then to his own great surprise,
  He felt himself grown sober.
He walked the streets of Richmond now,
  With many a stifled groan,
But all he asked as once before
  Was to be "LET ALONE."[3]

---

[1] Conspiracy to free prisoners, and burn Buffalo and other lake cities, was discovered October 10, 1863.

[2] A conspiracy to rescue the prisoners in the Ohio Penitentiary and at Camp Chase, came to light November 31, 1863.

[3] "There was a man which had a spirit of an unclean devil, and cried out with a loud voice, saying 'Let us alone!'"—LUKE iv. 33.

CHAPTER XXXI

Now all this time in Charleston town
  Reigned dreadful discontent,
For Stanton had some gunners down
  With Quincey Gilmore sent;
And Charleston to the rebels was
  A sort of forlorn hope,
Her attitude, together with
  A letter from the Pope,

Which Jeff had got, was now the last
  And brightest constellation
In Southern sky, so overcast
  By Yankee occupation.
On Morris Island Gilmore lands,
  On Wagner makes attack,[1]
And gallantly he leadeth up
  His white troops and his black.

Old Massachusett's Fifty-fourth [2]
  Stands boldly in the front,
And of the rebels' dreadful fire,
  Unflinching bears the brunt;
The colonel falls, and one by one
  Its officers are slain,

[1] July 17, 1863.
[2] Colored Regiment.

The men are slaughtered though they " fight," .
  And slaughtered all in vain.

The rebels sally from the fort,
  They dig a long deep pit,
And bury Gilmore's fallen men,
  Said they, " It doth befit
These ' freedom shriekers,' in their death
  To find ' amalgamation ; ' " [1]
So in this safe and pleasant way,
  They did insult the nation.

Quoth Gilmore, " It 's not over yet ;
  My Uncle Samuel says, sir,
In Charleston town he owes a debt,
  And *U. S. always pays*, sir ;
He 's waited now for several years,
  And interest has run,
And I 'll collect it ; "—so he trains
  His big Swamp Angel gun,

Right over to the town, and waits
  For his small guns to scrape
Fort Sumter's face, and pierce its sides,
  And knock it out of shape ;
And then he wrote to Beauregard,
  To give him time for running,
And on the morrow Uncle Sam [2]
  Began his little dunning.

And every day for one whole year,
  The music of the shell

<hr>

[1] Col. Shaw and his officers were buried in the same trench with his colored soldiers.
[2] August 23, 1863.

Reminded gentle Beauregard
  That when Fort Sumter fell,
And Jeff and he sat down to take
  A social glass of brandy,
That Jeff had sworn they 'd fixed the fate
  Of Yankee Doodle Dandy.

The rebels said they were not hurt
  By all the shot so thrown ;
I only know, in Charleston streets,
  With grass and weeds o'ergrown,
On rotting wharves, and battered walls,
  When down our troopers came,
They found, in plainest characters,
  Had treason signed its name.

CHAPTER XXXII

Wʜɪʟᴇ Foote was scolding in the house,[1]
  Disgusted with Bragg's fighting;
Old Abe his proclamation of
  Free amnesty was writing.[2]
The proclamation threw the rebs
  Of Dixie in confusion,
And Foote declared it was, in fact,
  Unwarranted intrusion.

And he *resolved* (his usual way
  Of venting his displeasure,)
There never could be hour or day,
  More ill-timed for the measure;
That Dixie's spirit still was high,
  Etcetera, and so forth,
They 'd fight, and in the "last ditch die,"
  Or freemen they would go forth.

But Longstreet up in Tennessee[3]
  Was sadly disconcerted;
His men the proclamation read,
  And scores of them deserted;
And Davis found his load of care
  Did steadily increase,

[1] Rebel House of Representatives, Dec. 15, 1863.   [2] Dec. 8, 1863.
[3] See Longstreet's correspondence with Gen. Foster, January, 1864.

For Dixie journals here and there
  Were calling out for *peace*.

The North Carolina discontent,
  Vance[1] said, was growing stronger,
Jeff must a remedy invent,
  He could n't hold out longer;
Wrote he, "The people are possessed
  In wishing for a peace.
'Tis strange, the more they are distressed
  Their clamors more increase.

"It 's come to this,—we cannot choose,
  We must negotiate
With Abe, King Jeff, or we shall lose
  Outright the Old North State."
"Negotiate," growled out King Jeff,
  "That is a famous joke, sir,
Vance must have slept, these last three years,
  And has but just awoke, sir."

He wrote to Vance (in confidence)
  "Three efforts I have made
To come to terms, but Abe has not
  The slightest notice paid
To my attempts; we have no choice,
  To fight 's our only course,
And I advise you, Vance, to try
  The argument of force."[2]

While Vance is trying Jeff's wise plan,
  He hears a heavy tramp

[1] Governor of North Carolina.
[2] See Davis' correspondence with Governor Vance.

Of Abe's five hundred thousand more
  In his instruction camp.[1]
And o'er the Mississippi comes
  A noise of cavalry, sir,
And bothers Vance, who "works his sums"
  Out slow and wearily, sir.

'Tis "crazy" Sherman in the West,
  Who leads a promenade, sir,[2]
(By crazy people, sometimes great
  Discoveries are made, sir;)
And Old Tecumseh on his raid
  Found rations were so handy
In Dixie's Land, he could subsist
  All Yankee Doodle Dandy.

He treasured up this little bit
  Of useful information,
And when there came a season fit
  He gave it to the nation.
But while he runs his sabre through
  The bubble of secession,
That other raider, Colonel Straight,
  From Libby makes egression.[3]

Through tunnel, patiently scooped out
  Beneath the sentry's beat,
One hundred captured officers
  Stand free upon the street.
The rebs on guard see dusky forms
  Diverging from the shed,[4]

[1] Draft ordered February, 1864. [2] Left Vicksburgh February, 1864.
[3] February 10, 1864.

[4] "One of the guards told me that they saw our men escaping through the tunnel, and that they did not prevent them, supposing it was their own men stealing our boxes."—*Deposition of Capt. A. R. Calhoun, June* 1, 1864.

Where Abe's great boxes of supplies
    Were stored ; they only said,

" Our boys are out again to-night,
    A-confiscating things."
And ere they turned again, the forms
    Had somehow taken wings.
And off through lane, and wood, and swamp,
    The scattered patriot band,
Hound hunted, sore and famished, all
    Are headed for " God's Land."

Some drop in faintness by the way,
    But Sambo's hut is handy,
And Sambo *never did* betray
    His Yankee Doodle Dandy.
He gives him *all he has* to eat,
    " For Linkum's sake " he said,
While Dinah bathes his bleeding feet
    And " shakes him up " a bed.

And Sambo guides him through the swamps,
    Across the bridge of logs,
And skillfully he teaches him
    To foil the rebel dogs.
So on they plod, so wearily,
    Till startled by a tramp
Of cavalry,—oh ! joy to see !
    The blue coats, from the camp.[1]

Now rest, poor battered patriots,
    From hunger, cold, and rags,
And learn to smile !   See, yonder wave
    The glorious Union flags.

[1] Gen. Butler sent out cavalry to meet the fugitives.

Drink deep of air and light once more,
  Then, now again so free,
Remember Libby and Belle Isle,
  And strike for Liberty!

Said bold Kilpatrick to his men,
  "Here is a chance, no doubt, sirs,
I don't see why we can't *go in*,
  Since Straight has just come out, sirs;
Let's make a dash for Libby, men!
  And rescue, ere they die,
Our gallant boys in Belle Isle pen."
  Four thousand throats reply.

And bit and bridle to their steeds,
  Impatiently they stand,
No second word Kilpatrick needs
  To speak to his command;
Young Dahlgren springs upon his horse,
  No thought of danger tames
His bounding heart,—he leads the way,
  He's off across the James.[1]

He sees but one absorbing sight,
  He rideth gallantly,
He'll reach Belle Isle before the night,
  And set the captives free.
His horses feel the goading spurs,
  They dash through sun and shade,
Through wood and field; and halt at last,
  In rebel ambuscade!

A flash of sabres, and a shot,
  A struggle in the dark,

[1] Leaves Culpepper February 28, 1864.

And Dahlgren's horse is riderless,
　　And he is lying stark.[1]
In vain Kilpatrick waits for him,
　　In vain his signal gun ;
No answer comes, 'tis all in vain,
　　Kilpatrick's raid is done.

He turns his horses round about,
　　And strikes for Yorktown Station,
And leaves the rebs in Richmond town
　　In dreadful consternation.
They ring the bells, and call to arms,
　　And Jeff sends off to Lee,
To say the " Yanks " are at the gate
　　With all their cavalry.

And Satan with a wicked frown,
　　Comes out of Castle Thunder,
Walks to and fro throughout the town,
　　And sends his slaves down under
The prison walls, to stow a stock
　　Of double proof gunpowder ;[2]
Says he, " When Yankees loud do knock,
　　We 'll answer them still louder."

The hours passed by, no knocking came
　　But that of their own hearts,
And rebels blushing in their shame,
　　And tingling with the smarts
Of passing fear, began to scold
　　King Jeff for being scared ;

[1] Dahlgren murdered March 4, 1864.

[2] Major Turner said in my presence, the day we were paroled, in answer to the question " Was the prison mined ? " " Yes, and I would have blown you all to Hades before I would have suffered you to be rescued."—*Affidavit of Col. Farnsworth.*

He might have known the Yanks were bold,
  And should have been prepared.

'Twas rumored Jeff had packed his trunks,
  And sent them off by rail;
'Twas vain the rebel press declared
  'Twas but an idle tale.
What! Jeff desert Virginia!
  Richmond evacuated!
'Twas in her sacred precincts that
  The "last ditch" was located.

For ever as the days rolled on
  The rumor was repeated;
And on reb visages forlorn,
  Suspicion grew deep seated.
In vain they choked the rising groan,
  Or tried to drown in brandy
The fear of being *left alone*
  With Yankee Doodle Dandy.

CHAPTER XXXIII.

King Jeff stuffs cotton in his ears
  To keep out rebel grumbling;
But there's a deeper noise he hears
  Continually rumbling:
'Tis Abram's trains of volunteers,
  And wagons heavy freighted;
Quoth Jeff, "Abe's armies it appears.
  Are being concentrated.

"'Tis clear the tyrant is resolved
  Upon a desperate course;
He's mustering all Yankeedom,
  And with tremendous force
He'll strike, to crush us by his *weight;*
  I'm not alarmed at all,
But I must trim my ship of state
  To weather such a squall."

So Jeff sends off for General Bragg—
  He couldn't find a wiser—
To come to Richmond for to be
  Jeff's right hand and adviser.
And Lincoln sent for General Grant;[1]
  Said he, "'Tis a relief, sir,
To make so sensible a man
  Our General-in-Chief, sir."

[1] March 12, 1863.

And Jonathan endorsed the move ;
  "'Twas true," the old man said,
" The army had for many days
    Been weak about the head."[1]
So Grant and Halleck coalesced,
    The experiment was fine,
And proved the *ornamental* with
    The *useful can* combine.

Grim Grant brought up his best segars
    To smoke the rebels out ;
He brought up, too, his son of Mars,
    "For *Sheridan*, no doubt,"
Said he, "we 'll need to send the rebs
    A-whirling down the valley."
Then Grant he sounds a bugle blast
    And Abe's battalions rally.

They do not cheer for little Grant
    Whene'er he comes in sight, sir ;
They only stand still more erect
    And draw their belts up tight, sir.
They 've heard of Grant, and know 't is true
    What all the rebels say,
That once at work, his task he 'll do
    If in no other way—

He 'll bridge the ditch with heaps of slain,
    Who perish in the strife ;

[1] " Halleck's Official Report had shown that operations were sometimes directed by the President, with or without the approval of his military counsellors, sometimes by one or another of his military counsellors without the approval of the President, and sometimes by the General in the field without the approval of any one.—*See* " *Twelve Decisive Battles of the War*," *page* 361.

But he 'll exact for every man
    The foe shall give a life.
" A life for life," said " butcher " Grant,
    " For six from six leaves nought, sir ;
But six from twelve 's another thing,"
    And so his reck'ning brought, sir,

This grave conclusion—" Stroke on stroke,
    Till Jeff repents his sin ;
An equal loss is victory—
    I can lose half and win."
Then Jonathan, he tells Old Abe,
    That Grant must have *carte blanche*, sir,
That if *nobody interferes*
    The rebs won't have a chance, sir.

Grant wrote to Sherman that same day
    To make a move instanter
On Johnston, who had stopped the way
    'Twixt him and doomed Atlanta.
So while in Richmond Jeff and Bragg
    Mourned over hopes departed,
" Demented " Sherman took his flag
    And into Dixie started.

CHAPTER XXXIV.

ONE Sunday morning, just as Abe[1]
 Was going out to meeting,
In came Old Jonathan and said,
 Without a word of greeting,
"Here, Abe, I 've brought our Betsey Jane,
 To speak a word with you, sir.
She 's true as steel, and good as gold,
 And what she *says*, she 'll *do*, sir."

"I 'm glad to see you, Betsey Jane,
 Be pleased to take a chair."
And Abe sat down between the twain
 With a bewildered air.
"There 's nothing wrong, I hope," he said,
 "This is so bright a day."
"*Yes*, sir," said Jonathan, "*there is*,
 The devil is to pay !"

And Jonathan, he struck his cane
 So hard upon the floor,
He startled Abe ; and Betsey Jane,
 (Who spoke no word before,)
Said, "Jonathan—you 're roused again,
 You 'll not be understood, sir,

[1] About the middle of May, 1864.

Be patient, man, and speak out plain
  Your anger does no good, sir."

"It *does* do good," roared Jonathan ;
  "I must n't make a noise ?
God help us ! Abraham," he groaned,
  "They 're *murdering* our boys !"
"Too many, sir," said Abraham,
  " Are counted with the slain."
"It is n't *that*.   They 're *starving* them
  In Southern jails," said Jane.

" We 're just up from Annapolis,[1]
  We 've seen such dreadful woe,
I 'm fearful I should speak amiss
  If I should try to show,
What I have seen, as to and fro
  The hospitals I 've walked, sir."[2]
" What do they say ?" said Abraham :
  Said Betsey Jane, " I 've talked, sir,

" To these poor living skeletons,
  Of friends—of going home, sir,
But on their pinched and pallid face
  A *smile* has never come, sir.[3]
Our words of kindness—all too late,
  Are powerless to save,
For food alone—crushed, desolate,
  They still have strength to crave.

[1] In the late (May, 1864,) temporary resumption of the cartel, boat loads of half-naked living skeletons, foul with filth' and covered with vermin, were landed at Annapolis.

[2] See Report of Commission of Inquiry, appointed by Sanitary Commission. Published by Littell, Boston.

[3] " As if they had passed through a period of physical and mental agony, which had driven the smile from their faces forever."—*Page* 5 *of Report.*

"From bed to bed, from ward to ward,[1]
  The same sad sight," said Jane,
"Blank, bony faces, staring out
  Above the counterpane ;
Beneath the sheet—oh, misery !
  Shrivelled to skin and bone,
Our boys—alive—some famine-wild,
  Some idiotic grown.

"The sunken eye, the blighted skin—
  Sand-bruised, and dead, and rough,
The bones protruding—sockets dry—
  Oh ! Abe, it is enough
To break one's heart to contemplate
  Such agony unspoken,"
"Hush ! hush !" said Jonathan, "there—wait—
  For Abe's is being broken."

Old Abe had sunk down in his chair,
  His head upon his breast,
His hands were clenched, and Betsey heard
  A groan but half repressed.
She opened up her reticule,
  "Here is a photograph, sir,
I 've brought to show you—it is *one*,
  There 's many more than half, sir,

"Of our exchanged, resembling it,
  For one may stand for all."
"Do they all *die* ?" said Abraham,
  "This *dead* form doth appall !"
"*That* is a *living* skeleton—
  My boy.   John was his name, sir ;

---

[1] See Report, as above.

His grandsire, Jonathan, and I
    Just from his bedside came, sir.

"He does n't know us, sir, as yet,
    He wails at every breath
For food; we dole it out, for food
    Is agony and death
To those so long kept starving, Abe,
    And Jonathan and I,
Have smothered grief as day by day
    We 've listened to that cry,

"Till Jonathan has grown quite faint,
    And sick with indignation,
And I have come to ask you if
    The honor of the nation,
Must be maintained at *such* a price ?
    If rebels, loathsome, vile,
Must hold our soldiers till they rot
    In Libby and Belle Isle ?"

"Ask Jonathan," said Abraham,
    "Whate'er *he says is law.*"
"I 'm thinking of Fort Pillow, Abe,[1]
    And slaves they took in war;
We *must* be just.   This foul abuse
    Is with a purpose done, sir,
It had its origin, Old Abe,
    When strife was first begun, sir."

"They say it 's dire necessity;
    They have n't food to spare."

____

[1] April 12, 1864, Fort Pillow was captured, and the garrison murdered after surrender.

"Good heavens, Abe !" said Jonathan,
  "Their *cattle* better fare.
Besides, they were not forced by want,
    When they their prisons made, sir,
To choose a pestilential swamp
    The site for their stockade, sir."

"It did n't add to their supplies
    To mark out a *dead line*, sir ;
And water 's free—and yet our men
    For *water* pant and pine, sir ;
The country 's full of forests, Abe,
    They grudge our boys the logs,
And fireless, and shelterless,
    They 've grovelled like the hogs.[1]

"No, Abraham, it 's done *to kill !*
    Old Winder's foul stockade
Has slain more men for Jefferson
    Than all Lee's cannonade ;
The only way that I can see
    This horror to abate,
Is to make Grant the remedy,
    You can't retaliate."

"Well, Jonathan," said Betsey Jane,
  "While Satan, sir, is stalking
All through the land, 'tis very plain
    I have no time for *talking.*

[1] "They lay in the ditch, as the most protected place, heaped upon one another and lying close together, as one of them expressed it, like hogs in winter, taking turns as to who should have the outside of the road. In the morning, the row of the previous night was marked by the motionless forms of those who were sleeping on in their last sleep—frozen to death."—*Sanitary Commission Report, page* 11.

I 'll go back to the soldier's bed,
    You 'll find out, I dare say, sirs,
Some plan to save them—*when they 're dead,*
    That 's *not* a woman's way, sirs."

" What would *you* do ?" said Abraham ;
    Said Betsy Jane, in answer,
" I would not waste most precious time
    In poulticing a cancer.
You *threatened* to retaliate,
    And won our grateful thanks, sir,
But after the report we found
    Your cartridges were blanks, sir.

" I would n't be surprised at all,
    Were Jeff now safe in jail,
You two would talk, and talk, and call
    A court, and give him bail."
Here Abram smiled. " Yes, sir," said Jane,
    " You *men*, with all your reason,
Are fit to twist and turn out Jeff
    As *innocent* of *Treason.*"

Old Jonathan uneasily,
    Was pacing to and fro
Across the floor. " Come, Betsey Jane,"
    Said he, " it 's time to go.
You 'd better speak to Stanton, Abe,
    These cruelties *must* cease, sir,
Our starving soldiers *must* obtain,
    Some way, a quick release, sir."

Then Abe called Stanton, who declared,
    Whatever folks might say,

That he, for one, would *not* consent,
  To give Jeff his own way;
" We 've thirty thousand stalwart rebs,
  Jeff wants them now at home—
For them he 'll fill our hospitals."
  Said Abe, " The boys *must come.*

" It 's no use, Stanton, we must fight
  The rebels at their *strongest*—
Give Jeff his reinforcements ; if.
  The right way *is* the longest,
It will not matter in the end,
  So History may tell,
Not that our work was *quickly* done,
  But that we *did it well !*"

Thus " man for man," the cartel ran,
  And sorrowful to know,
That never Charon o'er the Styx
  Steered such a load of woe,
As down the James to Jonathan,
  And Betsey Jane, who waited,
The truce-boat steamed, with nameless grief,
  And misery deep freighted.

CHAPTER XXXV.

When Jeff and Bragg, in Richmond heard
　　Of Sherman on the move,
That he had knocked his army from
　　The military groove,
And now was running from his base,
　　Three hundred miles away,
Jeff laughed, and Bragg he had the grace
　　Right saucily to say:

" Tecumseh 's on the war-path, Jeff,
　　Great warrior of his nation,
He 'll whoop when Wheeler's raiders cut
　　Through his communication."
But Sherman's lines were like the snake,
　　Which, when once cut in two,
Wriggles its ends together, and
　　Is just as good as new.

Down dash the raiders, tear up rails,
　　And burn a few cross-ties,
Up backs a *reconstruction* train,
　　The new made gap supplies.
So, leaving Johnston's cavalry
　　To sport at their own pleasure,
The ground 'twixt him and rebel camp,
　　Doth crazy Sherman measure.

He finds a mountain spur between,
    By Buzzard's Roost Gap cleft,
The pass was strongly fortified,
    He turns it to the left.
Now left—now right—now in advance,
    Till Johnston, all in sadness,
Finds out that crazy Sherman hath
    A method in his madness.

Quoth Jo, "It is not very clear,
    I must consult my map;
McPherson's getting in my rear;
    It 's very like a trap." .
He falls back on *Resaca.*   That
    Was just to Hooker's mind,[1]
And somehow in the falling back
    Resaca falls behind.

Jo does n't stop.   At Adairsville[2]
    Doth Newton touch his rear;
It shrinks away from his bold grasp,
    And rebels said 't was clear,
"That General Jo did drag the Yanks
    From their communication,
When they were where he wanted them
    He 'd deal annihilation."

Said Jo, "My Allatoona Pass
    Will brave the Yankee's might, sir;"
"Ah, ha!" said Sherman, "I 'm in haste,
    I 'll turn it to the right, sir;

[1] Battle of Resaca, fought May 15,.1864. Hooker drove the enemy
from several hills, and Johnston escaped in the night.
[2] Second of May, 1864.

If I can get to Dallas first—
  I do not care to banter—
But Jo will rather have the worst
  In racing for Atlanta."

Jo sees the game, he takes a stand
  With Hood in line of battle,
And day by day fierce skirmishing [1]
  Keeps up the musket rattle.
Jo thinks the Yanks "disorganized,"
  He makes a sudden rush,
McPherson's corps will be surprised,
· Jo will the Yankees crush.

With shout and yells, the rebels dash [2]
  On Logan's brave division
A lightning flash, and dreadful crash,
  And swift, with sharp incision;
The rebel ranks are mowed like grain,
  The rebel columns reel, sir;
They rally once, and once again,
  And meet McPherson's steel, sir.

The baffled foe drew back, and left
  His wounded and his dead,
And Sherman makes another flank:
  The rebs in Richmond said
The news was satisfactory,
  Their sanguine hopes did meet,
"That all Jo Johnston's victories
  Were won by his retreat."

[1] Near New Hope, Ga., May 25th.
[2] Battle of Dallas, 28th of May.

But as to Jo himself, he might
  With reason be confounded;
Now flanked to right, and now to left,
  And now well nigh surrounded;
He gains the mount of Kenesaw,
  Secure upon its height, sir,
While Old Tecumseh halts below,[1]
  With every camp in sight, sir.

Three weeks of skirmishing and mud,
  Till reb as well as Yank
Cried out, impatient of delay,
  " Why *don't* Tecumseh *flank* ?"
Said Sherman, " I 'm a man of sense,
  They 're very much at fault, sir;
I 've more than *one* way of offence,
  I 'll Kenesaw assault, sir."

He makes attack,[2] it 's no use now
  The blunder to detail;
Two armies[3] strike, apart, at once,
  And both the armies fail.
Half up the slope the veterans fight,
  Then broken, crushed, retire;
As well toil up the dreadful height
  Of Etna, when on fire.

Jo telegraphs a victory,
  And then sends off a letter,
To tell King Jeff he 's *flanked* again
  With Yanks at Marietta;[4]

[1] June 11, 1864.
[2] 17th of July, 1864.
[3] Army of the Cumberland and Army of the Tennessee.
[4] Sherman occupies Marietta.

That he is making greatest speed
  To get across the river,[1]
Ere Sherman's guns unlimbered be,
  And canister deliver.

Jeff frowned, and wrote to General Hood
  That he was sadly grieved ;
He always knew Jo was no good ;
  That now he was relieved,[2]
He hoped that *Hood* would imitate
  The gallant General Lee,
And never more insult the state
  With Fabian policy.

Said Hood, "My gallant boys in grey,
  There 'll be no more retreating ;
We 'll change our tactics, and to-day
  Will give the Yanks a beating."
They sallied from their works in force,[3]
  With frantic scream and yell,
And down on Sherman's startled troops,
  With desperation fell.

On, as a mighty avalanche,
  Crumbling, and caving runs,
So pressed they, melting as they went,
  Before Tecumseh's guns ;
On and over their own dead
  They never stopped or quailed,
Till Hood, in disappointment said,
  "Our bold sortie has failed."

---

[1] Johnston crossed the Chattahootchee, July 9, 1864.
[2] July 17th, 1864.
[3] July 20th, Hood sallied from his Peach Tree Creek line and attacked.

Hood does n't *fall back* ; has n't Jeff
  Expressed a prohibition ?
But, two days after his assault,
  He *changes his position.*
Behind a strong line of redoubts,
  He puts the army down;
He 's bound to keep Tecumseh out ;
  Of his Atlanta town.

Up comes the tireless Yankee host,
  Their coil is growing tight ;
Cried Hood, " To wait is to be lost,
  I *must* go out and fight."
He starts in desperate agony,[1]
  And out his chieftains go;
The army of the Tennessee
  Is there to meet their blow.

McPherson falls, but Logan lives,
  Is ready with his life;
" *McPherson and Revenge !* " he cries
  And leads the gallant strife.
Pressed back at every point, at last
  Hood calls his rebs inside,
The next contraction of the coil
  In terror to abide.

Tecumseh, as he presses, has
  A very strong suspicion,
That Hood, of his late rash sortie
  Will make a repetition.
He 's right ; for out Hardee and Lee,
  Their countless masses pour,

[1] July 22nd.

And dash, and break themselves in vain
    Against the Fifteenth Corps.[1]

In vain, in vain, they only swell
    Their aggregate of lost ;
Hood learns at last his lesson well
    But at a fearful cost.
He 'd let *offensive* work alone,
    He would most certainly,
But that he does n't like to own
    Jo's Fabian policy.

Tecumseh stretched out to the right,
    And made some demonstration
Along his line, but what he *sought*
    Was Hood's communication.
Hood's line was fifteen miles in length,
    'Twas thin as any shell;
When it might break in Sherman's grasp
    There 's nobody could tell.

All round and round his little cage
    Hood beat his puzzled head,
And dodged, in helplessness and rage,
    The shells Tecumseh sped.
" I *can't* whip Sherman in a fight,"
    Cried out despairing Hood ;
" Go, Wheeler, start this very night,
    And make a change for good.

"Take out your troops, and operate
    In Old Tecumseh's rear, sir,
So far as *I* can calculate
    The end is drawing near, sir.

[1] On the 28th July.

If I can't starve him off, why then
    He 'll surely starve me out, sir,"
So strangely, under pressure, men
    Do put themselves about, sir.

For Wheeler, off on useless raids,
    His cavalry doth goad,
And leaves Tecumseh unopposed,
    To cut the Macon road.
Cut off by east, cut off by south,
    And with the coil contracting,
Hood wishes, in his inmost soul,
    That Jeff *was less exacting.*

Once more he sends Hardee and Lee
    To pierce the living wall;
The rebel corps strike gallantly,
    But many thousands fall;[1]
Hood's army dwindles fast away
    Before his helpless gaze.
That night Tecumseh's soldiers lay [2]
    And wondered at the blaze

That turned the heavens, far and wide,
    Into a sea of fire,
And reddened, in Atlanta town,
    Its every roof and spire.
But Sherman, on the morrow, found
    His long campaign was done ;
He wrote to Grant, "Atlanta, sir,
    Is ours, and fairly won." [3]

---

[1] September 1, 1864.

[2] That night Hood blew up his magazine, burned his stores, and one thousand bales of cotton, and evacuated Atlanta.

[3] Sherman's troops took possession September 2, 1864.

11

CHAPTER XXXVI.

Tᴴᴱ meanwhile in Virginia,
  Across the Rapidan,
One bright May morning, our grim Grant
  His skirmishing began.[1]
Like fighting Jo he meets with Lee,[2]
  Down in the Wilderness;
He leads the battle gallantly,
  Our Jo did nothing less.

He deals, like Jo, his sturdy blows,
  He fights until the night;
His loss is dreadful, and the dark
  Shuts out a fearful sight.
And Grant, like Burnside, and like Jo,
  Feels many a chilling shiver,
But *unlike* them, straight *on* he 'll go,
  He wont recross the river.

Lee tries the tactics he had tried
  So lately on our Jo, sir;
He masses; down upon the left
  His heavy columns throws, sir.
Hour after hour the strife goes on,
  No ground is gained or lost,

[1] Crosses the Rapidan May 3.
[2] Battle of the Wilderness begins May 4.

They wrestle, almost man to man,
  God knows at what a cost.

For Hays sinks down beneath the flood,
  And many a noble life
Is quenched beneath the bitter waves
  Of that mysterious strife ;
The sun goes down upon the fight,
  It rises on the field
Where foe holds foe, as in a vice ;
  None conquer, and none yield.

The wounded stream out into sight,
  The living still go in ;
The tangled thicket grows alive,
  Whence issues fearful din
Of unseen battle.   Wadsworth falls !
  All honor to the dead
Who fell with him, as gloriously
  The hopeless charge he led.

The stretchers bear the dying out,
  They carry in more powder ;
The conflict thickens, now a shout—
  The battle-crash grows louder ;
With cheer on cheer, and stroke on stroke,
  With skill that is but folly ;
A grapple, wrestle, face to face,
  And volley upon volley.

The tide of battle to and fro,
  Sways like a pendulum,
Held fixed between, nor Grant, nor Lee,
  Doth nearer victory come,

The morrow !—not a cheer went up
  From patriot or from foe,
But all along the trampled ground
  Went up a wail of woe.

Full fifteen thousand weltering
  In that dark field of death!
No wonder Lee moved out of sight,
  And Grant drew quick his breath,
As " Forward !" was the order given
  Along his battered lines,
And friend and foe moved off, and left
  Their dead among the pines. .

A race to Spottsylvania next,
  Where Sedgwick gives his life,
And many a weary patriot
  Sinks in the bitter strife ;
Where Sheridan sets out to find
  The rebs, communication,
And does n't stop till he 's behind
  The works at Richmond Station.[1]

Where Hancock " finished Johnston up
  And then went into Early,"
And captured Stuart, who, it seems,
  Behaved quite cross and surly.[2]
Where " butcher " Grant and butcher Lee
  Piled awful heaps of slain,

[1] Sheridan's command gets between the first and second rebel line at Richmond, on May 11th.

[2] When Hancock offered his hand to Stuart, the rebel replied : " I am General Stuart, of the Confederate army, and under present circumstances I decline to take your hand !" Hancock replied, " And under any other circumstances, General, I should not have offered it."

God grant that never more may be
  Such butchering again.

Old Jonathan stands all aghast,
  With horror in his eyes,
As stroke on stroke is dealt so fast,[1]
  And piled before him lies
His bleeding sons ; he gasps for breath,
  But says to Grant, " Strike on, sir,
My boys have nobly met their death,
  Thank God that they were born, sir !"

And Betsey Jane, whose brow the pain
  Of *living death* had carved,
Moaned as she stooped above the slain :
  " They 're better *so* than *starved.*"
And Abram drew a long, long breath,
  And raised his drooping head—
" At last, I think, we 've surely come
  Out of the woods," he said.

The Devil quick recalled his imps,
  To view the situation ;
Said he, " I would n't have them miss
  This chance of education."
And Grant, he strokes his dogs of war,
  All grimly doth he smile, sir ;
And lights another fresh cigar,
  And up the James meanwhile, sir,

He sends Ben Butler with a troop,
  Who cautiously doth steam,
And lands his force near City Point,
  But Lee, he has a dream

[1] Battle of Spottsylvania, May 10th. Loss, 10,000 slain on each side.

That Ben at Richmond has a squint.
  He starts when Kautz strikes hard,
And cuts in two at Stony Creek
  The force of Beauregard.

Then Ben sends out some more brigades,[1]
  This doth the rebels goad;
And Beauregard, ubiquitous,
  Comes stalking up the road,
And finding there the little force
  That meddled with his track,
He roars, this small Napoleon,
  And drives the raiders back.

Now, Ben's a persevering man,
  Again to move he tries,
So Smith and Gilmore northward press
  And open wide their eyes,
When down upon them Beauregard
  Exasperated tramps,
With such momentum when he strikes[2]
  He drives them to their camps.

(Just here, Old Jonathan, distressed
  At news from New Orleans;[3]
Asks Abraham if *he* can tell
  What *that* confusion means?
That Abe has quite too many schemes
  He has some strong suspicions;
Too many irons in the fire,
  Too many expeditions.)

---

[1] May 7th and 9th.   [2] May 16th.
[3] Red River Expedition.

He says to Grant, " You 'd better spy
  The nature of the ground, sir ;
I think you 'll need right now to tie
  The loose strings lying round, sir,
In all directions.   There 's a snarl
  Down on Red River floating,
Where Porter doth amuse the rebs
  With his new style of boating."

So Grant drew out his telescope,
  And pointed it southwest,
" All right," said he to Jonathan,
  " Just set your mind at rest,
Your Porter won't be drowned this time,
  He 's resting on the *Banks*, sir ;
There is a chap named Bailey [1] there,
  Who well deserves your thanks, sir.

" He saved your fleet by building dams,
  It 's done in splendid shape, sir ;
Your army 's safe, let Banks alone
  For getting out of scrapes, sir ;
You just keep quiet, Jonathan,
  The signs are looking well,
I'll fight it out upon this line
  Though it should take a spell."

[1] Lieutenant-Colonel Bailey, Fourth Wisconsin Volunteers, who constructed a dam to raise the river and liberate the fleet. The passage of the boats was completed on the 15th of May, 1864.

CHAPTER XXXVII

Now, Grant had buried all his dead,
    And started in the night,[1]
To gain North Anna.   This, he said,
    If all his plans came right,
Would cut the rebels from their base,
    And cause a falling back ;
But Lee starts first, and in the race
    He takes the inside track.

When Grant came up on Monday morn,
    With many a dread suspicion,
He found the knowing rebs had won,
    And Lee was in position.
Now forward ! Birney stops to fight,
    But Griffin pushes o'er,
While rebel works on either side,
    Sweep all along the shore.

Hurra ! hurra ! Excelsior ![2]
    Bold Birney gains the ridge,
And Hancock with his fighting corps
    Is down upon the bridge.

[1] Starts night of 20th May, 1864.

[2] Two regiments of the Excelsior Brigade, the 71st and 72d N.Y.V.,
first reached the redan, making a foothold in the parapet with their
muskets, the brave fellows clambered up and simultaneously planted
their colors on the rebel stronghold.

So fighting here, and fighting there,
    They bear the starry banner
Across the stream, to find the rebs
    Intrenched upon South Anna.

Alas ! for Grant, where'er he moved,
    A stronghold came in sight ;
The rebs had well the time improved,
    Since Mac gave them a fright.
And all along in every way,
    That leads to Richmond town,
Redans, and pits, and batteries,
    Defiantly did frown.

Said Grant, "Lee waits for me to send
    And dash against his works,
The strongest yet.   I don't intend
    To humor all his quirks."
So quickly he withdrew his troops
    Unto the northern bank,[1]
And moves around upon the left
    (His usual way to flank).

He orders all his baggage sent
    To *White House.*   "Ah !" said Lee,
"Old tricks again—*Grant* wants to try
    The Chickahominy."
Grant pushes boldly, soldier-like,
    And it comes out, of course,
That all along the traveled pike,[2]
    He finds the rebs in force.

[1] Of North Anna, leaving the 27th of May.
[2] Mechanicsville pike.

11*

Said Grant, "Cold Harbor I must have;"
　　Said Sheridan, "I'll take it."
Lee felt the raider's sudden grasp,
　　And Hoke went out to shake it.
The blue-coats fight and hold their ground
　　Till up comes General Wright,[1]
And Smith with gallant eighteenth corps
　　Tramps bravely into sight.

They've traveled up from City Point,[2]
　　They do not stop or tarry;
They charge across the field of death,
　　The rifle-pits they carry.
Lee does n't like this sort of work,
　　He sends out just at dark,
And all along the Union line
　　He makes his wicked mark.

But still the "boys in blue" hold out
　　Till General Lee has learned
'T is not their way, by any means,
　　To give up what they've earned.
He draws his battered columns off
　　With mingled pride and sorrow,
"I'll try," said he, "another bout
　　With General Grant to-morrow."

"It's my turn now," says General Grant,
　　As o'er the field he glances.
On Friday morn,[3] at four o'clock,
　　His skirmish lines advances,

[1] Wright came up on the afternoon of June 1st.
[2] This corps withdrawn from Butler was just off a march of twenty-five miles.
[3] June 3, 1864.

He flings himself with all his might
  Against the rebs' position,
And torn and bleeding from the fight
  He comes to this decision—

The rebs have got a dreadful blow
  If *this* is the *reaction*,
I think I'll wait until I know
  If Lee wants satisfaction.
He had n't long to wait, the foe
  At eight o'clock came out,
And down upon the veteran left
  They bore with frantic shout.

On—on—they close the horrid gaps,
  The dark mass in the gloom, sir,
Unflinching bears itself right on,
  And out of darkness looms, sir,
Up to the very parapets
  Their bearing is superb,
But, lo! the patriot volunteers
  Their desperate valor curb.

Back ebb the rebels—out of sight,
  Back unto General Lee,
Who wonders all that weary night
  Whose is the victory.
At least, thought he, the Yanks have lost
  Full thirteen thousand lives,
" And I—oh, me!—here captain! bring,
  The moment he arrives,

" To me the latest scout come out
  From General Grant's headquarters,[1]

[1] It is said that by means of traitors in *our camps* every order of
Grant was immediately known to Lee.

And bid my Generals ready be
   To move their guns and mortars."
Now Grant had looked upon the field
   And shudderingly said,
We'd better take a little time
   To cover up our dead.

And then he lighted his segar,
   And smoked a day or two,
(While Sheridan rode wide, and far,
   And cut Lee's railroads through.)
Grant on the situation mused,
   And pros and cons debated;
It more and more unpleasant grew,
   The more he meditated.

"Lee runs no risk at all," he said,
   "Sometimes he fights in spasms,
But all the time in *my* brave ranks,
   I'm making fearful chasms;
I'll fight it out upon this line,
   Or what is just the same, sir,
I'll *skew* my line to meet the case,
   I'll start now for the James, sir.[1]

"Phil Sheridan will Hunter meet,
   And thus secure the Valley,
And cut off Lynchburg, while I cross
   And with the movement tally.
I'll land at City Point where Ben
   Has got a base for me;
Then what can stop our swinging round
   The stronghold of Bob Lee?"

[1] Crosses the James on the 14th and 15th of June.

With tireless heart, and steady tramp,
  The "blue coats" made their way,
From City Point across the wood,
  But oh! they found the "gray"
Were settled down in Petersburg;
  It was the same old tale,
A "*programme*" on the Union side
  Did never much avail.

Lee smiled, as it came out so clear,
  Grant's *coup-de-main* was blighted,
And Jonathan began to fear,
  Somebody was short-sighted;
"Well, well," growled Grant, "Lee knows quite
  His tactics do no good;   [well
I *shall prevail;* I thought to save
  Another sea of blood.

"But Lee will have it;" so there comes
  . Three direful bloody days[1]
Of desperate and vain assault,
  Till Grant the carnage stays;
Said he, "This knocking at his gate,
  May meet Lee's approbation,
It don't meet mine,—so boys we'll wait
  And try siege operation."

[1] From 15th to 18th of June, 1864, loss in four days, 10,000.

CHAPTER XXXVIII.

Ere Grant had borrowed Mac's old spades,
   And 'neath a scorching sun
The boys went digging for a shade,[1]
   Old Hunter took his run
Off South to Staunton, thence still down
   By way of Lexington,
To take a 'peep at Lynchburg town,[2]
   And here his sport was done.

For in the place a vet'ran corps,
   Just hurried there by Lee,
Stood waiting right behind the door,
   Old Hunter for to see.
When Hunter spied them through a crack,
   All fearful was his ire,
Cried he " I ammunition lack,
   Woe's me, I must retire."

Chagrined at such a cruel fate,
   His wits he could not rally,
But started for Kanawha's stream,
   And left exposed *the Valley*.
Cried Jubal Early,—" Here's my chance,
   To make the Yankees stare,
So, down the Valley I 'll advance,
   And raise the ' *annual scare*.' "

[1] Before Petersburg. [2] On the 16th June, Hunter invested Lynchburg.

Quoth Breckinridge, "I'll go along;"
  They did n't stay to dally,
But off—full twenty thousand strong,
  They thundered down the Valley;
Young Sigel felt at Martinsburg,
  The ground begin to quiver
Beneath their tramp,—and with a shrug,
  He slipped across the river.

At Williamsburg[1] and Point of Rocks,
  They crossed to Hagerstown.
Said Early, " Now the way is clear
  To win us great renown."
They burned up bridges, captured trains,
  And pockets they did pick,
Stole shoes, and hats, robbed roosts and pens,
  Played many a scurvy trick.

The Marylanders swore the foe
  Would all their cities sack,
And Bennett of the *Herald*, cried
  Most piteously for Mac.
But Abram wrote to Jonathan,
  Who started a town meeting;
Through all the streets he quickly ran,
  And set the drums a-beating.

And extra trains he loaded up,
  Which groaned as off they started,
They were so full; then Jonathan,
  When all his trains departed,
Went to the cup-board for his fife,
  (He always kept it handy,)

[1] July 3, 1864.

And whistled out, as for his life,
Old Yankee Doodle Dandy.

Now, Early meets the volunteers,
And calls them " Yankee cattle ; "
And thinks to *drive* them, but they make
Monocacy [1] a battle.
A yielding mass, these minute men,
They check bold Jubal's speed,
And his attack on Washington
They do so much impede,

That, when he comes up to the forts,
And sees the spires a-looming,
The old Sixth corps the town supports,
And there are cannon booming.
Poor Breckinridge ! within his gaze
The Capitol's proud dome,—
He sighs, and thinks of better days,
And faces towards home.

He carries off—fit trophies they,
The papers of Old Blair,[2]
And Breckinridge has had his day,
And Stanton his last scare.
Wright sallied out to haste the route,[3]
And ended speedily,[4]
Bold Jubal's raid he fain had made
Turn out a jubilee.

But Early was not satisfied ;
Quoth he, " I don't design

[1] Battle of Monocacy July 8, 1864.
[2] Breckinridge made his quarters at Blair's house on the Seventh street road, a few miles from the city.
[3] July 12, 1864. Rebels driven from Fort Stevens.
[4] Raiders cross into Virginia with their plunder, July 13.

To quit the vale, ere North I ride,
  And vengeance dire be mine."
He strikes at Averill and Crook,[1]
  And hurls them o'er the ferry;
And sends McCausland o'er the brook,
  Who makes himself so merry

With honest folks at Chambersburg,[2]
  "They cry out bitterly;"
Growls Grant, "We 're getting in a snarl,
  We 'd better go and see
What now is wrong; 't won't do, my Phil,
  To let the rebels sally
Across the river at their will—
  You just clean out the Valley."

While Phil makes ready we may now
  Reverse the steam of time,
And start our locomotive back,
  And in another clime
Just glance at traitors and their sport;
  The story comes in handy,
How rebels at a foreign port
  Thrashed Yankee Doodle Dandy.

[1] July 24, 1864.
[2] He burned the town, July 30, 1864.

CHAPTER XXXIX

WHILE Grant was sitting down to rest,
    The nineteenth day of June,
That Sunday morning, at Cherbourg,
    An old familiar tune
Is whistled on the quarter-deck
    Of Uncle Sam's Kearsarge;
Whence Winslow gazes on the bay
    Where many a Frenchman's barge

And yacht and boat expectant lie
    To view the coming fight;[1]
And yonder in brave Winslow's eye,
    With traitor flag in sight,
The Alabama slowly drifts—
    Hark! how the Johnnies shout,
And cheer the pirate as she shifts,
    And past the mole moves out.

"God speed the rebel!" with the bell
    That Sunday morning tolled;
The blessing of the Frenchman fell
    And o'er the waters rolled
To Winslow, on the quarter-deck,
    Who strove with sudden pain

[1] Trains came down from Paris bringing excursion parties to see the fight,

To catch one blessing on *his* flag,
  But listened all in vain.

The solitary Kearsarge waits
  The Alabama's motion,
Who with her consorts from the bay
  Steams out upon the ocean.
"Now, then," said Winslow, "out to sea!
  'Tis plainly my conviction
That Uncle Sam had better be
  Beyond *French* jurisdiction."

The Alabama follows fast,
  The Kearsarge turns about;
She 's free to strike the foe at last;
  No wonder that they shout,
Those gallant tars, whose starry flag
  Lifts proudly to the breeze;
And Winslow smiles, as on his bow
  The pirate bold he sees.

He 'll run her down; no, off she sheers,
  Her starboard guns awake;
With quick, sharp puffs, and dull reports,
  The Sunday silence breaks.
The shot above the Kearsarge speeds,
  And through the rigging tears;
There 's no reply.   The ship moves on—
  Down on the pirate bears.

Another broadside; still again
  The rebel challenge flies
Across the wave, and Winslow speaks,
  Defiantly replies;

Till Crapeau, gazing from the piers,
　Is startled at the thunder;
And for his darling pirate fears,
　And then begins to wonder

What sort of guns the Yankee bears,
　The contest looks unequal;
Perhaps their Sunday sport may prove
　Unpleasant in the sequel.
Then Crapeau sighs and rubs his eyes,
　And then his telescopes;
And prays the Virgin to devise
　A way to bless his hopes.

Still round and round the two ships whirl,
　And Winslow's guns are playing
Right through the Alabama's hull,
　In spite of Crapeau's praying.
A few more blows and Crapeau knows
　His hope will be a wreck;
Ah! ha! Semmes throws a Blakeley shell
　On Winslow's quarter-deck.

Three men beside the pivot-gun
　Are wounded by the shell;
"All right! since we are whipping her,"
　Cried Gowan as he fell.
They bore the seaman down below,
　But ever through the strife
He *cheered* at every telling blow,
　And smiled away his life.

"Don't hurry, lads, take steady aim,
　And point the heavy guns

Below the water-line; the decks
  Sweep with the lighter ones,"
Said Winslow, as the rebel shot
  Went screaming over head.
"The Alabama hitteth not,"
  The Johnnie Crapeau said.

The Alabama's decks are wet,
  Blood every plank o'erwhelms, sir;
Huge gaps are yawning in her hull,
  She does not mind her helm, sir.
The pirate quickly crowds all sail,
  Semmes does n't want to drown,
The Crapeaux on the shore turn pale,
  The ship is going down.

Down falls the bloody rebel rag,
  The rebel pirates bow
To Yankee flag;—an instant more,
  The doomed ship lifts her prow,
Her mainmast with the effort breaks,
  Her battered stanchions sever,
And with a lurch her way she takes
  Down out of sight forever.

"Quick! man the boats," brave Winslow cries,
  "Pick up the drowning crew;"
The pirate's consort Winslow spies,—
  "Your best for God's sake do,"
He shouts, "to save the sinking men!"
  The Deerhound picks up Semmes,
And takes him straight to Johnny Bull,
  Who Winslow's course condemns;

And smooths down Raphael's ruffled pride,
  And buys him some dry clothes, sir,
And gives him a new sword beside,
  And then quite plainly shows, sir,
The Kearsarge was a bigger ship,
  She was an *iron-clad*,[1]
And carried monstrous guns; in fact,
  Semmes' case was not so bad.

His ship was lost, but *he* was free,
  And John could build a faster;
And soon again upon the sea
  He 'd be the Yankee's master.
So Semmes he smiled—why not? and grew
  So very fat and hearty,
For Johnny Bull each day or two
  Gave him a dinner party.

[1] Winslow had thrown some spare *chains* over the side of his ship, and covered them with planks.

CHAPTER XL

"RICHMOND was *placid*," rebels said,
  Although 't was strongly hinted,
That even at this fountain-head
  Of treason, news was stinted.
Jeff might be posted—as to that
  The press could only say,
The little scraps that it could glean
  Came in a curious way

From Yankee papers, and, of course,
  Were not to be believed;
One thing was certain on that point,
  The town might feel relieved,
For Richmond never would be reached
  By Yankee shot or shell,
Her strongholds never would be breached,
  Whatever else befel.

"Richmond was placid." No news yet;
  'T is true, "the wires were broken,"
Such accidents *would* happen—this
  No evil could betoken.
The dearth of news was really strange,
  No rumor of advances
Or falling back, but now and then
  A train of ambulances

Would rumble up the quiet streets;
  And soldiers, bruised and bleeding,
Gasped stories of a mortal strife,
  Of men swept down while leading
The desperate charge; of stubborn fight;
  Of blood in rivers flowing;
Of cannon, with resistless might,
  Great swaths of *Yankees* mowing.

And then the *press*, in largest type,
  Would print, "FROM GENERAL LEE!"
And herald with a trumpet tone
  "*Another victory!*"
Still, still they came, those mournful trains,
  Came early and came late;
The press, amazed, in rebel strains
  Began to speculate.

That butcher Grant was hard at work,
  'T was very plain to see;
In fact, was butting out his brains [1]
  Against their General Lee.
'T was *just as well;* it was agreed
  The war *this year* must cease,
One way or other—as for them,
  They *always did* want peace.

The North was frightened at the blood
  Their butcher Grant was shedding;
The cry for peace rolled like a flood,
  And everywhere was spreading.
One way or other war *must* end,
  Their course none should condemn,

[1] Richmond *Whig*, July 21st.

Whate'er the North might choose to do,
  One way was left to them,—

And one alone.   Though Lee *should* fail
  To stand before Grant's fire,
Though his brave host should *not* prevail,
  And Lee himself retire,
Why, Beauregard was left; their lines
  Were manifold and strong,
The siege would Saragossa be,
  Or, Derry!   'T would be long

Ere vulgar Yankee foot should rest
  On soil more sacred now;
The laurels Grant won in the West
  Were withering on his brow;
That 't was n't Pemberton or Bragg,
  With whom he had to deal,
But Robert Lee—the difference
  He bitterly would feel.

And then the Drury Bluff affair
  (It seemed the wires were mended)
Was noised, and it appeared their joy
  Would never more be ended.
They cheered and shouted; true, some guessed
  The serious loss they 'd met,
But then—"One must," said they, "break eggs
  To make an omelette." [1]

Then came the Kenesaw's sad fight,
  And Richmond was ecstatic;
And placid rebels in its light
  Grew all at once emphatic.

[1] Richmond *Examiner*.

12

The "wires were up" for several days,
   All through bold Early's raid,
Which would have captured Washington
   Had Canby but delayed.[1]

[1] Nineteenth Corps, which had just arrived from the Gulf.

CHAPTER XLI

"'T was placid," too, in Canada,[1]
   Where Mr. Horace Greeley,
With rebel Saunders, and the like,
   Expressed himself quite freely;
They talked and talked, till even Abe
   They managed to beslaver,
And Jeff himself turned up his nose
   At *such* a peace palaver.

'Twas "placid" time at Petersburg[2]
   All through the hot July,
Till at its close, one early morn,
   Beneath a dim gray sky,
Secure, within their fort so strong,
   Lee's rebel soldiers sleep,
While o'er th' unconscious garrison
   The guard its vigils keep.

Deep in the bowels of the earth
   There darts a blazing line,
A serpent hissing from its birth,
   For Grant *has sprung his mine;*
A quiver! as the ground doth quake,
   The guards—one startled breath,

[1] July 18th, 1864. See page 301, McPherson's History of the Rebellion.
[2] July 30th, 1864.

The sleepers for an instant wake,
  And then—a crashing death!

Oh, horrors! is this crater hell?
  Dead, dying, living men,
Shrieking, fighting, burning! well
  May we let fall the pen.
Well may the stormers of Grim Grant,
  By untold woe surrounded,
Right in the awful chasm *halt*
  Affrighted and confounded.

Pushed on they huddle in the gap;
  The rebels are surprised,
But Grant's bold storming party is
  Completely paralyzed.
Now guns to right, and guns to left,
  And cannon straight before
Sweep—like a quick tornado blast,
  Into the chasm pour.

How any came out thence alive,
  Will ever be a wonder,
As well as whom to saddle with
  So horrible a blunder.
It *did* seem that the soldiers' lives,
  Quite soon enough were spent,
Without the wholesale butchery
  Of this experiment.

" 'T was placid," too, in Mobile Bay,
  'T was so, the rebels stated,
Where Farragut, full many a day,
  For iron clads had waited.

But on one hazy August morn,
  Placidity was broken,
The drum on board the flag ship beat,
  And Farragut had spoken!

But what he said, and what he did,
  We will not try to show it,
The theme so glorious we leave
  Unto a nobler poet.
Perhaps in time there may be born
  A soul by inspiration
Made worthy to depict in song
  The glory of this nation.

A note from Gideon Welles to Abe
  Came, in few words, to say
That Farragut had *anchors dropped*
  At last in Mobile bay.[1]
He said he had a toughish time
  In running by the forts
And rebel rams, as Abe would see
  By reading his reports.

He said "The iron-clads were *slow*
  In getting into line ;
They did n't act like wooden hulls,
  But then their crews were fine.
The Winnebago's turret was
  A little out of gear,
It would n't turn, and then the boat
  Was difficult to steer.

His gallant gunners he had seen,
  When shot and shell were thick,

[1] August 5, 1864.

Unflinching, though their hearts he knew
   Were like his own heart, sick
At sight of shipmates struck with death
   And decks all wet with blood.
He saw it all, with bated breath,
   He in the rigging stood.

He mentioned the Tecumseh's fate,
   "Torpedo struck," then said,
"The Hartford's loss was very great,
   She was the *ship that led.*"
A few more words about the fight,
   "In close proximity,"
The ships had with the monster ram
   They called the Tennessee.

How wooden hulls and iron hearts[1]
   Did once again prevail
'Gainst traitor souls, girt round about
   With stoutest coat of mail ;
And how the little Monitors
   Helped on the consummation,
And brought the white flag on, "The pride
   Of the Confederation."

"The wires were down" in rebeldom—
   'Twas long before they knew
From Yankee papers of this fight,
   And then "it was n't true."
The press implored its countrymen
   For such *lies* not to fret ;
"'T was past belief," that being so,
   They do n't believe it yet!

---

[1] From the moment the Hartford struck the Tennessee she never fired a gun.

There was another rebel ram
  Which also came to grief
By daring deed, (of many such
  Perhaps this was the chief.)
The Albemarle at Plymouth lay,
  Full eight miles up the stream,
With pickets all along the way,
  Yet up did Cushing steam.

Up, up, in silence, in the dark,[1]
  And his torpedo boom
He drove beneath the monster's ribs
  And sent her to her doom.
With thirteen men his boat went up,
  Two only did come down ;
The rest—they won a sailor's grave,
  But Cushing won renown.

[1] October 5, 1864.

CHAPTER XLII

And Washington was " placid," though
  A miserable faction
Had brought the bleeding country to
  What they called a " reaction."
The war had failed, they wanted peace,
  Abe had no policy;
Each day's events did but increase
  His incapacity.

Infirm of purpose, and stiff-necked,
  The nation understood
At last that Abraham was wrecked
  Upon his sea of blood.
Election time was close at hand,
  Lincoln repudiated ;
They 'd put a true man on the stand,
  So Mac they nominated.

They made a platform stout, *not* new,
  Without a single crack;
And on it, with conventional glee,
  They fastened little Mac.
They stuck beside him Pendleton—
  A curious grouping, rather;
Not all the glue in Christendom
  Could make them stick together.

For Pendleton was all for peace ;
  "So far, so good," they said, sir ;
For certainly he 'd get a vote
  From every copperhead, sir.
Then Little Mac thought well of war—
  Good in itself again—
War democrats would vote for him,
  But still it was n't plain

How they could steer their ship of state,
  Although a double ender,
Both ways at once ; just here the rebs
  Did signal service render,
For Stephens, with the best intent,
  Did prove it clear as glass,
If Mac was chosen President
  How it would come to pass

That they, the rebs, could slip with ease
  From their platform to Mac's, sir,
Or he to theirs ; the war would cease ;
  For why, they both would lack, sir,
The *casus belli ;* Mac's platform
  Was made of their *old* planks, sir,
Would hold all rebeldom ; for which
  He gave most hearty thanks, sir.

Whatever Mac himself might be,
  The *platform* was the thing
That never would coerce a State,
  And so, of course, 't would bring
Their independence.   Mac in power,
  'T was just the same as granted ;
State sovereignty was recognized,
  And that was all *they* wanted.[1]

[1] Extracts from Stephens' letter to T. J. Semmes, Nov. 5, 1864.

12*

As for McClellan's sentiments,
  As written in his letter,
About the Union as it was,
  Why, every reb knew better
Than for an instant to believe
  In such a repetition ;
The moment Mac tried that 't would bring
  Them foreign recognition.[1]

So (Stephens said) in every view
  He took of Mac's election,
He felt the South had much to lose
  In case of his rejection.
The action of Chicago was,
  In all their weary night,
To them, the rebels, and their cause,
  "The first ray of real light."[2]

When Jonathan read Stephens' views,
  "Well, now," said he, "that's nice !
I 'd like to give the democrats
  A little sound advice.
They want to save the country, eh !
  They 'd come in at the end
And steal the credit from old Abe—
  Well, now, I do n 't intend

---

[1] " Just as soon as McClellan should renew the war, with a view to restore the Union, the old Constitution with slavery, etc., etc., would England, France and other European Powers throw all their moral power and influence of their recognition on our side."

[2] Another extract from Stephens' letter to Semmes, Nov. 5, 1864 : " So in any and every view I can take of the subject; I regard the election of McClellan, and the success of the States Right party of the North, whose nominee he is, of the utmost importance to us. With these views, you will readily perceive how I regarded the action of the Chicago Convention as a ray of light, the first ray of real light I had seen from the North since this war began."

"To hold *my* tongue in all this noise,
  While treason works its way;
I think that I and my brave boys
  Have got a word to say.
Out of my way," cried Jonathan;
  His grown up boys, still bolder,
Brushed quick the carping crowd aside
  And took Abe on their shoulder.

They bore him straight through thick and thin
  Right through the White House gate,
Inside the door, and set him in
  The same old chair of state.[1]
"Now *you stay there,*" said Jonathan;
  "The day is almost won, sir;
Keep hold of hands, I'll stand by you
  Until the job is done, sir."

Abe said "There were much better men,
  But still it didn't seem
The wisest course to swap one's horse
  While crossing o'er a stream,
And so he'd do his best to bear
  The burden the meanwhile."
Then settled 'neath his load of care
  And smiled a weary smile.

Quoth Jonathan, "Old Abe is apt
  To be a little tender;
The nation needs some sterner stuff—
  Some iron-clad defender.
Then Jonathan he looked about—
  He spied our valiant "Andy"—[2]

[1] November 8, 1864, President Lincoln re-elected.
[2] Andrew Johnson elected Vice-President.

" *The very man*," said he, "to stand
  By Yankee Doodle Dandy."

Then Jonathan turned straight to Grant,
  "Now try the soldier's mettle,"
He said, "the new year 's coming on,
  And my accounts to settle.
I 'll have to square with Johnny Bull,
  Who all a-roaring stands ;
But I can't take another job
  Till this is off my hands."

Now Jonathan that very day
  Had stopped at Seward's door ;
And Seward made the old man stay
  To hear John Bull's last roar.
A certain lord, Wharncliffe by name,
  (Perhaps he *knew* no better,)
Had written Adams ;[1] so it came
  That Seward got the letter.[1]

'Twas all about a big *bazaar*
  Just held at Liverpool
To aid the rebs, and Wharncliffe, so
  Impertinently cool,
Proposed to send an agent out
  With lots of British gold[2]
To rebel prisoners, who, he feared,
  Were suffering with the cold.

Old Jonathan at this breathed quick,
  But not a word spoke he,
He grasped instinctively his stick
  Of stout old hickory ;

[1] Under date of November 12, 1864.   [2] £17,000 sterling.

Then thought of Libby, and Belle Isle,
  And then of Betsey Jane,
'Till his fierce anger settled down
  Into a leaden pain.

Of course the agent did n't come,
  For Seward boldly vowed
This insult to Old Jonathan
  Could never be allowed.[1]
So Wharncliffe (for humanity
  So deeply interested)
Found " ways circuitous" in which
  His guineas he invested.

But Jonathan was *hurt*, he said,
  That Abe had been *so* "*set*"
On treating well his prisoners ;
  He never *could* forget
This studied insult ; he would show
  John Bull, when it came handy,
There was a small account to square
  With Yankee Doodle Dandy.

[1] See page 460 McPherson's History of the Rebellion.

CHAPTER XLIII

Now Sheridan had been at work,
  And all along the border
"Had straightened things," that is to say,
  Confusion brought to order:
Now here, now there, he ever kept
  Bold Early in his sight,
But Grant still held the reins, and Phil
  Was "spoiling for a fight."

"Now, Phil," said Grant, "why risk a match?
  'Twould be a sad diversion
If you were whipped, for then we'd catch
  Another reb incursion."
"Pooh! whipped, indeed!" cried Little Phi'
  "That old scare of invasion,
I promise you my soldiers will
  Soon cure that inclination."

"Well then," said Grant, "go in, my boy!
  On Monday morn."—"All right, sir,"
Said Sheridan, and with his troops
  Was off before daylight, sir;
Straight for the Opequan he aimed,
  Where well he estimated
Bold Jubal and his traitor clan
  Down at the crossing waited.

He fell upon them like a blast ! [1]
  Unto their shot replied
So fiercely, it fell out at last
  That Jubal, stupefied
At such outrageous style of fight,
  Gave up his useless trying,
And found himself, with all his might,
  Through Winchester a-flying.

He did not stop for thirty miles
  Beyond that noted town,
And when he added up his loss,
  Ten thousand were set down.
Then Jubal felt his prestige ebb,
  His men he could not rally.
And *this* is *how* Phil sent the rebs
  " A-whirling up the Valley."

Quoth Phil, " These troopers will be back,
  Its just as well to know a
Little more about their track
  Across the Shenandoah."
He found the Valley rich with grain,
  " This is a tempting bait, sir,"
Said he, " the rebs will come again,
  Unless I devastate, sir."

Now Phil, whate'er he undertook,
  'T was plain enough to see,
That he was bound by hook or crook,
  To do it *thoroughly.*
So Phil he rode, with torch and blade,
  All up and down rode he :

---

[1] September 19, 1864, Battle of Winchester.

And—oh ! the wilderness he made
  Was pitiful to see.

Then down he camped at Cedar Run,
  He thought the rebs were "*settled*,"
But it came out that Jefferson
  Was only sorely nettled.
He sent to Early, Longstreet's corps,
  To turn his ebbing tide,
And out to crush Phil Sheridan
  Did General Longstreet ride.

He quickly slipped the mountain o'er
  And crossed the little stream,
Hid by the darkness and the fog,
  Before the sun did gleam ;
And down upon Phil's sleeping lines,
  With an unearthly yell,
In Phil's own style and quality,
  The rebel columns fell.[1]

They seized and turned whole batteries,
  They raised the victor's shout ;
Confusion spread—the troops gave way—
  In parts, it was a rout.
Phil Sheridan, at Winchester,
  ('Tis twenty miles across,)
Doth catch an echo of the guns,
  He springs upon his horse.

He hears the distant cannon boom,
  He doth his brave steed goad,
And with a glimmer of the truth
  Tears madly o'er the road ;

[1] Battle of Cedar Creek, October 19.

Mile after mile annihilates
  In his immortal ride!
He plunges in the sea of men
  And turns the backward tide.

"Now face the other way, my boys!
  You 're running off the track;"
He shouts above the battle's noise,
  "Hurrah! we 're going back!"
He swings his cap above his head,
  His face is all a-blaze,
The stragglers in astonishment
  Stop in their flight to gaze.

"Face about! face about! hurrah!
  Face the other way,
We 're going back, boys, to our camps,
  We're going *back!* I say.
This never would have happened, boys,
  Had I been only here,
Hurrah!! hurrah!!"—retreat is stopped,
  Up rolls a deafening cheer!

They rally as the cry goes on,
  "Phil Sheridan has come!!"
"We 're going to get a twist on them,
  We 'll drive the rebels home;"
"We 'll shake them from their boots, boys,
  Before the day is done, sirs;"
"We 're going back, boys, to our camps,
  We 'll have back all those guns, sirs."

The rebel host across the field
  On Emory bear down;

Hurrah ! the Yanks no longer yield,
  The rebels back are thrown.
"That's good," cries Phil ; "thank God for that,
  We 'll show them what we mean,
We 'll get the tightest twist on them
  That ever yet was seen."

Now Early sees that Phil's at home,
  He falls back, takes the spade ;
He thinks that Sheridan's assault,
  Of course will be delayed
Until his hungry men are fed ;
  His ranks demoralized
Must be recruited, or, he said,
  Must be reorganized.

Not so, " *Right now, and here*," says Phil,
  " We 'll wipe out our defeat."
By three o'clock his solid ranks
  Go out the foe to meet
With steady tramp ; an instant more,
  The firm advance is spent ;
A volley ! then the huge guns roar,
  The steady lines are rent.

They waver ; at the sickening sight
  Where most the thick shot crush
Among the broken ranks, doth Phil,
  Aroused to frenzy, rush.
" Why, boys ! *those cannon are our own,*
  Charge ! charge !" The crest, the wood,
The breastworks, but half done, they gain ;
  " So much," cries Phil, " is good.

"Still forward, boys!"   Phil's eyes flash fire,
  His voice, a bugle blast!
On through the thicket, o'er the ridge,
  They chase the foe at last.
Back through the blue-coats' pillaged camps,
  Back dash the rebs pell mell;
They're off for Jefferson's *last ditch*—
  For aught that I can tell!

Through Staunton to the mountain ridge
  They scatter through the gaps;
And Sheridan trots home again
  To get his shoulder-straps.[1]
And Jubal!—well! he will survive
  This last humiliation,
And die rejoiced he leaves alive
  The glorious Yankee nation.

[1] Sheridan was made Major-General for his gallantry on this occasion.

CHAPTER XLIV

The rebs at Petersburg had filled
   The crater, and the mine
Slipped into history, while Grant
   Was strengthening his line.
Attacking here, and feinting there,
   His aim at length he showed
By camping down, right fair and square,
   Upon the Weldon road.[1]

But Lee objected to the plan,
   So down on Reams' Station [2]
He dashed against the Second Corps
   In wild exasperation.
The shock was great, so great, indeed,
   As history is true;
Lee from the meeting did recede
   And Hancock fell back too.[3]

The rebs went back to Petersburg
   Within a mile or so,
And sent out troopers in Grant's rear,
   Which rapidly did go
To Coggin's Point;—surprised the guard,
   And in a bloodless battle,

---

[1] August 19th.   [2] August 25th.
[3] At nightfall Hancock withdrew his force, the enemy moving away
at the same time (Page 301 " Grant and his Campaigns.")

They captured some three thousand head
    Of splendid Yankee cattle.[1]

Refreshed with extra rations then,
    They grew so vigilant
They guessed and counteracted all
    The movements of Grim Grant,
Till tired out with dragging deep
    Through mud their guns and mortars,
Both armies, though awake they keep,
    They wink at winter quarters.

Grant built himself a wooden hut,
    At City Point located;
And Butler—while for his canal[2]
    He confidently waited—
Got up a new experiment[3]
    To test the strength of powder;
'T was *safer* than the July mine,
    Though its report was louder.

But no committee has, as yet,
    The problem undertaken—
To prove how much Fort Fisher was
    By its concussion shaken;[4]
We simply know the fleet itself,
    To Grant's dissatisfaction,
To Hampton Roads, by quickest route,
    Was blown by its reaction.

Now, what was right and what was wrong,
    There were enough to say;

[1] September 16th.
[2] Dutch Gap Canal, work on which was begun 10th of August.
[3] Transport fleet got under way 13th of Sept., 1864.
[4] Powder-boat exploded 24th Dec., 1864.

Grant did n't stop to quarrel long,
  He took a wiser way.
Before that Congress could invent
  A court of inquisition,
He up and fitted out and sent
  Another expedition.[1]

And while at Ben's discomfiture,
  Jeff's scowling phiz relaxes,
Brave Terry at the palisades
  Is hewing with the axes;
And ere the rebel jeers had died
  Upon that shore so sandy,
Our gallant boys all safe inside
  Played Yankee Doodle Dandy.[2]

And while they make themselves at home
  On sacred Southern soil,
We 'll travel back to see how Hood
  Broke through Tecumseh's coil.
We left him stealing in the dark
  From out Atlanta town,
To find a safer spot on which
  To set his soldiers down.

Tecumseh slipped into the place,
  He found it big enough
To settle in, but it was full
  Of useless rebel stuff.
Said he, "My gallant Yankee boys
  With traitors can 't be mated;"
He ordered[3] quickly that the town
  By rebels be vacated.

[1] Second expedition sailed Jan. 6, 1865.
[2] Fort Fisher captured Jan. 15, 1865.   [3] Order of 4th of Sept., 1864.

The mayor groaned [1] " 'T was barbarous."
  Said Sherman,[2] "It is war, sir.
When first you fired upon the flag
  The consequence I saw, sir."
Hood [3] said " It was iniquitous,
  And studied cruelty;
Transcending all he ever knew
  Of war's dark history."

Tecumseh took a dip of ink,
  (You see he was insane,)
Before the bar of history
  Bold Hood he did arraign;
" Who [4] was it, sir," said he, " that plunged
  In war our peaceful nation,
And bloody desolation wrought
  Without a provocation ?

Talk to marines," Tecumseh said,
  " But do not talk to me, sir,
Who knows the length and breadth and depth
  Of your hypocrisy, sir ;
I want the town now for my camp,
  The people cannot stay, sir."
And so Hood made a ten days' truce,
  And took them all away, sir.

[1] See letter of 11th of Sept. from the mayor and others.
[2] See Sherman's reply.
[3] See Hood's letter of the 9th of Sept., 1864.
[4] See Sherman's reply, same date (Sept. 9).

CHAPTER XLV.

Now Jefferson had chosen Hood
  Because he thought him fitter
To lead the chivalry than Jo,
  But truly it was bitter
To see Tecumseh, spite of all,
  The sacred soil bisect;
Jeff hastened from his capital
  Hood's errors to correct.

Poor Jeff! he has an awful task,
  The people round him crowd
In fear, and wrath, and criticism,
  Till clamors grow so loud,
That Jeff, who never looked for such
  Concomitants of treason,
In sore perplexity doth lose
  His temper and his reason.

His soul is fired, his swelling wrath
  Its culmination reaches;
He scintillates, that is to say,
  He takes to making speeches;
Before his burning eloquence
  The disaffected shrivel,
No one *could* stand such scathing fire
  Except his friend—the Devil.

The Georgians shrink abashed away,
  And in a martial mood
Come back again with small delay
  To reinforce bold Hood.
Militia men spring up, and Jeff
  Applauds the loyalty
Of forty thousand lank, long-haired,
  Full-blooded chivalry.

Then Jeff unto the Georgians
  Emphatically says,
"These barbarous invading Yanks
  Shall all, in thirty days,
Be driven like Napoleon
  From Moscow in retreat,[1]
Back to and out of Tennessee
  With horrible defeat."

Then Jeff he speaks to General Hood,
  Says he, "There is the foe, sir,
And Chattanooga is his base,
  Now out your columns throw, sir,
And cut him off from his supplies ;
  I think it will appear,
With his long train, the wisest plan
  To strike him in the rear."

Says Old Tecumseh, "There are signs,
  When Jefferson is wroth
And on a rampage, he designs
  A visit to the North ;
Now, Thomas, back to Nashville go,
  Keep everything there handy,

[1] Jeff's speech at Macon, Ga.

13

The hospitality to show
  Of Yankee Doodle Dandy."

Hood starts for Dallas,[1] and his horse
  Strike north of Marietta ;
And Sherman moves to Kenesaw,
  And sends post haste a letter
To Corse, at Rome, who hurries up
  His little preparations,
And off in Allatoona Pass
  Secures a million rations.[2]

It 's just in time, for up bold Hood
  Comes knocking at the gate ;
"You can't get in," says gallant Corse,
  "You 're just an hour too late."
Hood knocks away—within the works,
  Two thousand men and Corse,
Outside, a whole division stand ;
  Without the least remorse,

They cannonade two mortal hours,
  Then French sends in a note,[3]
That Corse, in just five minutes' time,
  (The knave's own words I quote,)
"Had best surrender, and avoid
  A profitless effusion
Of blood."   "Dear me," says Corse, "that reb
  Is under a delusion."

He sends an answer instantly,
  Resenting the intrusion,

---

[1] Starts October 1, 1864.

[2] Reached the pass 1 o'clock A.M., October 5; French's division (rebs) came up in one hour after.

[3] Half-past eight o'clock on the 5th of October.

And says his garrison are all
  Prepared for his effusion,
As soon as he can bring it on.
  Then shuts his gate again,
And up against it fiercely beats
  The rebel hurricane.

All day against the parapets
  In desperate attack
They dash, and surge, and rage, and yet
  Are constantly hurled back.
Tecumseh stood on Kenesaw,
  Beside his signal corps,
The little flags from mount to mount
  This silent message bore :

"Hold on, there 's help at hand, my boys !"
  And eighteen miles across,
The little fluttering flags waved back
  The answer of brave Corse.
Tecumseh's anxious brow relaxed,
  He once again breathed free ;
"If Corse is there, he will hold out,
  I know the man," said he.

The fight still rages, larger grow
  The awful piles of slain ;
One-third the garrison laid low ;
  The heroes who remain
Set firm their teeth, the last wild charge
  Defiantly they meet,—
Hurrah ! hurrah ! 'T is victory !
  The bugles sound *retreat !* [1]

[1] At night, 6th of October, the enemy were driven from every position, and Allatoona was secure.

"Well, you may keep your little pass,
  There 's plenty just as good, sir,
I 'll make Resaca do as well,"
  Says valiant General Hood, sir.
He strikes northwest, he has the start,
  But Sherman 's most as soon, sir ;
Hood comes upon Resaca first,[1]
  He thinks of Allatoona, sir.

He knows that Baum's small garrison
  Has got a brave defender ;
He flirts a line of skirmishers,
  And then demands surrender ;
Says he, "In case I am compelled
  To carry by assault, sir,
I 'll take no prisoners."   "If you *do*
  'T won't be," says Baum, "my fault, sir."

Well, just as Hood *was going* to win
  Resaca, and Jeff's thanks,
Tecumseh's generals began
  A pressure on his flanks ;[2]
He shrinks a little, Howard nears,
  Hood does a fight refuse, sir,
And off southwest his course he steers,
  A-down the vale of Coosa.

He wriggles round among the gaps,
  He will avoid a fight ;
So down Tecumseh takes his maps,
  (His cavalry in sight
Still hold the foe,) and studies out
  In novel strategy

[1] October 13, 1864.
[2] October 13, at Snake Creek Gap.

To leave to Hood the Northern route
  And start down for the sea.

"I might as well, as chase Hood round,
  Be laid upon a shelf, sir,"
Says Sherman, " I 'll give him a rope
  And let him hang himself, sir.
Perhaps he 'll choose to run headlong
  Into my lion's mouth
At Nashville!   Well, all right, my boys,
  Just point the colors South."

He sends his surplus stores all back
  To Chattanooga station ;
His sick go home, then all the track
  Of his communication
He tears relentlessly away,
  His captured posts he fires,
Sends up his last dispatch to Grant,
  And then he cuts the wires.

And by the lurid crackling blaze
  Of doomed Atlanta town,
His rear-guard marches to the tune
  The soldiers call " John Brown."
Far in advance and fearlessly,
  Along the road so sandy,
His bands the serried columns lead
  With Yankee Doodle Dandy.

CHAPTER XLVI.

WHEN rebels wise in Georgia
   Heard Sherman's drums a-beating,
. They flashed by telegraph the news,
   Tecumseh was "retreating ;"
But Governor Brown, a shrewdish man,
   By some wise intuition,
Looked shocked when word was brought to him
   Of Sherman's expedition.

As rumors thick and thicker grew,
   And touched on the romantic,
The rebels fell into a stew,
   The Governor he grew frantic.
He sent to Beauregard in haste,
   Who said the public weal
Required, first of all, that he
   Should publish an *appeal*.

So Beauregard and Brown sat down
   And straightway did concoct
Some proclamations, sent them out,
   And all the people flocked
(That is, as many as could read,)
   To get some information
Direct from these two clever ones
   Upon the situation.

Now Beauregard and Brown had called
  On *all* to volunteer,
And drive Tecumseh from the State,—
  Alack! it was n't clear
Who was to start on Sherman's track,
  As Brown implored they would,
When all the able-bodied men
  Had gone with General Hood.

This view of matters striking Brown
  His patriotism kindled,
And grew—just in proportion as
  His love for Davis dwindled.
Georgia should *not* be sacrificed
  To Jefferson's ambition;
Militia should not leave the State
  Against his (Brown's) volition.

He quick unbarred his county jails
  And set the convicts free,
And gave them guns to fight beside
  His other chivalry.
Jeff sent to Beauregard a force,
  The boys formed into ranks,
And, singing Dixie, out they went
  To exterminate the Yanks.

One thing alone was in the way
  Of this glad consummation—
Tecumseh had a wicked way
  Of baffling expectation.
His cavalry about his flanks
  Perplexed the rebs, because
They hid his march—no one could tell
  Exactly where he was.

If Sherman, on the road to right,
  Did start off with his drummers,
His cavalry would dash to left—
  And then those dreadful "bummers"
Were everywhere at once.   It soon
  Alarmingly was clear,
The rebels with Tecumseh's march
  Would hardly interfere.

The rebel press declared the news
  From Georgia could but cheer, sir,
The most despondent—what it *was*
  Could not at once appear, sir.
For reasons most prudential, Jeff
  Withheld his information,—
He was n't bound to furnish news
  Unto the Yankee nation.

But "Hood was managing the foe;"
  Then, later, it was stated
That Sherman, "cut off from his base,
  With terror unabated,
In disregard of strategy,
  War's principles defying—
Pursued by Cobb, in fearful haste,
  All ways at once was flying."

Tecumseh straight upon his course,
  Untouched by rebel wiles,
Cuts through the country clean a swath
  The width of forty miles.
The rebs declare that Macon is
  The object of his will;
They plant their guns in its defense—
  He enters Milledgeville!

The Legislature do not stay
  To vote Tecumseh thanks;
But *sine die* they adjourn
  In terror of the Yanks.
Now, then, the rebels have found out
  Exactly where he's going;
And to Augusta run with spades,
  And earth begin a-throwing.

They 'll stand a siege (I think 't was here
  They dug their last great ditch);
But one midday, to their despair,
  There came a little hitch
In all these preparations; for
  In just the neatest manner
Tecumseh crossed the Ogeechee
  And headed for Savannah.

"Destroy the roads!" cried Beauregard,
  "Harass him night and day!"
Well, some bold rebel put a few
  Torpedoes in his way.
Tecumseh, then, he ordered up
  A wagon from each corps;
And, heavy loaded with secesh,
  He sent it on before.

"Hang like a tiger on his rear!"
  Was Beauregard's wild cry,
"Hang it all, we can't get near!"
  Wild echoes did reply.
"Starve him out," said Beauregard,
  "Take everything away."
"Leave that to me, it's in *my* line,"
  Did Old Tecumseh say.
        13*

"Burn what is left," said Beauregard,
　"Make all the land a waste ;"
"It shall be done," Tecumseh said,
　"According to your taste."
So Sherman with a ready wit
　Kept Jeff upon the scowl,
And more, he kept his promises,
　And made "the Georgians howl."

On through the fields, past villages,[1]
　Through forests of dark pine,
With bugle call and trumpet tone,
　In unmolested line
The mighty spectacle rolled on
　With banners floating free,
Tecumseh and his gallant host
　Went "smashing to the sea."

At length a distant heavy gun
　Comes booming o'er the lea,
A signal from the waiting fleet
　Then down the Ogeechee ;
Tecumseh sends a messenger[2]
　For Abram's information,
And thus it was Tecumseh found
　His "lost communication."

Now, Hardee, round Savannah placed
　By Jeff to guard the city,
Saw coming up with rapid pace
　This man devoid of pity,

[1] "Sixty thousand men, taking merely of the *surplus* which fell in their way as they marched rapidly over the main roads, subsisted for three weeks in the *very country* where the Union prisoners at Andersonville were *starved to death or idiocy.*"—*Page* 203 *of Sherman and his Campaigns.*　　[2] December 9.

This "crazy" Sherman, bound to fight
  On very slight pretences ;
He shuddered, and slipped out of sight
  Within the town's defences.

Tecumseh closed up steadily ;
  Somewhat in trepidation,
He reconnoitered, and he mused
  Upon the situation.
"I can't lay siege without siege guns,
  There's plenty in the fleet,
But how to get them, there's the rub—
  And then the case to meet,

He first resolved to take the fort
  That kept Abe's vessels out,
Whose guns, according to report,
  Swept all the land about.
He sent for Hazen ; when he came,
  As Sherman had expected,
He was rejoiced that for the task
  His troops had been selected.

The morrow[1] Sherman takes his stand,
  Some three miles intervene
'Twixt him and Hazen's gallant band ;
  And out upon the scene
With anxious gaze he turns his glass,
  Then seaward for the fleet.
At last, a steamer's moving smoke
  His anxious glances meet.

"See! Howard—there the gunboat is,
  And there a signal flies."

[1] December 13.

"Have we the fort?"—"No! can you help?"
    Tecumseh quick replies.
"What shall we do?" comes waving back,
    There is no answer given,
For from the fort in thunder tones
    A plain response is driven.

The strife begins—sharpshooters try
    To clear the parapets,
And Hazen sees them in the marsh
    And secretly he frets.
It's heavy work, the sun is low,
    And there plain in his sight
This signal waves—"*You, without fail,
    Must take the fort to-night.*"

He knows Tecumseh's watching him,
    And with a swift invention
He forms his line, his bugler bids
    To sound the call "Attention!"
The warning note sweeps o'er the line,
    And in the distance dies.
"*Sound it again ! !*" then still once more
    "SOUND IT AGAIN ! !" he cries.

The gallant fellows clutch their guns,
    In wild excitement stand,
When, FORWARD !—and a shiver runs
    Along the expectant band.
Then, with a ringing shout they bound,
    The fort's hot fire they meet,
Torpedoes, hidden in the sand
    Explode beneath their feet.

Unheeding death above, below,
  Abattis frown in vain,
They tear it, tramp it, lay it low,
  And on they dash amain.
They reach the ditch.—As Sherman gazed
  He thought their course was stayed,
They only stopped, from out their way
  To wrench the palisade.

And steadily the flag moved on ;
  Now, shrouded in the smoke,
Now, waving free ; from first to last
  The blue line never broke.
Right up the rebel parapet,
  And ere the day was done,
The Stars and Stripes were firmly set,—
  McAllister was won !

So Sherman got his heavy guns
  And put them in position ;
Then, ere he opened, of Hardee
  Politely asked admission.
"*No, sir,*" said valorous Hardee,
  But while Tecumseh waited
He changed his mind, in three days he
  The town evacuated.[1]

Then Sherman wrote, and of his note
  This was about the drift :
He did Savannah to Old Abe
  Present—a Christmas-gift.
The rebs their injured feelings did
  In one short phrase condense,
They said, " Savannah never was
  Of any consequence."

      [1] Evacuated December 20, 1864.

CHAPTER XLVII.

"Now, what comes next?" said Abraham.
　While Grant and he decide,
We'll, just to see the end of Hood,
　Straight back to Georgia ride.
How he was reinforced we saw
　Upon a prior occasion,
And how he started out to chase
　Jeff's "phantom of invasion."

When Thomas saw that o'er the stream
　Of Tennessee he wended
His daring way, his eyes did gleam,
　And his suspense was ended.
He gathers up his scattered men,
　Falls back as Hood advances;
And gaily to its certain doom
　Hood's cavalry it prances.

The rebels were in ecstacies,
　They rolled the exulting cry,
"Hood ravaged unresistedly,
　And roared without reply."
'T was partly true—the stars and bars
　He impudently flirted
Before Pulaski.　Ah! but then
　Pulaski was deserted!

He galloped to Columbia,
  His troopers were elated;
No Yankee there to stop the way,
  Columbia was vacated.
Hood telegraphs—he knows 't will please
  King Jefferson to see,
How every day or two, with ease,
  He wins a victory.

A few more triumphs (sure to be)
  And he will have the whole
Of poor distracted Tennessee,
  Quite under his control.
He snapped at Franklin greedily,
  He bit upon a file,
For Schofield laid his chivalry
  In many a ghastly pile.

All day they struggled for the town,[1]
  At night Schofield retreated,
And Hood sent back to Jefferson
  " The Yankees were defeated."
The end was gained, delay was o'er,
  For Thomas now awaited
The rebels nibble at his trap,
  With *Nashville* it was baited.

Up tramps the sanguine traitor host
  And camp all round about,
Old Thomas thinks away within,
  He does n't yet look out;
He lets the rebels quiet stay
  Until they are quite rested,

---

[1] November 30, 1864.

And Hood has written Jeff to say,
"That Nashville is invested."

Then moves the lion from his lair,[1]
  He springs upon the foe,
In vain the victim in despair
  Writhes in its dying throe.
He crushes, crunches him between
  His heavy iron jaws, sir;
He tears him piece-meal with his sharp
  And glittering steel claws, sir.

Night falls.   The shattered army seeks
  Escape at early dawn.
All night a watch "Old Thomas" keeps,
  And with the opening morn
His cavalry to saddle spring,
  And winged artillery
Fly to the tune the bullets sing,
  To keep Hood company.

Day after day 't is all the same,
  This helter-skelter chase;
Till e'en the lion himself gave out,
  And wearied of the race.
Hood crossed the river Tennessee,[2]
  Two-thirds his men were gone,
And all his guns, and he himself
  As wretchedly forlorn

[1] December 15th, battle of Nashville.

[2] Dec. 16th. Another battle. Hood's loss, 13,189 prisoners, 2,207 deserters, 30 guns, 700 small arms. Dec. 17th. Hood driven through Franklin. Dec. 18th. Hood driven to Spring Hill. Dec. 19th. Hood driven to Duck River: 61 pieces of artillery captured out of 66. Hood's rear-guard crossed at Bainbridge, Dec. 28th.

As every rebel soul will be,
   When with returning reason
The glamour falls, and he can see
   His own bare fact of *treason.*
Hood's men deserted left and right,
   Wherever it came handy;
And never *did* come back to fight
   Old Yankee Doodle Dandy.

CHAPTER XLVIII

Now, Hood's disaster through the South
  Like bolts of thunder pealed;
It burst their clouds of falsity,
  Their nakedness revealed.
In anger, shame, and fierce despair,
  With wild discordant notes, sir,
Of helpless wrath, they rend the air,
  And Jeff is their *scape-goat*, sir.

Brave people! like the Jews of old
  They turn upon their leaders;
They stone their Moses, fret and scold,
  Magnanimous seceders!
In their "*united South*" 't was plain
  There was a fearful schism;
One-half the rebs pronounced Jeff's reign
  A curséd despotism.

They cried for a dictator—called
  Despairingly on Lee;
They swore by Jeff they were enthralled;
  They vowed they would be free.
Lee said one thing remained that might
  Bring Dixie some relief;
That was—ahem!—in fact, conscript—
  Arm Sambo, to be brief.[1]

[1] "I think the measure not only expedient, but necessary." See Lee's letter to Hon. E. Barksdale, House of Representatives, Richmond, of February 18th.

This was a bombshell in their camp,
　The " Southern heart " re-" fired,"
But nothing being left to burn,
　Combustion soon expired.
Their Congress took the subject up,
　And finally *did* reach [1]
A vote conclusive; though both Orr
　And Wigfall made a speech.

With " public spirit on the wane,"
　The ship of state a-leaking
And settling fast, the rats began
　A-running and a-squeaking. [2]
The *States* began to talk of " rights "
　Reserved for time of need;
They did n't like Jeff's government—
　Perhaps they 'd best secede !

Some said 't would be a wiser plan
　To call a States' convention ;
Savannah (tho' the Georgians
　Would scarcely like to mention
The fact) was getting on so well
　With Sherman's government,
The starving people eating corn
　That Jonathan had sent, [3]

And actually satisfied
　With Yankee subjugation—
Oh, horrible ! was this the end
　Of their Confederation ?

[1] The Negro Soldier Bill passed both House and Senate, February 23d, by *one* vote.

[2] Foote resigned in January, 1865.

[3] Immediately upon the capture of Savannah, subscriptions were taken up at the North, and supplies sent to the suffering.

And South Carolina she cried out—
 Demanded *some* protection,
For Old Tecumseh's eyes she felt
 Were turned in *her* direction.

Some swore they 'd send to Johnny Bull,
 And be his colony,
But as for treating with the Yanks,
 That was *too* dastardly ;—
Just here the Blairs came into town,
 The rebs all expectation,
Declared that Abe had sent them down
 For peace negotiation.

Then once again the " Southern heart "
 Puffed out a little smoke ;
Their vows about their last great ditch
 They never would revoke.
" What, trust the mercy of the Yanks !
 Better the Lion's jaw,
The adder's fang, the scorpion's sting,
 Shark's teeth, or tiger's claw." [1]

Where was the Devil all this time ?
 To mention him I 've feared,
He 'd grown so like the other rebs,
 His ear-marks disappeared.
I search the records of the day,
 But always off his track run,
I thought I had him once, dear me !
 'Twas only Dr. Blackburn. [2]

[1] Richmond *Whig*, January 20, 1865.
[2] The chivalrous gentleman who introduced yellow fever and cholera into the Union cities by means of infested clothing.

I followed what I deemed his tracks
  To some New York hotels ; [1]
The job was managed bunglingly,
  He would have done it *well,* sir.
I thought I had him on the lakes, [2]
  I wrongly did infer,
'T was Beal, a Southern gentleman,
  A rebel officer.

The atmosphere of rebeldom,
  So dark and darker grew ;
That isolated blackness had
  No chance of showing through ;
His very imps did fade from sight,
  Lost in the general level
Of Southern principles, that hid
  The blackness of the devil.

Some cried for this, and some for that,
  The panic wildly spread,
The rebel press in desperate strait,
  The wild confusion fed.
" They had been ruined by King Jeff,
  Their end, so undramatic,
Was close at hand, brought on by *him*
  Hap-hazard, wild, fanatic."

Now Jeff was very politic,
  A crafty man indeed,

[1] The diabolical plot to burn New York, was attempted to be put in execution on the night of the 25th November ; fifteen hotels and Barnum's Museum and shipping were fired.

[2] Beal, a rebel officer, captured and destroyed two steamboats on the Lakes ; also attempted to throw a train of cars from the track between Dunkirk and Buffalo. It was shown on the trial of Beal, that he had made three such attempts. He was hanged, and the Virginia Senate adopted resolutions recommending retaliation.

He sent for Stephens who, though sick
  As usual, came with speed ;
And Jeff before him laid a plan
  Suggested, some declare,
By that disinterested man,
  The mystical Old Blair :

That Stephens once again should go
  With Hunter, speedily,
And Campbell up to Fort Monroe
  Abe Lincoln for to see.
Jeff thought the times were riper now
  For a negotiation ;
That Abe perhaps would come to terms
  With the Confederation.

Well, Stephens went to Hampton Roads,[1]
  And Abe sent Seward down ;
Then went himself to have a talk,
  While Jonathan did frown,
And fretted till Old Abe came back,
  And said the talk was done ;
The rebels of two nations spoke
  But *he* of only *one.*

They wanted Grant to loose his hold,
  Give them a breathing spell,
And then when passions had grown cold,
  Why ! things would all be well.
Abe " could n't see " the rebel point,
  He told them *he* had *three ;*
" No other flag than Jonathan's !
  No truce ! no slavery ! "

---

[1] See page 566 of McPherson's History of the Rebellion.

The rebs went home, and told King Jeff,
  Said he, "It's an ill wind, sirs,
That blows nobody any good;
  I dare say we shall find, sirs,
That *this* will fan into a flame
  The smouldering Southern hearts;"
Then Jeff he called his trusty rebs,
  And gave them out their parts.

They held war meetings, up and down,
  They rasped the Southern heart
Till it grew hot, they vilified
  Till rebel souls did smart
Beneath fresh insults from the Yanks;
  They pledged anew their lives
Unto the cause,—oh never would
  They wear Old Abram's "gyves."

Then Jeff he made a little speech,[1]
  "He felt ecstatic joy
To see the courage of the rebs,
  Which nothing could destroy;
Let them stand firm in sun or shade
  Whatever was the weather;"
Then all the rebs for answer made,
  "*We will all hang together.*"

They threw their scabbards straight away
  And waved their naked swords,
"War to the death! no parley now,
  They wanted no more words!"
Said Jeff, "This Northern wind for once,
  Has blown as I expected;
Now, Beauregard, find out the route
  That Sherman has selected."

[1] February 6, 1865, in Richmond.

Now this was just the very thing
   Tecumseh had decided
Should *not* be done,—it was his plan,
   To keep the rebs divided.
So Slocum stretches with the left
   Along Savannah river,
Augusta-ward, while Howard's line
   Puts Charleston in a shiver.

Tecumseh pushes thro' the swamps,
   In almost all directions,
And baffles with his skirmishers
   Sir Beauregard's inspections.
At length he gathers up his host,
   Leaves Branchville on the south,[1]
And Hardee feels a-drawing down
   The corners of his mouth.

He leaves Charlestonians to their fate,
   Evacuates the place,
And Quincy Gillmore, neighborly,
   Doth put a pleasant face
Upon the matter; makes a call;[2]
   The Charleston people say
They're glad to see him, and they all
   Express a hope he'll *stay.*

They did n't mind his colored troops
   That bore the flag upright
Along their streets,—for on the whole
   It was a pleasant sight.

---

[1] Leaving the left wing to destroy the Charleston and Savannah railroad west of Branchville, Sherman with the right wing moved on Orangeburg thirteen miles north of Branchville between Charleston and Columbia.

[2] The whole Seventeenth Corps was in Charleston on Feb. 12, 1865.

They had been burned, and eaten up,
  And eaten up, and burned,
Until exhausted, they grew sane,
  And for protection yearned.

The rebs in Richmond said they thought
  That *this* evacuation
Was, on the whole, a *benefit*
  To their Confederation.
What *could they want* with Charleston ? sure
  That would be hard to tell;
'Twas full of starving women, and
  The city was a shell.

" If all the seaboard towns had been
  Long since evacuated,
It would have added to their strength," [1]
  And they insinuated
That Jeff some other useless posts
  Had checked upon his maps;
And thus they tried to engineer,
  Their horrible collapse.

The traitors were prophetic, for,
  In just about a week,
Their troops in Wilmington foresaw
  'T was best for them to seek
A safer spot (where that could be
  Was hard to tell, oh ! very.)
But off they went; their guns and things [2]
  They just transferred to Terry.

Tecumseh turns his columns straight
  Upon Columbia City, [3]

[1] Richmond *Despatch*, February 22, 1865.
[2] Terry entered Wilmington on February 22, 1865; fifty-one pieces of ordnance (heavy), fifteen light pieces and a large amount of ammunition were captured.   [3] Surrendered February 17, 1865.

14

The rebels drag their cotton out,
    And Hampton, without pity,
Applies the torch; the wind is high,
    The bales are everywhere,
The burning tufts of cotton fly,
    And why should Hampton care?

Columbia made desolate
    By Sherman,—"Yankee Hessian!"
Becomes a famous rebel text.
    The "hot-bed of secession,"
However, has had fire enough,
    Enough of brag and fustian,
Carolina sits a victim of
    Spontaneous combustion.

Tecumseh leaves the burning town,[1]
    Wade Hampton left before;
O'er roads, plantations, villages,
    His mighty columns pour.
His foragers like locusts spread,
    Devouring what they find,
Green smiling fields stretch on ahead,
    A blackened waste behind.

His cavalry with Wheeler play,
    Still squinting at Augusta,
And to impede his march *that* way
    The baffled rebels muster.
"Kil" tears roads up and bridges down
    Along his flashing way,
Tecumseh's Jack o'lantern he
    To lead the foe astray.

[1] Sherman having destroyed all that remained of Columbia that could be used for military purposes, marched on the 20th directly on Winsboro.

CHAPTER XLIX.

WHEN Jeff learned Beauregard had failed
    Columbia to hold,
His elongated visage paled,
    His traitor's blood grew cold.
He sent to Jo, in haste, to say
    His services were needed;
And Beauregard that very day
    By Jo was superseded.

Jo gathered up the scattered rebs
    At Charlotte, got them steadied,
For he was sure *that* was the point
    To which Tecumseh headed.
And so it was; through mud and mire
    For Charlotte straight he steers, sir,[1]
A day or two, then wheels about,
    And leaves it in his rear, sir.

Across Catawba's muddy stream,
    And on for the Pedee,
Tecumseh moves, and at Cheraw
    He comes upon Hardee,

---

[1] On the 22d February, 1865, Slocum continued his march to Charlotte; then, facing to the right, marched for the Catawba at Rocky Mount. The 20th corps crossed on the 22d, followed by Kilpatrick, and moved on Lancaster towards Charlotte. It was not until the main army reached the Pedee that the rebels discovered their mistake.

That is to say, his guns and stuff[1]
　　From Charleston brought with care;
Now Sherman has such things enough,
　　He spikes and leaves them there.

Kilpatrick with his cavalry
　　About his column hovers;
His movements from the rebel scouts
　　Right skillfully he covers.
But Jo sees Old Tecumseh's game—
　　Jo is a cunning man—
And off for Fayetteville he starts
　　To spoil Tecumseh's plan.

The roads are bogs, the streams are floods;
　　So long as it's daylight
Tecumseh flounders and he wades—
　　He corduroys all night.
Jo hurries up, Kilpatrick tries
　　Three roads at once to hold;
Wade Hampton's troopers gallop up;[2]
　　Kilpatrick's boys so bold,

Caught napping, run and leave their guns—
　　The rebels stop to plunder.
Kil drives his men back into line;
　　Before the rebs can wonder,
Is down upon them, has his guns
　　Turned in their very faces,
And deals a fiery welcome out
　　At "hardly twenty paces."

---

[1] At noon, on the 3d March, Blair's (17th)corps entered Cheraw, capturing twenty-five pieces of artillery and much ammunition which had been brought from Charleston when that city was evacuated.
　　[2] March 10.

The rebs retreat, come back and fight,
　Their little dash is foiled ;
Wade Hampton draws his troopers off,
　His little sport is spoiled.
To gather up his broken boys,
　Was now the work of "Kil ;"
Then off—he heads Tecumseh's troops
　And enters Fayetteville.[1]

Now Sherman when at Laurel Hill [2]
　Had sent a messenger
To hunt him up a base—at least
　We may so much infer ;
This courier to Wilmington
　Had waded with a line,
To tell Old Abe "his troops were well,
　And they were doing fine."

When Sherman enters Fayetteville,
　There up the Cape Fear river
Comes puffing Uncle Sam's gunboat
　An answer to deliver.[3]
Quoth Sherman, "Jo is making up
　A heavy concentration
To fall upon us, by and by—
　I 've no disapprobation,

"But I must send dispatches down,
　Old Abe has troops to spare ;
I 'll move on *Goldsboro* at once,
　If *Schofield* meets me there."

[1] On the 11th of March,
[2] March 8. The whole army was massed on the 12th.
[3] On the 12th March the army-tug Davidson and the gunboat Eolus
reached Fayetteville from Wilmington.

So down the muddy swollen stream,
  The little tug departed;
And took Tecumseh's note by steam,
  But Schofield, sir, *had* started.

The rebels tried to hold him back,
  They pressed upon his flanks;
At Wise's Forks they made attack;[1]
  Repulsed, with broken ranks,
They crossed the river, burned the bridge,[2]
  And ran to General Jo,
Who massed his troops—*where* we shall see,
  As future movements show.

Then Schofield made himself a bridge,
  And crossed the very day[3]
Tecumseh off for Raleigh starts
  Where reb headquarters lay.
Now Hardee out from Fayetteville
  Had run into a mire[4]
At Averysboro.   Up rode Kil;
  Hardee would *not* retire.

Kilpatrick then to Slocum sent,
  That he "the rebs must rout;"
So in the swamp bold Slocum went,
  And Hardee he came out.[5]
Then said Tecumseh—"To the right,
  For Goldsboro make haste, sirs."
Said General Jo—"Now, boys in gray,
  We have no time to waste, sirs."

[1] March 8.   [2] Across the Neuse.
[3] On the 14th March, 1864.
[4] "Hardee halted in the Swampy Neck, between Cape Fear and South Rivers. He had 20,000 men and must be dislodged."
[5] March 16.

Jo falls on Slocum heavily;[1]
   If his wise plan don't fail
He has the Yanks at last.   He strikes
   Tecumseh in detail.
His move is quick, 't is bold, but oh!
   Tecumseh's bolder, quicker;
Kilpatrick hears the cannon roar,
   His squadrons gather thicker.

Then thunder-laden clouds do roll,
   In wilder storms they burst;
And Davis's immortal corps,[1]
   All heroes, for the first
Dread charge stand ready; as from rock
   The rebel hosts rebound.
Six fierce assaults the heroes meet,
   Yield not an inch of ground.

That night Joe fell to using spades,
   But spades Tecumseh spurned;
The morrow,[3] from his parapet,
   Jo saw the tables turned.
Instead of striking in detail,
   Jo finds the job extensive;
Tecumseh's battle-line is formed,
   And *Jo* on the defensive.

Tecumseh does n't force a fight—
   A man he of reflection—
With Schofield, pressing up the Neuse,
   He'd rather make connection.
He holds his army well in hand,
   And closely watches Jo,

---

[1] March 19.   [2] The 14th Corps.   [3] March 20.

To see, outside his parapets
  If he his face will show.

The meantime Schofield hurries up
  In Goldsboro' *commands*,[1]
And Terry halts ten miles above,
  And then they all shake hands.
They hold the river all the way
  Straight down to Wilmington,
The railroad track to Newbern town,
  And *that* campaign is done.

Now, what will General Johnston do?
  Let go his parapets?
He has an ancient fear of traps
  That Old Tecumseh sets.
Tecumseh gives a little tap
  Upon his outer gate;[2]
Jo gives an answer to the rap,
  But then—he does n't wait.

He leaves his pickets and his dead,
  And slips across the creek;[3]
The rebels down in Richmond said,
  In just about one week
That General Jo would have the Yanks
  All buried in the mud,
So rank and rapid on "*their Jo;*"
  Their hopes forlorn did bud.

Well, Sherman's boys with constant use
  Had worn their shoes quite thin;

[1] March 21st, occupation of Goldsboro', and junction of the armies
of Sherman, Schofield and Terry.
[2] The "Noisy Battle" of the 21st of March.
[3] Mill Creek.

They must be shod, before they can
   Another march begin.
Tecumseh leaves the job to Meigs,
   (Who never said, "I can't, sir,")
And then he slips on board a boat,
   To visit Abe and Grant, sir.[1]

And while the plans for future work
   Are laid for his inspection,
And Grant and he make new campaigns
   Converge in Lee's direction,
And Abe *begins to see the end.*
   Along the war's red track
Where the Potomac Army fought
   We'll turn our glances back.

[1] City Point, 27th of March, 1865.

14*

CHAPTER L.

WHEN Thomas hoodwinked General Hood,
  And managed him so handy,
That in the end he understood
  Old Yankee Doodle Dandy,
He back to Nashville went, and found
  A note from Grant did wait
To tell him, Schofield must come round,
  And so co-operate

With Sherman;(how his part was done
  We have already seen).
Grant also said, some cavalry
  Might brush up neat and clean
Those crumbs of the rebellion left
  Outside his concentration,
That steadily was grinding down
  The doomed Confederation.

While Stoneman utterly destroys
  The road Jo Johnston uses[1]
To bring supplies to his gray boys,
  And Jo thereby confuses ;
(This line Jo hoped to keep intact
  In case of a defeat,

[1] Railroad from Greensboro', N. C., through Salisbury to the Catawba.

(322)

In the contingency—in fact—
  Of having to retreat.)

While Canby sweeps along the bay
  And joins with General Steele,
To clear the rebel virus from
  The city of Mobile ;[1]
While Wilson with his cavalry[2]
  Through Alabama rushes,
That besom of destruction, PHIL,
  Through Old Virginia brushes.

He bolts post haste from Winchester,[3]
  His troopers ride so hard,
That Jubal Early in his works
  Cannot their speed retard.
They clatter up and *over* them,
  Right over men and guns,
And wagon train and battle-flags,
  Before their ride is done.

Phil tears down bridges, burns cross-ties,
  Destroys canals and locks ;[4]
His thundering squadrons shake the ground,
  Till Lynchburg feels the shocks.[5]
The web of treason, cut all round
  Hangs by a single thread ;
If Lee don't creep on that to Jo,
  Grant has the spider's head.

Will Lee wait for the narrowing coil
  To crush him where he lies ?

[1] March 28th, defences of Mobile attacked; city occupied April 12th.
[2] Leaves Nashville with 15,000 men on the 17th of March, 1865.
[3] February 27th, Phil took 1,600 prisoners, 11 guns, 200 wagons and
17 battle-flags. [4] James River canal. [5] Within 16 miles of Lynchburg.

Or will he leave Virginia's soil,
  When hope of victory dies?
Grant fears he may escape to Jo,
  And to the mountains flee;
Then Sherman's troops are working up—
  Grant thinks the victory

Belongs to the Potomac boys,
  Who 've toiled so long and well;
If they don't win ere Sherman comes,
  'T is easy to foretell,
Tecumseh 'll steal the laurels from
  Their weather-beaten brow.
Grant bites another fresh cigar,
  And says he 'll strike right *now*.

He wrote his orders out that day,[1]
  But Lee was desperate, sir,
He could n't brook an hour's delay,
  He would decide his fate, sir.
A coup-de-main—Fort Steadman fell,
  Its guns are turned about;
Hartranft's recruits rush *in* pell-mell,
  And push the rebels out,

Turn back the guns, sweep down the foe,
  And Meade starts into life;
And, forward! is the order now,
  And in the bloody strife,
Five thousand rebels bite the dust;
  Here, on his visit brief
Tecumseh came and went, then Grant
  Turned over his last leaf.

[1] March 24, 1865.

CHAPTER LI.

Phil from his raid comes up to Grant
    With many a travel stain;[1]
"Now, Phil," says Grant, "your horses pant,
    But you must ride again."
"All right!" cries Phil; "an hour's rest
    Will do for my brave ranks, sir."
"Then off," says Grant, "and do your best
    To find out Lee's right flank, sir!"

Phil gallops, stretching to the left,
    For Lee's hid flank he feels—
The rain! it rains, and in the mud
    He has to leave his wheels.
His horses flounder—on they go,
    Phil spurs them through the mire,
He nears Five Forks,[2] he sees the foe,
    He rideth into fire.

He fights, is driven, fighting, back,[3]
    Defeat he *won't* confess;
The morrow o'er his last night's track
    His gallant troopers press.

[1] March 27th.   [2] March 30th.
[3] The rebels drive Devin's Brigade. The cavalry is driven back to Dinwiddee.

Again the foe push heavily,
  Phil rather has the worst,[1]
It does n't matter, in the end
  He 's bound to come out *first.*

He grapples with the saucy rebs,
  Advances left and right,[2]
He charges *through, beyond* their works—
  The traitors take to flight.
His cavalry dash o'er the road,
  They seize and turn their guns, sir;
Dread fear of Phil the rebels goad,
  Demoralized they run, sir.

Farther to right, along Grant's line,
  A heavy cannonade
All day rang out the traitor's knell;
  And as the shadows fade
And die before the morrow's sun,
  A mighty living sea
Rolls out, engulphing as it runs
  The lines of General Lee.

In vain the drowning rebels strive;
  They cannot break the wave;
They only drop from its embrace
  Into a traitor's grave.
On! on! moves Grant, and Phil rides back
  On rebel flank and rear;
Till in dismay they turn and flee
  In pitiable fear.

In Richmond ('twas the Sabbath day)
  There was sufficient reason

[1] March 31, at Boydstown plank road.   [2] April 1. Battle Five Forks.

Why Jeff should go to church and pray
  For the success of treason.
And there he sat, his traitor soul
  As bare before his God
As were his victims bones, that lay
  Unburied on the sod.

"Spare us, good Lord!" ascended high
  Before Jehovah's throne,
Together with the battle-cry,
  The soldier's curse and groan.
"From all sedition (hear Jeff's prayer
  As he repeats it thus),
From all rebellion, (doth God hear?)
  Good Lord, deliver us!

"To show thy pity upon all
  Prisoners and captives, we
Beseech thee!"   (Though the heavens fall,
  Doubt not Jeff's piety.)
"Hear us, good Lord!"   The prayer went on,
  Devotion did increase;
Till from Jeff's holy lips went up,
  The cry, "Grant us Thy peace!"

A bustle at the church door—then
  A messenger from Lee
Slips up to Jeff, (his fervent prayer
  Is answered speedily):
"The enemy have pierced my lines,"
  (So General Lee had stated
In his dispatch); "Richmond must be
  At once evacuated!"

Why doth King Jeff turn pale, his face
　　A look of terror wear?
Each eye in all that holy place
　　On Jefferson doth glare.
What will their king decide to do
　　Now, will he die, or run?
He takes the train [1]—'t is sad, 't is true,
　　His brilliant reign is done!

The engine screams, the rebels pitch
　　Their archives on the train,
Jeff starts to find his last great ditch,
　　Ne'er to return again.
The people shriek, they wring their hands,
　　They curse Jeff without pity.
The fleeing soldiers burn their stores,
　　And set on fire the city.

Powder explodes and shells go off,
　　Fear takes the place of wonder;
Flames unresisted sweep the streets,
　　The starving take to plunder;
Crime unrebuked stalks through the town;
　　Lee's army in retreat,
All night files out to find King Jeff—
　　All night the tramp of feet

Keeps time with wildly throbbing hearts;
　　But, when the morning came,
And Weitzel brought the old flag back,
　　The rebel hearts grew tame.
The black troops marched in steadily,
　　The people never *sneered*;

[1] Leaves for Danville at 8 o'clock, P.M., April 2.

And Sambo trampled out their fire,
  And then, indeed, they *cheered.*

I do not know, I rather think
  The old flag brought a calm
To Old Virginia's troubled breast,
  And acted like a balm
To broken-hearted and oppressed.
  I know they ceased their vowing
About their ditch ; and what was best,
  The farmers set to ploughing.

CHAPTER LII

Wʜᴇɴ Lee fell back before our Grant
    He knew not *where* to go ;
Dim prospects of a junction made,
    With rebel General Jo,
Led him to take the Danville road,
    But swift disintegration
Among his ranks, ere long revealed
    A nearer destination.

For restless Sheridan struck out,
    Then followed Ord and Meade ;
They take the shorter, inside route,
    And make the greater speed.
Phil strides across the track of Lee,[1]
    Lee sheers a little west,
Ord heads him, gets a heavy blow,[2]
    Which he returns with zest.

Phil slashes at the fleeing foe
    He cuts off quite a slice ;[3]
Lee can't escape, for his attempt,
    He pays a fearful price.
Grant says, it is in fact a shame,
    It shall be understood,

---

[1] Jettersville, March 4.   [2] Farmville, March 6.
[3] Sailor's Creek, on the 6th, captures 7,000 prisoners.

That Lee alone must bear the blame
  Of useless waste of blood.

He writes a note to say this much ;
  Lee civilly replies,
And asks for terms, and they are such
  The rebel chief complies ;
But not until Phil Sheridan,
  Has made a final dash,[1]
And brought a score or so of guns,
  Out of the general crash.

The white flag comes across at last ;[2]
  A soldier's heart is tender ;
Grant does n't make it very hard
  For rebels to surrender.
They stack their guns, and stake their word,
  (The terms we need not bandy,)
"They 'll never more strike *(overtly)*
  At Yankee Doodle Dandy."

Tecumseh he was making haste
  To execute *his* plan,
To slip his troops 'twixt Lee and Jo ;
  But ere his march began,
He heard the noise at Petersburg,
  Knew Grant could manage Lee ;
He gave a little nervous shrug
  And changed his strategy.

He drives his columns straight at Jo,[3]
  Defying hostile rains ;
Just here, comes word of Lee's last gasp ;
  Tecumseh drops his trains,

[1] On the 8th, at Appomattox R.R. [2] April 9. [3] Starts April 10, 1865.

And pushes through the deepening mud;
  Jo wades a day ahead;
" I 'll have a brush with General Jo
  To-morrow," Sherman said.

Tomorrow brings a flag of truce,[1]
  Jo is a man of sense—
He 's cornered,—" Will Tecumseh please
  Relieve him from suspense." .
And while Tecumseh draws a plan,
  Which Jo will *not* refuse,
We 'll see how Abe and Jonathan
  Received the glorious news.

[1] April 14.

CHAPTER LIII.

OLD Abe was down with General Grant;
  He was a happy man
When he dispatched, that April day,
  The news to Jonathan.
The tidings flashed from wire to wire,
  O'er each, and every route,
It set the *Northern heart* on fire,
  And burned its anger out.

The people laughed and cried for joy,
  They all ran out of doors;
They hung their flags across the streets,
  With cheers, and cannon roars;
And Jonathan, who never did
  Do anything by half,
Declared the time had come for him
  To kill the fatted calf.

And all the neighbors cried "Amen!"
  And made so great a noise,
In their excess of joy, they drowned
  The groans of Grant's poor boys.
They grew so very merciful,
  (What sins that virtue covers)
They buried justice with their dead,
  All for their " erring brothers."

(333)

And Jonathan when he had made
  An end of celebrating,
And future plans and projects weighed,
  Said he, " Old Abe is waiting ;
I 'll take the train this very night,
  His face I long to see ;
In joy or grief, in dark or light,
  I know Abe thinks of me."

But Betsey Jane slipped up the stair,
  When Jonathan had gone,
Alone,—for she had treasured there
  All that was left of John.
The ornament from off his cap,
  The metal letter C,
Some yellow worsted stripes, for John
  Was in the cavalry.

She rubbed the little sabres bright,
  " *He* said the fatted calf."
She groaned as on her troubled sight
  There fell *John's photograph.*
She traced along the skeleton
  Where once his young blood ran
In full round veins—she saw the bloom
  Upon those cheeks so wan.

" *Men can forget,*" said Betsey Jane,
  " This haste my heart benumbs,
And God himself doth *not forgive*
  Until repentance comes."
She pressed her lips in agony,
  Against the photograph,
And murmured brokenly the words,
  " *Starved ! starved !*" and "*fatted calf.*"

CHAPTER LIV.

While Jeff fled o'er the Danville road
  With all his traitor crew,
And Grant in Dixie smoked, and smiled
  At the dissolving view
Of treason, chivalry and brag,
  Old Abe came back to town;
And Major A., with his old flag,
  To Sumter he sent down.

The very flag, four years ago,
  The Major furled in sadness,
Shall now to South Carolina show
  The fullness of her madness.
And when it floats in purer air,[1]
  Whence treason's clouds have vanished,
Thank God, ye rebels, and take care
  It never more be banished.

Then Stanton stopped the draft, and Abe,
  Who repossessed the forts,
Returned to Welles his blockade fleet,
  And closed the Southern ports.
And then the people called him out,
  ('T was with a serenade,)

[1] The old flag was raised on the fort April 15, the day Mr. Lincoln
died.

And pelted him with cheer and shout,
  Until a speech he made.

He said "The boys who did the work—
  · The soldiers and not he—
Must have the credit and the thanks,
  For hard-earned victory.
They 'd conquered Jeff and rebeldom,
  At *that* they had n't stayed ;
They 'd fairly captured *Dixie tune*—
  He 'd like to hear it played."

And so the band clashed out the air,
  And then it came so handy,
They could n't help but change the tune
  To Yankee Doodle Dandy.
"Now, then," said Abe, "we owe it all,
  Not to the dead or living,
But to Jehovah.   Let us call
  In general thanksgiving

"Upon His name, and His alone,
  Who with a mighty hand
Has swept the flood of treason back
  From our beloved land.
God help the mourners who have laid
  Away their holy dead ;
God bless the dying and the maimed,"
  Sad Abram Lincoln said.

CHAPTER LV.

THE train that bore Old Jonathan
  Wound steadily along;
The pulses of the brave old man
  Beat rapidly and strong.
He felt as he had felt in youth,
  Long, long before the war,
Those good old times come back; in truth,
  With his mind's eye he saw

When men would talk of rusty guns
  As he of his flint locks
In dusty garrets; and their sons
  Would gather fruitful shocks
Of corn from Southern battle-fields,
  Till war's last trace should fade,
In wonder, when some furrow yields
  A rusted bit of blade.

Time heals all wounds, thought Jonathan,—
  Now, brother armed 'gainst brother,—
To-morrow, in the wiser man,
  Will learn to love each other.
And then he thought of dear Old Abe,
  In times gone by so sad;
"I'll cheer him up," said Jonathan,
  "And make his old heart glad."

The train lurched on ahead, then stopped;
  The clock was just upon
The stroke of eight, as Jonathan
  Arrived in Washington.[1]
He bounded up the Avenue—
  He could n't step as fast
As his heart beat—to right or left
  A glance he hardly cast.

He ran against a group of men,
  Who stared at his quick pace;
He looked at one, he slackened then,
  The horror on the face
Struck like a chill: "Ah! I forgot
  The dark side of our joy;
This man has heard, perhaps, just now
  About his brave *dead* boy."

A bit of crape tied to a door
  Just fluttered in the breeze,
And caught his eye—"one mourner more"
  In that black crape he sees—
Another! all along the street
  Hung out the sign of grief;
A flag, *half mast*, his gaze did meet;
  Said Jonathan, "*some chief*

"Has fall'n in this last great blow,
  I 'll ask Abe for his name."
His step had grown, despite him, slow;
  To Jonathan there came,
He knew not how, or why, a weight
  That crushed down all his pleasure,
And made his very footsteps keep
  A melancholy measure.

[1] April 15, 1864.

He turned up from the avenue ;[1]
  The town was *very* still ;
He came upon a silent throng;
  Almost against his will,
He pressed his way. Ah! *now* he 'll *know*,
  The dead man in his shroud ;
His own, and Abe's beloved flag,
  Is carried through the crowd.[2]

A sob! and Sambo at his side
  Groaned out a well-known name ;
And Jonathan with one quick stride
  Up to the bearers came.
" Good God!" the sight went from his eyes,
  His stricken heart stood still.
He staggered, deaf to others' cries,
  He moved on without will.

They bore on through the White House gate
  Old Jonathan's best friend,
And left him lying there in state :
  " Just God, is *this* the end ?"
Groaned Jonathan, when he had gazed,
  Upon the sad, dead face ;
And mercy, outraged in his heart,
  To bitter wrath gave place.

In every house there was one dead,
  Throughout the mighty nation ;
And every man bowed low his head
  In awe and desolation.
Men *pray*, when smitten with the dart
  Of unforeseen affliction ;

[1] Up 10th Street.

[2] From the house of Mr. Peterson, on 10th Street, opposite Ford's Theatre.

But from the nation's broken heart
    Went up a *malediction.*

Then Jonathan took up his dead,
    The funeral procession
Wound wearily, and weary sped
    In mournfullest succession.
Day after day, as through the land
    The sad train took its way,
And Jonathan to his old home
    Brought back the lifeless clay.[1]

As Betsey Jane looked on the brow,
    And traced deep lines of care,
"No traitor's stab can reach *him* now,
    Their thrusts *we* still must bear.
Because he *rests,*" said Betsey Jane,
    "I envy him his lot;
The bullet of the murderer
    Has reached the *tired spot.*"[2]

*   *   *   *   *   *

The tale is told,—King Jeff still lives
    God's purpose to fulfill;
And wanders, like that other Cain,
    Whom nobody should kill.
Old Jonathan has been quite weak;
    I think it won't be long
Before his mind again he'll speak,
    In language rather strong.

"With malice tow'rd none," said Abraham
    "With charity for all;"

1 Abraham Lincoln was buried in Springfield, Ill.
2 One of Mr. Lincoln's expressions.

But oh! it comes into my mind
  A worse thing might befall
Than has as yet come on the earth,
  Should Satan deem it handy
Again to set his Judases,
  On Yankee Doodle Dandy.